JOURNEY TO SAND CASTLE

By

Leslee Breene

Books by Leslee Breene

Starlight Rescue

Hearts on the Wind

Leadville Lady

Foxfire

"I had a dream last night as I lay beneath the pines… I'd dreamed of home and family there beneath the Spanish Peaks. On the trail from Santa Fe, where plains and mountains meet. And the rivers rush through canyons and the air is fresh and sweet. I carved my life in granite, I let my roots run deep. I found the only peace I've known there beneath the Spanish Peaks."

~ Jon Chandler, *The Spanish Peaks*

Journey to Sand Castle is dedicated to the victims and survivors of Hurricane Katrina, and to the survivors of all natural disasters who have overcome with renewed spirit and courage.

Acknowledgments

Special thanks and recognition to the following whose contributions aided in the completion of *Journey to Sand Castle*.

The San Luis Valley: Sand Dunes and Sandhill Cranes. Text by Susan J. Tweit, The University of Arizona Press @ 2005

People Magazine - Sept. 12, 2005, *Nightmare* by Alex Tresniowski, Bob Meadows and Daniel S. Levy - Pgs. 64-70

Great Sand Dunes National Park & Preserve, Colorado, including map and illustrated *Life Zones of Great Sand Dunes*.

Bill Barwick: *Carolyn in the Sunset*, words and music by Bill Barwick @ 2000, from his CD "Sons of the Tumbleweed," www.BillBarwick.com

~Crystal~

Chapter One

Monday, August 29, 2005

Wailing wolves—that was the sound of it. Then louder—like a mammoth jet hovering in the turbulent skies. *Katrina.*

Tess Cameron stood riveted behind a boarded window of her empty Jefferson Elementary School classroom. Peering through a crack in the boards, she saw ragged rooftops and debris hurled through the streets. A shattering sound from the floor above her sent chills along her arms. Shards of glass whipped past the window like jagged missiles.

Showing no mercy, torrents of rain beat down from the angry sky. She imagined other parts of the city near the levees where flood waters would climb quickly to heights above a man's head. Her skin flushed clammy to the touch. Her legs went weak beneath her.

How high would flood waters climb here? She didn't know how to swim. Fear pumped her heart like a sledge hammer until it felt like it might pump right out of her chest.

Hours later, a gray watery silence smothered the city.

* * *

Tuesday, August 30

Tess rubbed her eyes, gritty from lack of sleep, and faced the tide of new evacuees streaming into Jefferson's gymnasium. Wet and bedraggled, their bodies as well as their spirits were devastated by the deluge. Masks of anxiety covered their faces. Now homeless and separated from their families, they had nowhere else to go for shelter but here.

It was a miracle the two-story school was intact. Perhaps because it was built of brick, built to withstand strong winds. Although all types of litter covered the grounds and several windows on the second floor were shattered, the interior had not been flooded.

When she'd arrived Sunday afternoon, offering what aid she could give to her neighbors and young students, Tess had had no idea Hurricane Katrina would leave such destruction behind. But then, just beginning her second year in the New Orleans area, what would she know about hurricanes? A former Air Force brat, she only recalled survival skills which involved adapting to wherever her family was transferred around the globe.

"Can you help us?" A young woman with disheveled brown hair and haunted eyes hurried toward her, a toddler straddling one hip. On her heels followed two young boys and a small, almond-skinned girl. There was something familiar about the girl.

"Over here." Tess pointed to cots set up against a gymnasium wall. "You can have these. There are blankets and some snacks for the children."

The woman's face crumpled. "My cousin is missing—her car was washed away. Can y'all get any information about her?"

"I'm sorry. We haven't been able to contact the local authorities yet. You know the power's out—" Tess stopped in mid-sentence. A rambling explanation would not make this anxious woman's situation any better. "What is your cousin's name and address?" She slipped a ballpoint pen from her clipboard. "I'll pass it along as soon as I can."

"It's her mother, Carrie Pearl," the woman said in a low voice, referring to the small girl with large, red-rimmed eyes who hovered behind her. "They've been livin' with us until she could find a place."

A strange tingle darted along Tess's spine as she jotted down the information. "Carrie's a teacher here at Jefferson, isn't she?"

"Yeah. That's her girl, Crystal. She doesn't know what happened." The woman shifted the toddler in her arms. "I haven't told her yet. I don't know how to tell her."

Although Tess didn't know Carrie well, her reaction to the bedraggled child now climbing onto one of the cots was one of immediate sympathy.

"And what is your name?"

"Winona Bingham. My husband's in Houston lookin' for a job." She glanced around at her two boys, their grim faces revealing the nightmare they'd lived through. "I wish we could have got out with him, before the storm hit."

"I can understand that." Tess set the clipboard down on a folding chair and passed a few bags of chips to the hungry children.

The toddler on Winona's hip, scantily clad in T-shirt and diapers, began to whine, grasping at her mother's arm. "Do y'all have any baby formula?" Near desperation tinged Winona Bingham's request. "All I had time to bring was a few diapers and a change of clothes."

The agony of what this mother had suffered was one more notch on a belt of misery, her plight similar to other evacuees Tess had talked to during the last twenty-four hours. They had lost everything. "We don't have baby food. But we do have some bottled water back in the locker room. Wait here."

Taking up her clipboard, Tess maneuvered through the crowd of arrivals to the locker room at the rear of the gym. "Carrie Pearl is lost in the flood," she told the assistant principal, John Lincoln, a usually jovial black man in his late thirties.

John's lower lip curled downward. "No way. Carrie's a teacher upstairs in the music department."

Tess shook her head in dismay. "Her cousin just came in with her three kids and Carrie's little girl."

"Geez. That's tough. Keep a list and we'll turn it over to the police...whenever we can reach them. All the lines are down. The cell phones don't work." John's dark-eyed gaze roamed the room while several volunteers rationed food supplies, salvaged from the school cafeteria, to take back to the gym. "Hey, remember that stuff is scarce as hen's teeth. Make it last."

Tess reached for four bottles from a locker. "How's the water holding out?"

John raked a hand through short black hair, sweat beading his upper lip. "Not much left. And there's no way to run over to the market for more with flood water up to your elbows."

A knowing sigh escaped her. "I've got to locate some baby formula."

His shoulders sagged. "Haven't seen any. I'll keep my eyes open."

"Thanks, John." Carrying her precious water bottles, Tess returned to the gym and its occupants rife with grief and uncertainty. No food, no power, no running water. A roof overhead and a cot was all the school had to offer.

And, from the looks of the crowded gymnasium, available cots were running short fast.

Chapter Two

Later in the afternoon, Tess located a few jars of apple sauce in a cafeteria cupboard. "It's all I could find," she said, handing Winona Bingham the jars and a plastic spoon.

"Thanks." Exhaustion pulled Winona's features taut. Her baby slept fitfully on the cot next to her, miniature fingers clinging to her mother's hand. "You don't have a hamburger stashed somewhere, do you?" The sudden sharp laugh belied her obvious hunger.

"Sure wish I had a stack of them." Winona's question stood heavy between them. When would help reach these people, bring food and medicines? Some of the elderly were in wheelchairs, desperate for medications they'd left behind in their families' immediate effort to escape the hurricane's wrath.

Small hands tugged at her pant leg and she glanced down into wide eyes, the shade of amber topaz, in the face of Winona Bingham's ward. "Do you have anything to eat?" The child gazed up at her with such trust as if all she had to do was ask this grown-up person and her request would be granted.

A mixture of regret and sadness bunched up inside Tess. Whatever edible food was left in the cafeteria kitchen had been handed out. The vending machines had been pillaged, with Principal Skeller's permission. No food deliveries could be expected while most of New Orleans' streets lay under water.

But Tess did remember one thing. The chocolate nut bar hidden in her school room desk drawer. Only to be recovered for an extreme hunger attack. It looked like now was the time.

Bending down to Crystal's eye level, she said in a soft voice. "If you come with me, I think we might find something."

The topaz eyes lit up with a hopeful spark. "Okay."

She nodded to Winona over on the cot, took the child's hand and led her down a dim hall. "My name is Ms. Cameron and I teach at this school," she said as they walked.

"My name is Crystal. My mommy teaches here too."

An uncomfortable twinge jerked Tess's insides. "Oh, she does? What does she teach?" she asked in a gentle tone.

Crystal looked up at her from beneath a tousle of mahogany curls. "She teaches music. Mommy's not here." What must have been a quick flashback of fear sent a tear trickling down her cheek. "She drove the car away." The child forced a smile. "But she's coming back."

Tess swallowed over a lump in her throat. "We all hope she will come soon, honey."

Entering her neat first grade classroom, Tess went to the front, also hoping the candy bar was still in the desk. That no sneaky-fingered thief had bypassed her locked upper drawer and found her buried treasure. With bated breath, she opened the lower drawer and slipped her hand inside. Crystal watched with fascination. "What's in there?"

"We'll find out." Tess's fingers skimmed over a story book she'd been reading to her class, around several glue sticks, a box of paper clips, and back toward the corner. She felt the slick paper wrapper. A little thrill skittered up her fingers.

She grasped the found treasure and held it up to Crystal. "What does this look like?"

Crystal let out a shriek of delight. "A candy bar!"

Her own stomach growling from its forced two-day fast, Tess ripped off the wrapper. The aroma of milk chocolate and salty peanuts invaded her senses. She looked from the candy to Crystal's expectant face. "Can I have just a bite?"

Crystal's brows lifted. "Okay."

Breaking off a small piece, Tess popped it into her mouth and gave the rest to Crystal. The sweet reward disappeared inside rounded cheeks followed by chewing pleasure. A gulp. Then a pink tongue licked dusky lips. "That was gooood."

Tess smothered a wry laugh. "We're like two mice scrounging crumbs from the giant's table."

Crystal grinned, showing perfect white baby teeth.

But the bite hardly satisfied. It only made her more ravenous. What she wouldn't give for a double cheeseburger or a plate of calorie-bursting fried chicken!

She curled her fingers around Crystal's firm little arm. "Please don't tell anyone about our treat, honey. You know there are a lot of hungry people out there in the gym. I don't have any more candy for them."

Crystal bowed her head slightly, ebony-fringed eyes staring at the floor. "Okay."

Fighting morose feelings, Tess retrieved the story book from the drawer, spied several others stacked beneath the windows. "Let's go see if anyone wants to hear a story before it gets too dark," she offered, heading over to the books.

In a corner of the gym, under windows letting in the best afternoon light, Tess gathered a group of children around her at a low table. She read from several illustrated books, until her voice became scratchy and her head bobbled like a helium balloon. Even with the windows opened, the air in the gym was cloying. Heat and humidity weighed heavily over her and the nearly one hundred people crammed together in frustrating proximity.

Winona Bingham's two boys interrupted Tess with frequent outbursts of "I don't like this book," to "When can we leave this place?" Too tired to run off their natural energy, they occasionally pounded the table or each other.

She responded in brief sentences, trying to keep order amongst the other restless children, until the afternoon light dimmed.

If only we could give them a nourishing meal, a promise of returning to their homes.

Finally she sent them all back to their parents or guardians and sought out the principal. Entering Ken Skeller's office, she found him slumped over his desk, running his hands through disheveled, thinning hair. After sending his family off to relatives in South Carolina, he had been at the school all weekend directing volunteer efforts. Even though she wanted to turn around and leave the overworked man alone, she couldn't. "Any word on when we'll get these people evacuated, Ken?"

Like an athlete biking up a steep mountain, he looked at her through glazed eyes. "I wish I could tell you. No agency has gotten back to me yet. Cell phones aren't working. The flooding is far worse than we all first thought."

She nodded, commiserating with his obstacles. "Anything I can do, just holler."

"Sure thing, Tess."

She picked up a flashlight from the front desk on her way back down the hall. Hunger gnawed at her shriveled stomach as it pushed against her spine. Stars shifted in front of her for a moment and a wave of nausea sent her down on one knee. She reached out and leaned against the cool wall. So this was what those poor orphans and refugees in third world countries had to put up with, most days of their lives.

Perspiration moistening her face and neck, she took a deep weary breath and pulled herself to her feet. *Got to check on them once more before I crash on my cot.*

Smells of stale sweat and sounds of crying babies mingled with the raspy moans of elder adults held captive in their wheelchairs filled the darkening gymnasium. Fresh tears pricked her inner eyelids. These people were growing more anxious by the hour.

When would help come? Would it be too late for some when it did?

* * *

Wednesday, August 31

The day passed slowly like a train engine running out of steam. Tired and growing short-tempered, Tess attended to the senior evacuee's needs as best she could. Finding a pillow for someone's back or helping another to one of the restrooms, which were now running over and reeking of human waste, was all she could manage.

Gagging and choking on her own dry heaves, she went to find refuge in an empty class room to pull herself together. No shower for three days, no food of any substance for almost that long. No clean clothes. She hugged herself in misery and stared through a cracked window. Although this middle-class neighborhood was farther west on higher ground than the flood area, the surrounding streets resembled a war zone.

Dear God. Where are you?

She straightened her stiff back and wiped moisture from her eyes. She must fight off the cynicism, the urge to make a run for it. The grapevine had it that many survivors had found shelter in the city's Superdome. More victims, more chaos—still no food. There wasn't anywhere to escape. Unless she could find someone with a motor boat. Fat chance.

The growling pain started in her stomach again. Images of food drifted before her eyes. A huge plate of bacon and scrambled eggs. A stack of giant blueberry pancakes running over with butter and syrup. Orange juice. A man-sized cafe latte.

* * *

"Y'all have got to help us. My baby's very sick!"

Tess looked up from the table where she'd been reading, in a grating voice, to a rag-tag group of children into the despairing face of Winona Bingham.

"She's got a terrible fever."

Winona's plea jolted her. Another sick child.

Light-headed, Tess pushed up from her chair. She went over and felt the child's forehead and found it warm and clammy. Her eyes, though puffed from crying, looked clear. "I'm not a nurse, Winona, but it could be she's just getting a cold."

"We need help—now!" Winona glared at her from desperate eyes then burst into sobs. "Our home is gone. I can't reach my husband—"

"Here, let me hold the baby. You need to get some rest."

Winona shook her head, swiped at her nose with the back of her hand. Still she gave no resistance when Tess scooped the baby from her limp arms. "I don't know what we're going to do."

"I have an idea," Tess offered, feeling stronger. "Let's go out to the playground for some fresh air. "Bring the children."

Crystal jumped up from the table, an instant spark animating her wide eyes. "I want to go, too."

Like a pied piper, Tess led them across the gymnasium and out into the hot sultry day. At least a change of surroundings might get their mind off the fears of what tomorrow would bring.

Crystal tagged along beside her. "Any more candy bars?" When Tess didn't answer, she scurried away toward a swing set that was miraculously still standing.

The two women found an upright wrought-iron bench facing the school yard and sat down.

Winona swatted at a darting fly and exhaled a ragged breath. "She takes to you."

Tess observed Crystal settle into a swing, chattering to a girl next to her. "She's a lovely child. Where's her father?"

"I don't know. Carrie never talked much about him, except once she said that he was a musician. A jazz musician, I think, from back east."

Tess smiled. "Hmm. Well, she is a music teacher. That would make sense." She scanned the yard to be sure no child wandered off the grounds. "Too bad he's not here to see her grow up."

Winona snorted a short laugh. "I'm betting it was a one night stand. He probably doesn't even know about her."

"That would be a shame." The thought of being left behind to raise a child after her own divorce gave her an uncomfortable twinge. Tess gently bounced Winona's baby girl on her knee and saw a flash of light brighten her dull blue eyes.

"I just hope they can find Carrie..." Winona's shoulders shook with a sudden spasm; tears rolled down her cheeks. "I pray she isn't dead."

* * *

"Here comes Santa Claus." A welcome beaming smile followed John Lincoln's announcement, along with a cart loaded with sandwiches, juice, and sodas.

"Where did you get this?" Tess demanded, her voice dry and hoarse, but her spirits rising. Other famished volunteers gathered round in the locker room.

He gestured to the rear open door where a crew of people brought in boxes on more carts. "The Jefferson Community Food Bank. They got through to us by rounding up some trucks."

She couldn't recall when she'd been more surprised or grateful. "Bless you all." She patted one sweet-faced black woman on her shoulder.

"Y'all have my permission to eat first," John said, his haggard features reflecting the other volunteers' hunger and fatigue. "But make it fast, so we can get the rest out to our guests in the gym."

They all nodded. A feeding frenzy followed. The first solid food they'd eaten in three days.

Tess pushed a loaded cart out to her designated area of the gym. Squeals of surprise came from the children; murmured "thanks" echoed from the adults. A wave of gratitude passed over her just to be able to bring these people something worthwhile.

Later in the volunteers' area, Ken Skeller announced he had finally made contact with the district's rescue team. "They tell me the Guard will start evacuating us early tomorrow."

"Tomorrow?" Tess's knees threatened to buckle beneath her.

"Where to?" a fellow teacher asked.

"Houston. Maybe Denver."

That Tess didn't know a soul in either city didn't bother her right now. At least they would be leaving this devastated place. She needed to make a phone call. Her mother, remarried and living in Germany, would be worried sick. In two or three weeks, she could return to New Orleans and... And hopefully, the water would be pumped out of the city and the school system could rebound.

Settling into her cot at nightfall, Tess drifted into the first peaceful sleep she'd had since before the wild witch Katrina screeched through the city.

* * *

Thursday, September 1

Morning came early. Launching her body into action on the fourth day, without the customary shower and cup of coffee taken for granted in her former life, Tess entered the bustling gymnasium. Occupants were grabbing up their meager possessions. A ragged line of people moved toward the school's front entrance.

To the side of the gym, an elderly man wearing a flimsy bathrobe slumped in his wheel chair. Her breath quickening, Tess hurried over to him and pressed fingers below the man's ear, seeking a pulse. And found none.

She craned her neck toward the entrance where National Guardsmen were in view. "I've got an emergency!" she hollered to one of them.

Realizing her CPR experience was rusty, Tess leaned over to the man's face. His features hung drooped, mouth open. His chest was still, his skin cool to the touch. A terrible dread swept over her. It was no use.

A tall, red-haired Guardsman appeared within seconds, repeated the search for a pulse, couldn't find one, and proclaimed the man deceased. In a rush, he pushed the wheelchair away.

Tess stood in the middle of the gymnasium, her mind swimming like a fish trying to escape an undercurrent. Voices and colors surrounding her melted together. *I've got to focus, pull myself together.*

Houston. Wasn't this group going to Houston? Winona Bingham and her family would be headed there.

She must catch her before she left. Say goodbye and wish them well.

Shaking off the temporary shock of the evacuee's untimely death, she moved toward the line of people in the front of the gym.

She looked for Winona, searching the haggard faces of women with children. Dark, shoulder-length hair, medium height, holding a year-old toddler. Two boys and a girl. So many mothers; so many children. No match.

Buses waited outside. People boarding. Which one would Winona be on? Wouldn't she have tried to seek out Tess before she left? No. Not enough time.

If I just had a cup of coffee. Some orange juice.

Out of breath, she stopped and leaned against a wall near the entrance. Sweat dampened her brow and upper lip. Absently she swiped at her forehead, pulled fingers through her short, dark, oily hair. Her reflection in the large side window scared her. An eerie phantom stared back into her eyes.

Other evacuees milled around in haphazard groups. Maybe Winona hadn't left yet. Maybe more buses would arrive later for Houston.

Impulsively Tess swerved back into the gym. It seemed important that she at least say goodbye to Winona and her clan. They had bonded during these last days, sharing the conversations of women, even though their lives were totally dissimilar.

She made her way to the rear side wall where the Binghams had stayed. Her hopes fell when she saw their empty cots. Then rose when she caught sight of little Crystal sitting with her legs dangling over the far cot. But as she came closer, her gut told her something wasn't right.

The child was sobbing, heart-wrenching sobs that shook her body and wrenched Tess's heart.

"Crystal." Tess sat down next to her. "Where's Winona?"

The child shook her head, misery etched on her tear-stained face. "Don't know...."

Bewildered, Tess slipped one arm around her then glanced down at a folded piece of paper pinned to Crystal's blue T-shirt. "Here, let me see this." She removed the pin and unfolded the paper. Out fell a billfold-size photo of Crystal and Carrie, and a ten dollar bill. Hastily she read the scrawled note, her vision blurring, a hot ember burning in her chest.

Tess,

Sorry—we can't afford to keep Crystal with us.

She likes you. She is a good little girl.

Call her grandpa in Sand Castle, Co. He's her only living kin. Jud Pearl – c/o Jud's Tobacco Shop.

God bless you, Winona

Tess gaped at the note then at the orphaned child next to her. Left behind like a stray puppy—with little more than the dirty clothes on her back.

We can't afford to keep Crystal with us.

Crystal looked up at her, tears glistening in her wide topaz eyes, and hiccupped. "Where's my mommy?"

The earth careened on its axis, out of control. A tightness gathered in Tess's throat. How in the world could she tell this sweet child that her mommy was gone, lost in the flood?

Tess took a shaky breath, tears welling in her own eyes. Holding Crystal close, she said, "I don't know, honey. But I do know she loves you..." Her voice cracked. "Very much."

"I want her. I want my mommy."

Tess gently wiped the child's face and running nose with the corner of a blanket, looked into eyes of innocence and trust. Stunned at her sudden dilemma, she reflected on

27

her previous wandering past. She had only been responsible for herself then. Conflicting emotions tumbled through her mind.

Did she have a choice? Really?

Tess wrapped her arms around Crystal's small shoulders. Whatever troubles awaited her, she could not abandon this little soul.

For now, all they had was each other.

Chapter Three

Weary from the past week's hurricane debacle and carrying their only possessions, the planeload of evacuees spilled out onto a runway at DIA and walked to the awaiting shuttle. Bright sunlight and a warm, dry breeze welcomed them.

Shielding her eyes as she gazed toward the distant blue-green Rockies, Tess expelled a relieved breath. "Hello, Denver." At least they had made it this far, the first leg of their journey west.

"Who's Denver?" Holding Tess's hand, Crystal looked up at her with a puckered frown.

Tess smiled for the first time in a week. "Denver is a city, honey. A place where people live."

"Are we gonna live here?"

"We're going to stay here awhile. Some people are going to help us." Yes, they needed all the help they could get after the harried confusion getting out of New Orleans. So many needy folks, so many questions about each one's future. So few answers.

First of all, she had notified the Louisiana Center for Missing Persons, revealing what little she knew of Carrie Pearl's disappearance and providing Carrie's father's name and address in Colorado.

Without any legalized papers to show that she was Crystal's guardian, Tess had been afraid the local authorities would not let her take the child out of state. But with the mass chaos of hundreds of different disastrous situations, all she'd been required to do was show her identification and fill out a form telling where she was evacuating with the child. The former Lowry Air Base, Denver.

She would rather have driven to Denver, but her car was still parked in the Jefferson school lot. No one was driving anywhere on the flooded roads of New Orleans but authorized search and rescue boats and military vehicles. All she could do was lock it, remove what belongings she could carry, and leave in a rush with the others. Free to take "disaster leave."

What seemed like hours later, a crowded bus delivered them to Lowry. Former Air Force housing on the base would be a temporary home for her and Crystal. A friendly gray-haired woman greeted them and directed the group to a large processing center.

A warm lunch was served in an adjoining cafeteria. The aroma of beef stew, served in generous portions, made Tess almost giddy. Her mouth watered in anticipation as she heaped other side dishes on both her tray and Crystal's.

"Do they have shwimp gumbo?" Crystal asked as they moved along the cafeteria line.

Smothering a smile, Tess shook her head. "Don't think so. You'll like this Denver stew, maybe even better."

Crystal leaned in toward her plate and sniffed. Her eyes brightened. "I think I'll like Denver stew."

They sat at one of the long tables across from a middle-aged black couple. The wife kept patting her husband's cheek. Then he would glance over at her and chuckle. As Tess crammed food into her mouth, she couldn't help but notice how their recent dire circumstances hadn't seemed to faze them.

"Y'all from N'Orleans, too?" the husband asked.

"Yes. I'm Tess Cameron, a teacher on disaster leave."

The couple nodded in commiseration.

Suddenly the wife beamed. "We're on our honeymoon."

Tess took them in, sitting so close to each other. That explained their unabashed affectionate behavior. Nice, while it lasted. "Oh, that's great. Bet you're not too happy with your travel agent."

The husband winked. "We thought we were going to play on the beach in Florida, but Katrina changed our minds."

Crystal cocked her head. "What's a honeymoon?"

"It's when two people get married," Tess offered.

Crystal screwed up her little nose. "Married?" She dragged out the two syllables.

Tess should have known better than to further this subject. Marriage was definitely a tough arena to negotiate. Especially when the newlyweds across the table were studying her now. Probably noticing she wore no wedding band.

Obvious interest filled the wife's question. "Is this your little girl?"

Brain lock. Tess flinched then grappled with an answer while Crystal looked up at her in that trusting way, topaz eyes focused. "Well, no, she's..." My niece? No. Companion? No. Charge? No. So cold. "I'm her teacher and we're on our way to visit her grandfather."

The couple gazed at her, strained smiles transfixed on their faces.

The unanswered questions were too personal, too emotional to reveal at this time to people she'd barely met. Slipping her arm around Crystal's shoulder, she said, "Finish your cake, honey."

* * *

Tess gave the operator her telephone card number and waited to be connected. Thankfully she'd come away from ravaged New Orleans with her billfold and two credit cards intact. Not many were so fortunate.

On the other end of the line, she heard the first ring.

From the corner of her eye, Tess watched Crystal play nearby in the receiving center with several newly arrived evacuee children. Surely Crystal's grandfather would welcome the news that his granddaughter was alive, that she'd survived Hurricane Katrina.

The second ring.

How would she ask for bus fare to Sand Castle from a stranger? She hated asking anyone for money. But this was different—this was Crystal's kin.

The third ring.

How old was Jud Pearl? Was he able-bodied? Perhaps lame?

The fourth ring.

This was a mistake. Crystal hadn't seemed to remember her grandfather at all. Why should he even believe Tess's story when she told him?

She started to place the telephone back in its cradle.

"Hello?" A male voice came over the wire–gritty, perhaps angered at being wakened from a late nap?

Her own voice went dry. "Hello. Is this Jud Pearl?"

"Yeah." In the background, a radio blared a tinny country ballad somewhere far away in the San Luis Valley.

"This is Tess Cameron. You don't know–"

"Who?"

Tess cringed, but plunged ahead. She repeated her name. "I'm calling from Denver. I've got your granddaughter Crystal with me. We've just been evacuated to Denver from New Orleans."

A long pause accompanied by static.

Tess cleared her throat. "I'm sorry to have to tell you this, Mr. Pearl, but your daughter Carrie is missing-"

Was that a snorting response coming over the wire? "My daughter's been missin' for five years."

"You don't understand." Words tumbled miserably in her brain. The receiver on the other end made a hard clunking sound in her ear.

Something mean twisted in her gut. She'd blown it. With a heavy heart, she hung up the phone.

Her glance slid over to Crystal, blending in with the other displaced children. Abandoned. Orphaned. Tess's throat constricted. Not even the child's grandfather wanted to know of her existence.

What could she do about it?

* * *

The long, narrow room where several women and children slept was dark. Except for the light above the door leading to restrooms in an outer hallway. Tess lay on her cot, staring into the darkness, fighting the whirling thoughts in her brain.

What do I do next? If we stay here, it's probably too late to find a teaching position in Denver. What will happen to Crystal?

After a somber dinner with the child, she had given her a much-needed bath then climbed into the shower herself. Her first hot shower since before the hurricane. She'd scrubbed her body until her skin tingled. Then lingered, rinsing with cool water. A luxury that was marred by this afternoon's failed telephone conversation with Crystal's gruff and heartless grandfather.

As angry as she still was at Winona Bingham for leaving Crystal behind, Tess could understand how the woman hadn't been able to tell Crystal the truth about her mother. At dinner she had been a coward herself, unwilling to speak about the unreceptive Jud Pearl.

Now she flopped on the cot, her eyes burning behind her lids.

A whiney moan came from the nearby cot where Crystal slept. Then a high-pitched wail. "Mom-my. Mom-my!"

Swinging her bare feet to the thin carpet, Tess stumbled over to Crystal. The child thrashed from side to side, her skin beneath the light undershirt uncomfortably hot and clammy to the touch. Attempting to calm her, Tess stroked the thick curls. "It's all right, Crystal. It's all right."

Shaking with wrenching sobs, Crystal clung to her. "Mommy..."

A light flicked on across the room revealing half a dozen pairs of eyes squinting open from sound sleep. "Is she okay?" a large black woman asked, her round face etched with concern.

No, she's not okay. Glancing at the woman, Tess could only shake her head.

Crystal's tears continued. "I want to go home."

Her heart aching, Tess held Crystal close. "I know. You had a bad dream."

The woman heaved herself up from the cot, carrying some tissues in her hand. "We know how y'all feel. We'd like to go home, too." Tears glistened in her kind gaze as she leaned over them.

Crystal rubbed her eyes with small fists. "I want my mommy."

The woman's features screwed up into a frown. She stared at Tess, mouthing the words, You're not her mama?

Moisture clogging her throat, Tess whispered, "No."

"My mommy's lost..." Crystal whimpered.

"I'm so sorry, baby." The woman handed the tissues to Tess. "I'm Ms. Celia. Anything I can do to help, you let me know."

Tess nodded as she wiped Crystal's nose. "Thanks."

Ms. Celia plodded back to her cot and several children across the room. The light went off and the room once again plunged into darkness.

Her small body tense, Crystal buried her face in the crook of Tess's neck. "I had a bad dream... You went away...and I couldn't find mommy."

Crystal's nightmare tore at her insides. Rocking Crystal in her arms, she crooned, "Don't be afraid now. I'm here."

Small arms clung to her still. "Don't go away. Sleep here."

The cot barely held both of them. Tess tugged the thin sheet up to her waist and lay with her legs straight downward. "Okay," she murmured, "but don't push me out of bed."

A muffled snicker against her neck. Minutes passed, and then soft even breathing. Inhaling Crystal's sweet little girl's smell, Tess's mind swirled with a crazy mix of hope and fear. No one had ever needed her this much.

How had she ever let herself fall into this dilemma? She: A rolling stone that gathered no moss, a free spirit that traveled alone? Never in her thirty-two years had she pictured herself becoming a mom. Certainly not with her former husband. All she'd wanted was to break loose from him.

Yet, if Carrie Pearl was truly gone, could she leave Crystal with a stranger or strangers?

Was she up to taking care of a ready-made daughter herself?

Tess released a sigh on a ravaged breath. Tomorrow, she would have to think of something.

* * *

Stiff and cranky was not a good way to meet the new day. Tess fumbled around searching for her underwear, dressed herself and Crystal in fresh clothes donated from generous contributions. The thought of real food and hot coffee for breakfast pumped up her spirits a notch.

"I want pancakes," Crystal chirped, skipping into the cafeteria hall, last night's bad dream seemingly forgotten. For now.

During the morning meal, they sat with other families from New Orleans that were still stunned from their recent loss.

"I'm gonna be lookin' for a chef's position," a thirty-something man told the Hispanic man seated next to Tess. "Should be some jobs available at the hotels over by the airport."

The Hispanic, a father of four, glanced over his mug of coffee at his wife across the table. "I need construction work, man. Don't think we're going back to Louisiana any time soon."

Tess munched on a piece of lukewarm toast, swallowing hard. "Denver looks like a nice place to live. The people have been so friendly and helpful."

"Will you stay here?"

She watched Crystal finishing her syrupy pancakes. "I haven't decided yet."

Her decision to stay or leave really depended on a crusty old coot from out on the Colorado plains. Before she made any plans, she knew she had to try once more to reach Jud Pearl. Rising from her chair, she excused herself from the table.

On the first ring, Tess clamped her jaw, determined.

By the second ring, she knew what she would say to old Jud Pearl. She would not let Crystal down without giving it her best shot.

"Pearl's Tobacco Shop." The same male voice but with a more receptive tone. She hoped.

"Mr. Pearl, this is Tess Cameron again. I wanted to let you know that your granddaughter Crystal is staying in Denver with me in temporary housing."

A long pause.

Her chest felt like someone had lassoed her and was tightening the rope. "You do know that you have a four-year-old granddaughter...Mr. Pearl?"

"Nope. No, I didn't know."

The air in this mile-high city was thin, but she hadn't thought it was this thin. *How could he not know?* "Well, Mr. Pearl, I wish you could see her...she's beautiful. And even after what she's been through...the hurricane, losing her home...her mom—"

"Hold on, girl. Hold on." The voice sputtered, gruff but now more interested. "You say she's got nobody? Where is her mom? Where is Carrie?"

Tess clutched the phone, attempting to keep her cool. "I don't know. I was told she was driving a car that washed away in the Katrina flood waters."

A choking sound traveled over the wire.

Tess closed her eyes, hoping she'd struck a sympathetic cord. "Mr. Pearl, you are Crystal's only living immediate family. Won't you consider letting me bring her up to see you?"

"This town ain't much. I don't have nothin' to offer." The gruffness had evaporated from his voice replaced by a forlorn drawl.

"Crystal needs you, Mr. Pearl. She needs to know her grandfather. I can bring her to Sand Castle on the bus." Tess worried her lower lip, waiting for the reply she prayed would come.

"Well..." The old man cleared his throat. "Guess you could do that. Tell me where yer stayin' and I'll wire you the bus fare."

Her heart did a double somersault. "She'll be so happy when I tell her. You're going to love her..."

"Don't get yer hopes up, now. I don't get along much with kids." The old raspy critter voice. "If you come, ya'll have to find yer own place to stay. I don't have room to put ya up."

Tess shook her head, not knowing whether to thank the old coot or tell him she didn't give a gosh darn whether he liked kids or not. "That's okay." She'd find a way to take care of Crystal somehow, if it didn't work out. She gave him the information then ended the conversation. "We'll come up as soon as you'd like."

Back in the communal room where she and Crystal were staying, she shoved their meager belongings in two donated backpacks. A few pairs of shorts, T-shirts, light jackets, not counting the clothes on their backs. Staring at Crystal's backpack, the thought that it contained no dolls or toys, possessions every child should have, made Tess's heart ache.

Scampering into the room from the hall, Crystal stopped short when she saw the packs sitting on their narrow beds. "Where are we goin'?"

The lilt in Tess's voice was as bright as she could muster. "To see your grandfather."

Topaz eyes widened in her small, curious face. "Where does he live?"

"In a town by the mountains."

Crystal's lips came together in a pout. "No. I don't want to see him. I want to stay here."

Tess reached out to touch Crystal's shoulder. "But he wants to meet you."

"No!" Defiant eyes bored into hers. "I don't want to go." Backing away from Tess, she flung herself against the wall, crocodile tears slipping down her cheeks. "I want to stay *here*."

A heavy vise clamped onto Tess's chest, the past week's unbelievable events racing across her mind. Tragic for any adult to remember, let alone a small child. An orphaned child. Two rescue shelters in that brief space of time. No wonder she didn't want to leave the first place that provided safety, food, and other survivors of the storm.

Tess struggled to pull out the right words that would make sense, that would assure Crystal. Sitting down on the edge of the bed, she forced a smile. "Of course, you like it here. The people in Denver have been very kind to us."

Crystal stared at the floor, nodded her small head. "I have some new friends."

"Yes, Frankie and Shanelle," Tess agreed, referring to two of Celia's children. "But you will make new friends where your grandpa lives."

Once again, the lower lip jutted out. A new, glistening tear slid over Crystal's cheek.

Tess reached out and drew Crystal into her arms. "We'll take a fun bus ride there...and, I know you like popcorn, huh?"

Crystal glanced at her, her expression dubious, but not quite so disagreeable. "Yeah."

"Well, I'll buy you a big bag of popcorn to take on the trip." She finished with a squeeze and a kiss to Crystal's temple.

The lower lip retracted, feathery eyebrows raised. "With buttah on it?"

A smile and a hug. "You bet. With buttah on it."

The sigh of resignation came next. "Well...okay."

Inwardly Tess sighed, relieved for the moment. At least they had come to a tentative agreement. What was waiting for either one of them at the end of the bus trip, she could not predict nor make any promises.

After breakfast the following morning, as they were leaving the dining hall, Celia's son, Frankie, came scurrying up to them. "Hey, Crystal," the six-year-old called, his dark eyes bright with urgency. "Do you want our cat?" The small squirming cat he held meowed in protest.

Tess had seen the children playing with the three-legged, short-haired tabby during play breaks outside the facility, but thought it lived here on the base.

Crystal scooped the cat from him, cradling it next to her chest.

Taken aback, Tess shook her head vehemently. "Thanks, Frankie, but Crystal really can't have a pet where we're going."

Her chin beginning to tremble, Crystal stroked the cat.

Gently lifting the cat from Crystal, Tess proceeded to hand it back to Frankie, who shifted from one energetic foot to the other. "You tell your mom thank you, but–"

"We can't keep her," Frankie said. "Mama wants you to take her."

A commotion to her left and Ms. Celia shuffled over to the group, a hot pink T-shirt covering her swaying wide hips. "Did Frankie tell you we got a new apartment?" Her large hands came together in a praying position. "Thank you, Lord!" Her exuberant gaze lifted skyward, then back to Tess still holding the bewildered cat. "We can't keep the kitty; no pets, they said. Wouldn't Crystie like a new little friend?" Ms. Celia'a luminous brown eyes fixed questioningly on Tess.

Oh, brother. A cat of all things. Tess didn't really like cats. Feeling like a skinny bag of bones in her hands, the feline meowed up at her. Its agate-green gaze probed hers. "I don't think so. How did it lose its back leg?"

Ms. Celia's expression saddened. "The rescue shelter told us she was in a car accident and she nearly died. She's a good natured little thing. Very sweet. She's a year old, with all her shots, and she hardly eats anything."

Crystal reached up to stroke the cat. "Can we keep her? Please, can we keep her?"

Tess gingerly looked at the cat as it tilted its petite head and wiggled long white whiskers. "Well, it's not that I have anything against cats. But I don't know where we'd find a place for her."

As Crystal continued petting the small creature, the cat nestled against Tess's breast. And purred.

"I'll take care of her," Crystal promised in her serious child voice.

Tess closed her eyes, sensing a weak gene in her DNA. The gene that couldn't say no.

"She comes with her own travelin' cage." Celia offered up a ready-made cat cage, complete with blanket and various toys.

"You said the cat has its shots?"

Ms. Celia nodded, smiling.

"She likes me," Crystal added, her eyes wide with anticipation.

A soft heart was something Tess had always scoffed at. No such thing. Live by your own rules. Keep things uncomplicated. She'd be crazy to take a cat on this long road trip. Simply crazy.

Even as she answered, Tess sighed in resignation. "Well...okay. I guess we can make room."

Crystal leaped up like a little frog and bundled the furry creature into her arms. "Thank you. Thank you!"

"What kind of cat is she?" Tess asked Celia.

"Just a tabby. We never got around to calling her anything but kitty-cat."

Crystal nuzzled her new pet's pink nose. "I'm going to call her Miss Tabby. Now, Miss Tabby," she addressed the cat, "How would you like to meet my new grandfather?"

Tess turned away, gazing out the dining hall windows toward the mountains. And how would Grandpa Pearl like to meet Miss Tabby?

Chapter Four

Splashes of sun filtered through pillow clouds over the vast open plain of the San Luis Valley. A valley so wide it took her breath away. Outside the bus, afternoon winds blew across shrub and sparse grasses, painting the landscape shades of ochre, yellow and pale green. To the east, the magnificent Sangre de Cristo Mountains rose in the distance. To the west, the San Juans stretched like a guardian wall for miles ahead.

A complete contrast of climate and mood from where they had just come. Here, little water, lots of sand and endless blue sky. Behind them, ruin; ahead, if they were lucky, an open door.

Inside the bus, Tess shivered beneath the constant air conditioning. Crystal played with the striped tabby in the window seat next to her. Since reboarding in Salida after a lunch stop, Tess had allowed her to remove the cat from its cage for some exercise. The two were bonding nicely as only small creatures could. Shutting out the rest of the world and its woes.

Tess removed a light sweatshirt from her backpack and slipped it over her head. "Are you cold?" she asked Crystal.

"Uh-uh." Batting her long lashes up at Tess, she draped the cat around the front of her neck like a fur collar. In her new, bright yellow top and cotton slacks, she made a striking image. Hair in barely manageable curls, skin the hue of lightly toasted almonds.

Smiling down at the child, she pointed out the window to the rising mountain range. "Look at those purple mountains. How tall do you think they are?"

Crystal lowered the cat to her lap and looked out in that direction. "Don't know. But they almost touch the clouds." She frowned. "Is that where we gonna live?"

"Not in the mountains but near them."

Crystal considered the idea. "Will Winona be there?"

Here came those same questions again. Tess slipped her arm around Crystal's narrow shoulders. "No sweetie. Remember, Winona and the boys went to Texas to find their dad. He had to get a job there."

"Why?"

"So they could find a new home."

"Why?"

"They couldn't stay in New Orleans because the storm washed away so many houses."

"Is my mommy in Texas?"

It felt like someone had just kicked her in the stomach. Answers were quickly becoming harder to come by. "I don't think so," was all she could manage.

"Can I see everybody in Texas?" Crystal persisted.

Tess's throat ached. "Maybe...some day you will. But now," she said, her words rushing forward, "you're going to a new place, too. You're going to meet your grandfather—and you'll be busy with new friends."

Crystal sank lower in the seat and pulled at Miss Tabby's ears until she meowed sharply. "Will grandfather like me?"

Tess laced her fingers through Crystal's. "Does a bear like a honey pot? Of course, he will."

As if satisfied for the moment, the child returned to her play friend but soon lost interest. It was time for Miss Tabby to go back in her traveling cage beneath the seat.

From her backpack, Tess pulled out a coloring book and crayons, a gift from the volunteers at Lowry, and watched Crystal color with bold hued crayons. An uneasy feeling nagged at her; questions darted around in the back of her mind. How welcoming would Jud Pearl be of his never-before-seen granddaughter? A bi-racial child with an unknown father.

From the window, the giant San Luis Valley loomed ahead of them. Did the warm winds carry happy tidings or an ill omen? Were people from the West so different in their views than people anywhere else?

What makes you think you can do this?

A certain queasiness curled into a ball inside her. Howard had spoken these words to her on the day she'd walked out of their apartment to start a new life, without him. Leaning against the bedroom doorframe, his lower lip tilting upward in a cynical smile, her ex-husband had mocked her as he often had when he thought he held the winning hand. She squeezed her eyes shut against the painful image.

Two years had passed since her hard-fought divorce. And she'd moved on, to regain her self esteem, to support herself. But the sharp-edged memory still caused her throat to close in need of fresh air.

"How long 'til we get there?"

Crystal's question compelled Tess to retrieve the Colorado road map stuck in the seat pouch in front of her. "Well...we're turning onto the Six Mile Lane," she said, peering ahead to more open golden plains as the bus took them closer to the Sangre de Cristos. "Shouldn't be too much farther."

Munching on her half-finished bag of popcorn, Crystal was still full of questions. "Will we see some buffalo?"

"Could be. They live out here."

Intent on spying some of the foreign creatures, Crystal stared out the window, long enough for Tess to apply some lip gloss and gather her thoughts, but not quell the unease that had settled in the pit of her stomach.

* * *

Whatever her preconceived idea of Sand Castle might have been, its stark simplicity surprised her, after coming from the lush greenery of New Orleans. The dusty town, surrounded by scattered trees too scraggly to cast much shade and low-scale buildings, reminded her of the western movies she'd seen in her childhood. Trucks of a certain vintage and a few SUVs traveled the road. A hardware store, two western-style motels, a setback grocery store, small coffee shop, and leather goods business dotted the main street. Around the corner from a gasoline station, the Greyhound driver ground to a halt in front of a one story building which obviously served as Sand Castle's bus station.

Would Jud Pearl be waiting inside for them?

Tess gathered up their belongings, took Crystal by her small warm hand, and followed the few passengers deboarding the bus. From the front window of the weathered building, Tess caught sight of their reflection: an intent thirtyish woman with short unruly hair and a precocious four-year-old carrying a three-legged cat in a cage. Quite a trio.

No one inside the station identified himself as Jud Pearl so Tess approached the bus station attendant, a rotund man wearing a faded green baseball cap.

Five minutes later, after learning that Pearl's shop was two blocks south, next to the Java Jug, they headed in that direction. The early afternoon sun beat down on their uncovered heads, the cat Tess now carried in its cage meowed mournfully, and Crystal dragged along beside her. Guess she'd hoped for too much, to expect ol' Jud to welcome them as they got off the bus.

"Where we goin'?" Crystal whined.

"Up the block to meet your grandfather."

"I'm thirsty."

"We'll get something to drink in just a while."

They reached the end of the block and crossed the street, walking past an ice cream parlor.

"I want some ice cream," Crystal demanded.

Tess prayed for patience. It wouldn't be long before the kid met her kin and she could make plans to ease out of the picture. Once a rolling stone always a rolling stone.

Finally she saw the sign—Jud's Tobacco Shop—up the street and hurried their pace.

"Don't pull so hard." Crystal's voice held the same fear Tess felt but would not admit.

Ahead a tall man wearing a light colored western hat and denim jeans stepped down from a newer model truck parked in front of the Java Jug. He paused at the curb to let them pass. Touching his hat brim, he said, "Afternoon, ma'am." His voice was tinged with a slight drawl. Tess acknowledged his polite manner with a nod then forged ahead. As he ducked into the café, an intoxicating aroma of brewed coffee escaped from inside.

In the next few seconds, her hand was on the door handle of the tobacco shop, her palm clammy, her brain blanking out the smooth introduction she'd planned. Then they were inside. The heavy door banged shut behind them. Cigarette smoke assailed her nostrils as she blinked and gazed into the hazy interior.

The place was small: an aisle with a straight shot to the back with a counter on one side and shelves filled with various tobacco products on the other. Except for her and Crystal, the store was empty. A twangy western ballad drifted from the rear.

"I'll be right with ya," a crusty voice called from the back room.

Setting the cat cage on the worn hardwood floor, Tess glanced into Crystal's wide eyes. Her eyebrows arched and her chin lifted as if to say, What now?

Tess smiled stiffly and straightened just as a gray-haired man and a scruffy yellow dog swung from the back room into the shop. She stepped toward the man, taking in his wiry build, draping mustache and beard-stubbled jaw. "Mr. Pearl?"

The man frowned, more like scowled, at her. "Yeah?"

"I'm Tess Cameron," she began as the yellow dog loped past her, jowls jouncing, to sniff at Crystal, who put her hand out toward him.

"I–we just got off the bus from Denver– "

Jud Pearl squinted from her over to Crystal, his frown deepening. "Who is she?"

With a bright smile, Tess said, "This is your granddaughter, Crystal." She turned to the child and motioned for her to come over to her.

"She can't be no granddaughter of mine," the old man shot back, his voice tinged with a sarcasm that caused an angry heat to flare up Tess's neck and face.

At that moment, the dog broke into a barking spasm. The cat hissed at him from its cage.

Crystal let out a shriek.

Pearl pointed a knobby finger. "Hey, get that cat outta here."

Tess ran to the cage and picked it up as the guard dog growled low in its throat, eyeing her with suspicion. Crystal broke into tears and grabbed onto her leg. "I want to go home!" she wailed.

Mortified, Tess pulled the door open. "I'll be back," she called over her shoulder as she scooted Crystal and the caged cat outside.

"Old coot," she muttered under her breath once they were out on the sidewalk. She'd brought Crystal all this way just to come face-to-face with a prejudiced old fart.

"Huh?" Crystal wiped her eyes with the back of her hands. "What's a 'old coot'?"

Tess shook her head. "Nobody we want to know."

The child looked up at her, obviously puzzled. "Was that man my grandfather?"

"You know, I'm not really sure it was him." She glanced at the large front window of the Java Jug next door. The memory of brewing coffee beckoned. "Hey, let's go into the café and get something good to drink while we think about it."

Crystal nodded agreeably, following Tess through the door. "Miss Tabby don't want to go back to that place. She don't like that big ugly dog."

"Doesn't," Tess corrected as they slipped into a red, faux leather booth. "Miss Tabby *doesn't* like that ugly dog." When she set the cat cage on the floor beneath the table, her hand shook. Well, this wasn't turning out to be such a warm reception. And darned if she had a clue of what to do next.

Taking in the customers seated around the comfortable, western-style café, Tess noticed a few obvious tourists wearing visors and walking shorts, and other male locals. At a table in the far corner about six men relaxed over a late lunch, several wearing western, brimmed hats. What did they do for a living around here?

When a large-boned, busty blonde waitress approached, Tess ordered a root beer for Crystal, some water for Miss Tabby, and a café latte for herself. While Crystal hummed a little tune and fiddled with the salt and pepper shakers, Tess contemplated their immediate future in Sand Castle. She wasn't about to go back and confront Jud Pearl right now, even if she did have a scrap of proof that Crystal was indeed his granddaughter. In her billfold was the photo Winona had left behind of Carrie hugging Crystal in front of a Christmas tree, dated December of 2004.

Then again, they were stuck here for at least a while. And reality was knocking on her front door. Also in her billfold was a mere twenty-eight dollars, plus some small change, and a credit card. She had to keep the balance manageable since she currently had no means of support. If she was going to stay here and make her case for Crystal with the crusty old man, she needed to find a job.

The waitress brought a tray with their drinks and a plastic bowl for the cat's water. "Thanks so much," Tess said, smiling up at the middle-aged woman. At least someone was hospitable in Sand Castle. She read the waitress's name on her name tag. "Say, Jerri, would you know if there are any available jobs in town?"

The woman's dark eyebrows slanted into a V. "Hmm, nothin' in town." She thought for a moment. "Do you cook?"

Are you kidding? "Well, I –"

Jerri nodded toward the table of men in the corner. "Grant Wilder's been lookin' for a cook out at his ranch. The pay is pretty good."

Tess must have displayed a dubious expression as she took a mental note of how many meals she'd actually cooked in the last year.

With a wink, Jerri added, "He's kind of quiet, but I hear he's a nice guy to work for."

Tess mulled over the comment about the pay being pretty good. "Which one is he?"

"The only guy who took his hat off at the table. In the blue shirt."

The waitress hustled away to another customer, leaving Tess to observe the rancher in the blue denim shirt, sitting in profile to her. She recognized him—he was the one who'd paused at the curb as she and Crystal hurried by to see Jud Pearl. Collar-length, light brown hair, in his mid-thirties, long legs disappearing under the table.

Suddenly the room became very warm and her hands perspired. Who was she trying to fool? She was no cook.

She glanced across the table into Crystal's wide eyes, the sweet trusting glance of an orphaned child. Well, it looked like she had no choice.

She fluffed her fingers through her hair, hoping it didn't look too disheveled, and slid out of the booth. Her donated tank top was a bit too tight and her chinos wrinkled. Nothing she could do about it. "Stay here. I'm going to talk to a man at that table about something important."

With feigned self-confidence, Tess walked toward the all-male table. The image of a seagull tip-toeing over to a bunch of conversing crocodiles crossed her mind. The blue-shirted man glanced up as she approached. "Hi," she said. "Are you Grant Wilder?"

He immediately unfolded himself from the chair and stood. "Yes, ma'am," he answered in a low voice, a curious smile at the corners of his mouth. "What can I do for you?"

A sudden silence at the table made Tess acutely aware that all ears were tuned to their conversation, even though all eyes politely gazed in other directions.

She cleared her throat. "I'm Tess Cameron, from New Orleans. I understand you have a job opening at your ranch?"

He cocked his head, the afternoon light from the front window revealing a day's tawny beard stubble along his jaw and fine lines fanning out from his hazel-gray eyes. "I sure do." He glanced behind them to an empty booth. "We could talk more about it...over there...if you'd like."

It seemed ridiculous, with her education credentials and job history, that her head felt as light and transparent as a soap bubble. Applying for domestic work on a ranch couldn't require that many skills. "Fine," she said.

In the booth, the leathery upholstery conformed to her derriere, smooth and cool. The minor discomfort was

51

having to look directly into the rancher's face at such close proximity. Tess hadn't had occasion to carry on conversation like this with any male under eighty since her divorce. "What kind of job is it and what is the pay?" she shot out, more quickly than she'd intended.

Grant Wilder leaned back against the booth, his large tanned hands resting on the table. "Well," he drawled slowly, "I need a cook, breakfast and lunch, someone to keep the place straightened up." His hazel eyes gazed matter-of-factly at her. "You have some experience at cookin'?"

Momentarily taken off balance, Tess studied the plastic table cloth. "Well, I can fry an egg and make a pretty tasty stew." She glanced back up at him, hoping he didn't notice her knees knocking beneath the table. Actually she was used to eating on the run, grazing as her Midwestern farm cousins would call it. "I helped my mother bake pies...."

His expression bordered on the amused. Was he going to make a smart remark? Like how long ago was that—twenty years? Instead he asked, "You're from New Orleans?"

From the corner of her eye, Tess saw Crystal lift the cat cage from beneath the table and set it on the seat next to her. She and the cat seemed absorbed in each other. Thank goodness she wasn't hanging on her, making annoying demands as so many kids her age would have. "Yes. We just arrived an hour ago."

Wilder half-turned and looked over at Crystal and her companion. A light smile creased his face. "Your kid?"

"No. I'm her temporary guardian until she can be reunited with...a relative here."

We watched the news about that hurricane down there. Sounded like a lot of destruction." When she merely nodded, his eyes softened. "So, you need a job—and a place to stay?"

Lord, she hated him to think she was begging. Truth was, she sure didn't want to have to start paying motel bills on her dwindling funds.

"There's a cabin near the house where you could stay...if we agree on the job." He licked his lips in a thoughtful way. "My truck's outside. If you and the girl want to ride over there with me, you could give the place a look. I'll bring you back, if it doesn't work out."

She found herself bobbing her head. It was the best offer she'd had all day, and the day was growing short.

He slapped his cowboy hat on his head and tipped the brim forward. "Well, let's go."

After he made room behind the seat for their backpacks and the cat cage, Tess boosted Crystal into the front seat of the truck, a newer model Silverado. She climbed up and stretched the seat belt across them. Having quickly explained that they were going to visit a special place where there were a lot of animals, Crystal had tacitly agreed. Any concern that she might balk at the idea, now disappeared.

"This is a big truck!" Crystal exclaimed, scanning the wide windshield. "Look at how high we are."

Grant Wilder turned the key and the engine rumbled to life. His glance slid sideways. "Must be your first truck ride."

Crystal nodded vehemently. "Uh-huh."

He drove a few blocks then turned the truck onto the main road. "This your first trip to see the mountains?"

Crystal peered up beneath the brim of his hat. "Uh-huh. Mommy took me to the ocean once."

An unformed question appeared on Wilder's face. Tess was thankful he didn't ask it. Now was not the time to bring up Crystal's mom. The sad mystery remained as to whether she had survived Katrina.

Changing the direction of the conversation, she asked, "Do you have children...to help you with the ranch, Mr. Wilder?"

His eyes focused on the road. His knuckles seemed to tighten on the wheel before he answered. "No. Never had any."

An awkward pause followed. "I never did either," she volunteered, gazing out the window at scrub oak and the mountain range ahead.

Did her potential future employer have a wife? She bit back that question. Too personal. She would soon find out. If he did, she obviously didn't do much of the cooking.

He turned on the radio to a western music station. The song had a good beat to it. She didn't recognize the female singer. Just as she started to tap her toe, he flicked the radio off.

"You want to stay around here for awhile, or are you just passing through?"

His focus was still on the road. The question was a difficult one. "That depends."

"On getting a job?"

"No. It hinges on Jud Pearl."

For some reason, her answer jump-started his attention. He swung his hazel-gray gaze over to her. "Jud Pearl?"

A red flag went up. Better not give away too much of their business, before she'd had a real chance to talk to the old coot. "We came here to--"

"We came here to find my gran–" Crystal blurted.

Tess hugged her around the neck, interrupting. "Remember our secret, honey."

Gossip in small towns, she'd heard, traveled like wildfire and she didn't want their sensitive mission to be revealed just yet.

Crystal jutted out her lower lip. "What secret?"

"I'll tell you later," she whispered. Glancing at Grant Wilder, she was relieved to see him concentrate on the road and not their business.

Ahead the afternoon light accented the mountain range in shades of soft blue. She pointed to a taller mountain on the right. "What peak is that?"

"It's a beauty, isn't it? That's California Peak. One reason why my granddad settled here."

Tess smiled. "I can see why. What a beautiful place to be...so far away from civilization."

"Not anymore. But I wouldn't want to live anywhere else." Grant turned onto the highway, driving parallel to the mountains, with clusters of tall pine bordering the road.

"What kind of a ranch do you run?"

"I'm an outfitter. During the summer, I hire my horses out to camping parties. And I work construction jobs the rest of the year to keep the place going." His sideways glance caught her eye. "Do you ride?"

That question threw her. "Not really. Not since I was a kid." She did a double take. Cooking was one thing–riding horseback on a mountain top was another.

A short distance up the road, Grant turned and drove under a large, weathered, overhead sign that read, Wild Pine Ranch.

This was going to be a challenge. She'd never worked on a ranch before.

In a sudden barrage, apprehension peppered Tess's thoughts. What hurdles lay ahead for her and Crystal at the Wild Pine Ranch? And, could they surmount them?

Chapter Five

They drove down a dirt road, through scattered towering pine, like an oasis in a desert. Ahead, an opening revealed a large ranch-style frame home set back from the road. A sprawling horse corral and a two-story, faded red barn beckoned from beyond bordering trees. A Mexican man, wearing denim work clothes, waved from the corral as he led two mahogany horses from the barn.

Grant waved back. "That's Juan. He's my foreman and right hand man. He knows horses inside out."

Tess nodded, observing about twenty more horses grazing in a nearby open field.

"Can we pet them?" Crystal asked, looking longingly out the wide windshield.

Tess squeezed her small hand. "Maybe we'd better watch them first. They're pretty big."

"Here's the house." Grant pulled the truck to a stop at the edge of a wide front yard and they all climbed out.

With Grant leading the way, Tess followed, carrying Miss Tabby in her cage, Crystal on her heels. She noticed a porch swing, painted white, and a large terra cotta planter sitting next to it with the straggly remains of summer flowers.

Crystal eyed the swing, moving invitingly in the slight breeze. "Can I swing on it?"

"Maybe, in a while..." Tess answered, unsure if she should let her stay outside by herself.

"Sure she can. I bet your kitty would like to get some fresh air," Grant said.

"Okay, but don't let Miss Tabby out of the cage. She might run away."

Grant swung the big outer door open and Tess stepped inside onto a knotty-pine floor. She blinked, her eyes adjusting to the semi-dark.

He led the way into an open great room. "I hadn't planned on havin' company, but make yourself at home."

"Thank you." The make-yourself-at-home was a nice touch. She hadn't heard that offer in a very long time.

The great room was comfortable, complete with worn, man-sized furniture, a cowhide footstool and leather recliner. Western memorabilia and framed photographs decorated the dusty end tables and shelves. Thick ashes were piled in the floor-to-ceiling stone fireplace. She breathed in a stale smell that begged to be aired out. A closed up kind of smell. It was a home designed for comfort, but seemingly neglected for some time.

Grant removed his hat and hung it on a nearby hat rack. His sandy-blond hair seemed molded to his head. "Imagine you'd like to see the kitchen." He strode across the floor, down a hall, and through a doorway.

She followed, thinking he was a man of few words. He got right to the point.

Entering the kitchen, she was instantly overwhelmed. It was king-size. She took in the light wood cabinets, dark granite counter tops. The large gas range. The big window over a double stainless steel sink drew her. She looked out at a breathtaking view of the Sangre de Cristo peaks. One could stand here watching the rising sun every morning.

"How about somethin' cold to drink?" Grant opened the refrigerator door and stuck his head inside, his wide shoulders blocking her view of the contents. "A Coke?"

Her throat was parched from the ride out of town. "Sure."

He opened two cans of the soda and handed her one, a kind of shy smile at the corners of his mouth.

"Thanks." The cold drink slid down her throat real easy. It felt rather strange, yet good to be sharing a moment with someone adult, a completely new male adult, away from the ravages of Katrina and its aftermath back in New Orleans. Of course, she couldn't put those exact thoughts into words. Instead she said, "It's...good to be somewhere new."

One of his eyebrows lifted, a look of understanding passing over his face. "I'll bet."

Grant moved over to the stove. "This is a real fine range. I put it in myself."

Tess stared at it. The digital window in front. Lots of push-button pads. Could she measure up?

Suddenly he said, "My wife used to whip up some great meals on it." Then he stepped back a bit, his expression going stiff.

Used to? He could be divorced. His former wife was a good cook. Tess's stomach twisted uncomfortably, at her own apprehension and his obvious reluctant comment.

"Got any good cook books?" she quipped, glancing at an adjacent shelf.

He pointed to an overhead cupboard. "There's some stuck away up there."

She hoped he didn't notice her deep sigh of relief. "I'm pretty good with recipes–aside from the usual stuff."

That brought a semi-satisfied nod.

"And I'm a whiz at baking chocolate chip cookies," she added.

Grant broke into a grin that made her think she'd reached first base. "I never turn down a homemade cookie."

She took another sip of her Coke, reflecting on what her job would require. "So, how many meals a day would you want me to fix?"

He cocked his head. "How about breakfast and lunch? There'll be Juan and his son Carlos, and me. You can have dinner on your own–either fix it here–or in the cabin."

Ah, the cabin. How quaint would that be? Hopefully it had running water and indoor plumbing. "Yes. I'd like to see it."

"You got it." He went back toward the fridge. "Do you want to take Crystal something to drink?"

"Sure. Do you have any fruit drinks?"

He pulled a small bottle of juice from a shelf. "Apple okay?"

"That's great." When he handed her the bottle, his roughened fingertips brushed hers creating a strange sensation in her. Yes, a man who lived on a ranch would have work-roughened hands. His were also generous.

Leaving the kitchen, they passed a side room, obviously used as an office. Her glance took in clutter. "Your office?"

Grant half-grinned over his broad shoulder. "Sorry, should have closed the door. Don't like to advertise my mess to visitors."

She smiled to herself, reminded of the old saying about bachelor pads.

Then Grant halted directly in her path. Tess stopped in the second before colliding into him. "You have any office experience?"

"Well, I am...or was until recently...a teacher. Why?"

He swiveled his tall frame around to face her. "A teacher... You must be organized."

Uh-oh. Why couldn't she have said she'd been an artist or a taxi driver instead?

A thoughtful expression reflected in his eyes. "I sure could use some help in there. Like straightening the files, answering the phone. Keeping up the calendar. I'd pay you extra for that, of course."

Tess glanced at the piles of paper and general disarray. It was a boar's nest. She squirmed. "Well...I..." Then again, a computer with a large monitor sat on the desk. It would be a definite means of locating information on Carrie, and Crystal's birth record. And extra pay sounded good. "Could I use the computer to do some research on Crystal's records?"

Grant nodded agreeably. "It's a deal. Better look at the cabin, though, before you decide."

His boot heels clicked across the hard wood floor. She tagged along, hoping for the best.

Located about a half acre behind the main house, with a tall pine in the front yard, the cabin beckoned. A real log cabin like she'd seen on the labels of maple syrup bottles. Only larger.

"This is a cute house," Crystal said, toting a curious Miss Tabby still in her cage.

Just ahead of them, Grant pulled the screen door open. "It needs some airing out."

Tess and Crystal walked over a circular, braided rag rug into a cozy front room. A small stone fireplace with windows on either side greeted them on the opposite wall. A blue-and-green plaid couch and an overstuffed side chair sat before it. Beyond the front room was a kitchen and, on the other side, a door opened into a bedroom.

Grant moved into the bedroom and opened a window. "The place hasn't been used for a while. Our handyman, ol' Tom Bick, lived here till he died a couple years ago."

Tess stood in the doorway, looking at the single bed, figuring she and Crystal could sleep in it all right. The attached bathroom had a shower. The kitchen was rather dark and small, but seemed adequate. A pine table and chairs fit next to the wall in one corner.

Grant observed her sizing up the place. "Well, what do you think?"

"Does the stove work?" Tess asked, taking a peek in the oven.

"Should. Put it in myself."

She'd heard that before.

"I'll have to connect the refrigerator. Easy to do." He pushed his hat brim higher on his forehead.

Tess nodded slowly. "What do you think, Crystal? Would you like to stay here a while?"

Crystal had plopped onto the sofa with Miss Tabby. She wrinkled her nose. "It's kinda dusty..."

"We can clean it up pretty quick." Tess smiled. "Maybe Mr. Wilder would let you pet one of his horses."

Crystal darted a questioning look at Grant. When he nodded in the affirmative, she said, "Well, okay."

Tess turned to Grant. "Guess it's a go. Did you say the cabin comes with the job? Or do you require a deposit?"

"Cabin comes with it. We can take things month-to-month. See how it goes."

"That's fine with me." There was no telling when or if her old job would be available. And at least she wouldn't get trapped into signing any lease. She dropped the backpacks she'd carried from the truck onto the side chair. Grant set to work hooking up the refrigerator.

"Well, would you like me to start by cooking dinner tonight?" Tess asked after he'd finished. Her offer held a bravado she didn't feel. What in the world could she fix, right off the top of her head?

He waved off her question at the front door. "Couldn't have you do that. I'll be the chef tonight. Hope you two like buffalo burgers."

Crystal's eyes grew bigger. "Buffalo burgers?"

Grant grinned, reminding Tess of a modern-day John Wayne, big and broad shouldered. "You're gonna love 'em, honey. They'll build up your muscles." He winked. "See you about six."

He swung out the door and headed toward the main house.

Looking after him, Tess shook her head, wondering what she'd gotten herself into. Never mind tonight. Tomorrow, she'd be expected to cook breakfast for three hungry men—besides Crystal and herself. She'd better grab a few of those cook books in the kitchen cupboard. And hope the kitchen gods chose to smile down on her.

* * *

"Mr. Grant is a good cook," Crystal announced as they got ready for bed later.

"Yes, he is. I know you liked your buffalo burger." She realized she'd forgotten to pick up a few of those cook books in the kitchen. Oh well…too late to plan a menu tonight.

Tess tugged on the second pillow case and tossed the pillow onto the bed. The sheets she'd found in the small linen closet smelled musty, but they would have to do until she could do a wash in the main house.

Her body suddenly felt bone-tired. The unbelievable events of the last ten days weighed on her like a boulder dragging her down beneath a deep, dark sea.

After they both climbed in under the covers, she whispered to Crystal. "Don't forget to say your prayers."

A sigh and a pause next to her. "I don't know how."

Tess frowned up at the shadowed ceiling. "Didn't…didn't your mom ever say a prayer with you at bedtime?"

"Uh-uh."

This would be a challenge. The past week had probably been the toughest in Crystal's young life. Tess had to admit, although she thought of herself as a spiritual person, moving from one Air Force base to another as a child had prevented attending any church on a regular basis. Right now, she didn't have a clue of what to say to God. "Well—put your hands together—like this."

Crystal folded her hands on her chest, imitating Tess. "What do I say?"

"Hmm." She cleared her throat, thinking. "You know when people talk about Jesus...?"

"At Christmas time. He was a baby in the manger with the sheep and cows."

"Yes. Then, Jesus grew up to be a man. He loves children. Pray to him to watch over you."

"You mean Jesus is like an angel?"

"That's right. The most important angel in heaven."

"Is he watching over Mommy?"

A lump formed in Tess's throat, making words difficult. After a moment, she said quietly, "Yes...wherever your mommy is, Jesus is watching over her."

She wanted it to be true. She wanted to ease Crystal's mind. At any rate, she wanted to believe that every soul had a chance to move on to a higher place. Tess closed her eyes, listening to Crystal whispering in her sweet child's voice. She stroked Crystal's arm. "Goodnight."

* * *

Hours or minutes later, the moaning came at the edge of her consciousness. Then stronger sobbing. Heat burrowed into her side.

"No...no...no!"

Like talons, small fingers grasped Tess's arm. Blunt objects kicked at her legs. She jolted halfway up from the narrow bed, her senses reeling.

Crystal clung to her, half crying, half whimpering. Another nightmare.

"What's wrong, honey?" Her own voice sounded rough as sandpaper.

"The water is coming," Crystal sobbed in her ear. "I'm afraid."

Wrapping her arm around the child, Tess comforted. "No water is coming here."

"The big rain storm– It will wash us away."

"No, baby. We're safe in Colorado. We're far, far away from the big rain." She began to rock Crystal, back and forth like she used to rock her dolls to sleep at night. The nights when the airplanes flew over the newest air base and she was afraid.

In her arms, Crystal's small body shuddered then calmed.

Tess hummed a song she'd heard in Sunday School years ago about angels. She sang a verse then made up a phrase or two. Rocking away the pain.

Long after Crystal's breathing eased and she'd fallen back to sleep, Tess stared into the corner of the unfamiliar room. Unwanted images of Katrina's devastation drifted before her. Houses ravaged. Through a bus window—a body floating face down in someone's yard. Cars strewn everywhere, some ending up on rooftops, some in tree branches.

Carrie–where did the storm take you?

A loneliness, an emptiness, seized her. Her heartbeat quickened. Would Jud Pearl see her again?

She had to talk to him. And soon.

A wild animal howled at the pale moon somewhere in the valley. A coyote?

Willing her eyes to close, she breathed deeply. The child sleeping next to her needed to find a normal life, a sense of security. She would try her best to make that happen.

She needed to be a pillar of strength to help Crystal. But where could she find a safety net in case she stumbled in the effort?

* * *

Morning came too early. Only a faint light peeked through a crack in the curtain when the distinct chirping of birds reached Tess, cocooned in the bed covers. Yawning broadly, she stretched and rolled over onto Crystal, who groaned in half-sleep. She frowned at her wrist watch lying on the bed stand. Five past six.

Yikes! Grant had said the men came in for breakfast at six-thirty.

She jerked upright, tossed her legs over the side of the bed. "C'mon, sugar." She gave Crystal's bottom a quick shake. "We gotta get rollin'...up to the big house." She shuffled over to the narrow bureau and pulled two sets of underwear from the drawers.

Then, scooping Crystal from beneath the top blanket, Tess guided her into the bathroom.

"I don't wanna go to the big house," Crystal mumbled.

With forced enthusiasm, Tess said, "Of course, you do. Breakfast is waiting." Breakfast was waiting all right—to be made. She turned on the shower spigot, stripped off her nightshirt and Crystal's, and hustled them both inside the stall. Ordinarily, she would have showered Crystal first, but this was no time to be modest. Using an old bar of soap, she lathered a clean wash cloth and scrubbed Crystal, much to her squeals of protest, and then herself.

"You have bumps," Crystal said, touching the side of Tess's left breast.

Right, that was about the size of them. "They're called breasts." She quickly rinsed the soap off Crystal's back.

Crystal giggled. "When will I get breasts?"

Tess attempted a straight face. "When you get to be a grownup."

Ten minutes later, hurriedly dried and dressed, they made their way across the back yard to the house. Crystal insisted on bringing Miss Tabby, in her cage, as the cabin's kitchen cupboards were bare.

No one answered at the back door, which she found unlocked, so they entered. Tess went right to the kitchen and started getting out some pans. The coffee maker and a can of ground coffee sat in a corner of the counter, and the filters were stashed in a drawer below. Grabbing a teaspoon from a flatware drawer, she stopped and reconsidered. Didn't men like strong coffee? She put it back and took a large tablespoon instead.

How long had it been since she'd actually made a pot of coffee? Couldn't remember.

Starbucks on-the-run had been her mainstay for the last several years.

By the time Tess had plugged in the coffee maker and absconded with eggs, milk, orange juice and bread from the refrigerator, she heard the low timbre of Grant's voice drifting in from the outer great room. Other male voices accompanied his. A streak of jitters scampered down her arms, causing her to overshoot the side of the mixing bowl as she cracked an egg. The yolk slithered onto the counter in an amoebic puddle. "Shoot!"

"Hey, looks like our new cook's already at work," Grant said, striding into the kitchen. "Coffee smells good."

Quickly wiping up the egg with a nearby hand towel and trying to smile instead of grimace, Tess glanced up. Her new employer's sandy-blond hair appeared combed with an egg beater, his features tanned and almost roguish. A towering figure of a man, Grant stood gazing expectantly at her from across the kitchen island. "What's for breakfast?"

"Ah, thought I'd just fry some bacon and scramble some eggs," she answered, self-conscious as she slapped a hunk of bacon in a heated pan. The bacon instantly smoked and bubbled, sending her in search of the overhead fan button. Aware of her own disheveled hair and lack of makeup, Tess wished she'd had time to make a better appearance this morning.

"Sounds good. I'll wait with the men in the other room. Call us when it's ready."

She nodded, leaving the bacon to finish setting the long table by a bay window. "Can you put the coffee mugs around at each plate, honey?" she implored Crystal.

"Okay." The child left the cat in its cage and, on tiptoe, set the mugs around the table.

Tess was dishing up when Grant stuck his head around the corner. "Can I help?"

She released a nervous sigh. "Sure. I could use some help making the toast."

At last, the meal was ready. Grant introduced Juan and Carlos, quiet dark-haired men, who then sat down at the table. Pouring coffee into the men's mugs, Tess wondered where Crystal should sit. The child stood to the side, watching the adults with large, questioning eyes.

Before she could ask, Grant pulled a cushioned chair away from the table. "Here, join us Crystal. We all need to get acquainted."

Grateful for Grant's thoughtful gesture, Tess served the platters of steaming eggs and bacon. Everything seemed to be going well until she sat down herself and tasted the coffee. And almost choked. Black as pitch, bitter as gall, it stuck in her throat.

Grant heaped sugar into his mug and stirred.

It was kind of him not to remark on her obvious lack of coffee making skills. Embarrassed, she said, "I'll get some milk." Quickly finding the milk carton, she returned to the table.

"My grandfather couldn't drink his coffee without milk and sugar," Grant remarked, filling his mug to the brim. The other men did the same.

"Miss Tabby would like some milk too," Crystal said.

Tess raised one brow. "If you say please."

Crystal jumped out of her chair, smiling. "Please!"

"I'll get a bowl for her." Tess got up and found a small bowl in a cupboard.

When they had finished breakfast, Grant pushed his chair away from the table. "I've got to help Juan with the horses this morning," he commented in her direction, "but I'd like to drive into town and get groceries this afternoon. Do you and Crystal want to come along and help?"

Tess nodded. Driving back to town was a good idea. Maybe she could stop in to see Jud Pearl. "We'd love to help with the shopping."

Grant paused at the kitchen doorway. "You did a good job on breakfast."

She wasn't so sure. "I hope to do better, but thanks."

Juan and his son Carlos smiled politely as they followed Grant out of the room. A second later, she heard Juan remark to Carlos when he thought they were out of earshot. "Bet I could have tarred the barn roof with that coffee."

Chapter Six

As the road brought them closer to Sand Castle, anxiety became Tess's albatross, settling into her stomach like an immovable rock. Her mission, as her job-oriented father used to call his ordered tasks, was also intractable. To see Jud Pearl again and convince him, first of all, to believe that Crystal was his blood kin. Secondly, to *accept* her as such.

That she dreaded this mission was a fact she tamped down inside herself.

Behind the wheel of the truck, Grant spoke over Crystal, seated between them. "Feel free to add to the list," he said, referring to the grocery list he'd handed her just before they started out. "Whatever you all like."

"We like buffalo burgers!" Crystal announced. "And ice cream."

"So do I," Grant agreed. "I've got frozen buffalo, but we need more ice cream."

Tess's anxiety eased for a moment. The kid knew how to make brownie points. "Okay." She pulled a pen from her small back pack. "Think orange juice and cereal might be a good idea."

Grant turned off the exit onto the town road. "Did you say you wanted to run an errand first?" He glanced sideways at Tess. She noticed he had shaved since this morning and put on a clean shirt. To his credit.

"Yes. I really need to stop in at Jud Pearl's shop."

His eyes crinkled up at the corners. "Don't tell me you're a smoker, Tess?"

"No," she said emphatically. What the heck, she had to reveal at least part of her reason to see the old man. She'd been tip-toeing around it ever since he hired her. "I have some important...ah...family business to discuss with him."

69

He nodded in understanding, his eyes shaded beneath his hat brim. He found a parking spot a few spaces down from the tobacco shop and pulled in. "How long do you think it'll take?"

Tess pressed her lips together, the tamped down anxiety rising in her chest. "Not long, I hope." She glanced over at Crystal, eager to get out of the truck and release some pent-up energy. "Would you mind keeping an eye on her for a few minutes? "

"No problem. Maybe we'll check out the ice cream store."

"Yea!" Obviously smitten, Crystal flashed a sparkling smile at Grant.

"Thanks...a lot." Tess connected with his hazel gaze, sending him a look of appreciation. "I'll be as quick as I can."

Entering the tobacco shop took more courage than she had acknowledged. At the end of the counter, the old man stood finishing a sale to a customer. His grumpy yellow dog lay curled up in the opposite corner. It looked at her with fleeting interest. Who knew what kind of mood the proprietor would be in today.

She fingered the photo in the side pocket of her back pack then strode up to the counter with an ease she didn't feel inside. He turned rather stiffly, his small eyes showing recognition, his hair shaggy, his long gray mustache drooping at the sides of his mouth.

"Hello, Mr. Pearl," Tess chirped before he could boot her out. "I was in the other day and we talked, but I didn't get to show you something that should be of interest."

The frown in his receding forehead deepened. "What's that?"

She whipped out the photo and handed it to him. "It should convince you that Crystal is truly your granddaughter."

Gingerly he took the photo and reached for a pair of glasses near the cash register. He stared at the picture of Carrie and Crystal for a long moment.

Tess's palms sweated. How could he not believe after seeing for himself? "They do have a resemblance, don't you think? The shape of Crystal's face, her smile—"

"That's Carrie, all right. But this don't prove anythin'. She was–is a teacher, ain't she?"

"Yes, she was."

"Well, this could be one of her students." He shifted his weight from one foot to the other. "Shoot, she could've just got herself in trouble with some black man. Or maybe this girl lost her folks in Katrina and yer tryin' to pawn her off on me."

Hackles rose on the back of her neck, but she fought against the urge to spit out a sarcastic remark. "Did I tell you that Carrie's cousin, Winona Bingham, left the photo with Crystal?"

"That name don't sound familiar to me." He scratched his unshaven jaw. "My younger brother's kid was named Winona... They stayed in Louisiana years ago, after me and my wife moved up here."

"I know this is a very difficult situation, for you and for Crystal. The storm has left thousands of families separated and lost. But, I can tell you honestly that I would never go to this length, put my own life on hold…" Tess's voice cracked. "And come this far on a guess."

Jud stared at the floor. The dog in the corner stretched and yawned.

"I haven't been able to get onto a computer or call anyone in New Orleans to follow-up on Carrie yet. Or locate Crystal's birth certificate. But I will soon."

He gave a short laugh. "Good luck. Things are a fine mess down there about now."

Starting to pace, wondering what to say next to persuade him to give her a chance, Tess glanced out the front window and saw Grant and Crystal enjoying their ice cream cones outside on the sidewalk. "Please come here, Mr. Pearl. You can look and see the resemblance for yourself."

Old Jud took his time, first straightening some tins of chewing tobacco on the counter, before slouching up to the front of the shop. Squinting through his glasses, he leaned forward. "Is that Grant Wilder?"

"Yes. I've taken a job as cook and office assistant at his ranch. Crystal and I are staying on the property, for now."

Jud swiveled, observing her with new interest. "Grant's a good man. Honest. Hard workin'."

Before she could comment on her gratitude, Jud added, "It's been tough on him since losing his wife a few years ago."

Losing his wife?

"I didn't know..." She saw Grant lean back against his truck's front grill, and a sudden empathy tightened her chest. Losing a loved one to death had to be more painful than losing them to divorce, especially when you no longer loved them.

Finishing her cone, Crystal looked through the window at Tess and waved.

"I know Crystal would like to come in and say hello," Tess exaggerated.

Jud's reply was gruff. "Well, bring her in here. I don't see so good with these old glasses."

She opened the door and beckoned Crystal inside. Entering the shop hesitantly, Crystal eyed the dog in the corner, now snoring raggedly. She hovered near Tess and slowly looked up at Jud.

His mustache twitched as he sized her up. "What's yer name?"

"Crystal," came the small voice.

"What's yer mama's name?"

A tiny frown creased Crystal's brow. "Carrie."

Tess slipped a protective arm around Crystal's narrow shoulders.

The child looked up at her. "Can we go now?"

"Pretty soon, honey." As much as Tess wanted Jud Pearl to come around to the truth, she would not let him intimidate his granddaughter.

Crystal studied Jud. "Who are you?"

Obviously taken off guard, Jud took a step backward, his grouchy expression faltering.

Behind his glasses, his eyes got watery. "I–" With a shake of his shaggy head, he turned away.

Disappointed and dejected at his response, Tess took Crystal's sticky, ice-cream hand and headed out the door. What was the old goat thinking? Was he really all that hard-headed, or was he simply confused?

Outside, Grant was still leaning back against the truck, his arms folded over his broad chest. Tess averted her eyes, wanting to avoid him and the entire situation she found herself in. She wished she could take the next bus out of Sand Castle and pretend none of this burden ever happened or existed.

But Crystal was tugging at her hand. "Is that crabby man my grandfather?"

Startled at Crystal's question, Tess glanced up into Grant's surprised expression and expelled an exasperated breath. "That's what we want to talk to him about– when he's ready."

Hurriedly she pulled open the truck door and boosted Crystal inside. She climbed up beside her, fuming at her untenable position.

Grant slid in behind the wheel. He didn't seem in any hurry to turn on the ignition, just sat for a minute, his hat slanted over his forehead. Finally, when she was near bursting with frustration, he half-turned and looked at her. "You want to talk about anything?"

"Yes, I do." She reached into the side pocket of her backpack, fished out the photo, and handed it to him. "You've lived here for some time." She pointed to Carrie. "Do you recognize this woman?"

Grant's eyes widened in recognition. "Carrie Pearl." He shook his head in amazement. "I haven't seen her in years-"

"That's Crystal's mom."

He handed the picture back to her. "And Jud won't accept it?"

"Not yet." She gave Crystal the photo to hold. She wanted to tell him more about Carrie's disappearance during the flood but couldn't in front of Crystal. "He's driving me up a wall."

"Think we'd better drive over to get some groceries first."

Still in a huff, she darted a glance back at him. "Yeah," she agreed as he started the ignition. Her anger eased for the moment.

On the way home, Crystal curled up in her lap and fell asleep. Gazing down at her, Tess fought back the renewal of unresolved emotions. An unbidden tear slipped down her cheek. She swiped it away and stared out toward the Sangre de Cristos.

Grant interrupted her mood. "Hey, this started out a pretty fine day. Don't let old Jud get you down."

Tess shrugged uneasily. "With that man's attitude, I doubt if he'll ever believe Crystal is his granddaughter."

In his quiet mannered way, Grant said, "I believe you."

Her throat constricted. Sympathy only made her more vulnerable. "Thanks. Now, all I have to do is prove it to him."

* * *

Later in the afternoon, while Crystal took a nap, Tess went up to the main house to use Grant's computer. He had some work to do with Juan, but had invited her to feel free to search the Internet as long as she needed.

Setting some of the stacked papers aside, she quickly got online, glad that his software was familiar to her. Finding the Louisiana government offices page was one thing, but seeking information and finding it was another. She clicked on several links, but realized finding answers about Carrie Pearl was going to be an arduous task. It seemed thousands of people were seeking loved ones lost during Katrina. New Orleans was a disaster zone and Baton Rouge had become the makeshift search center. She filled out a missing persons form and submitted it, hoping someone somewhere could help her.

Tess rested her elbows on the desk, her head in her hands. She rubbed her temples, slid her fingers through her hair. The fear that Carrie may never be found trickled into her mind. Denial of her death was childish. Even Crystal had seemed reticent to bring up her mother's whereabouts today. And Jud had hardly leaped for joy when he'd viewed the photo, which made him appear callous. Couldn't he have shown some emotion? The photo didn't convince him. No, he wanted proof. DNA proof.

Now, that may never be a possibility.

Her eyes burned. She rubbed them, exhaled deeply, and sat up in the chair. To her left, on a crowded shelf just above the computer screen was a silver-framed, five-by-seven photo of a man and woman, happily embraced. The man was Grant, standing behind a lovely blonde woman, his arms draped around her. Captivated for some unknown reason, Tess gazed at the picture. She lifted the frame from the shelf, studying the young woman's features: high forehead, light green eyes, heart-shaped face. And a perfect cook.

An unfamiliar twinge of discomfort zigzagged through her. Was it insecurity? Envy? A brief memory of Howard floated before her eyes. His handsome arrogant face. When had he last embraced her in such a loving way?

The sound of boot heels on the office hardwood floor made Tess jump.

"How's it going?" Grant asked then halted just behind her.

Tess swiveled in the chair, holding the photo awkwardly. "I just noticed–"

His expression beneath his hat brim sobered. "That's me with my wife Laura. She...died a few years ago."

Heat burst up Tess's neck to her face. She started to replace the photo, but Grant took it from her and set it back on the shelf. His sudden entrance had put them both in an embarrassing, uncomfortable position. "I'm really sorry...I never meant to intrude."

"No problem," he said, brushing aside the uneasy moment. "Some people are arriving for a camping trip the end of the week. I've got to make a call and firm up some details."

Tess jolted from his chair. "Oh, sure. Thanks for letting me use the computer."

His gaze softened. "Did you have any luck?"

She shook her head, not wanting to admit her early disappointment. "No, not yet. But I've just started."

"Right. There must be lots of web searches you can check out." He settled down into the chair and reached for the telephone.

Tess excused herself and backed through the doorway. *Lots of web searches you can check out.* Lots of searching ahead. Lots of chaos and red tape. And waiting.

She tore out the rear screen door, banging it shut behind her.

* * *

"Can we pet the horses?" Crystal looked up at Tess, her eyes shining like bright amber buttons.

Smiling, Tess took her hand as they left the cabin and headed over to the large corral beyond the cottonwood trees. "I'll bet we can find at least one that won't mind."

Tess had brushed the child's hair, carefully pulling it up into a ponytail, the thick texture still a challenge to manage. Crystal had played most of the morning with Miss Tabby, but became bored with being inside. Seeing the horses from their front window, Tess decided it was time to introduce themselves to a few of the other residents on Wild Pine Ranch.

Inside the corral, Carlos stood brushing a tall Appaloosa. Two other smaller brown horses lingered beside the barn door.

Crystal broke free of Tess's hand and romped ahead, her ponytail bouncing, the new blue jeans given to her back at Lowry snug across her nicely rounded bottom. "Hi, Carlos," she called, waving.

Tess sprinted to catch up as Crystal reached the corral fence and peered through the space between the rough-hewn slats. "Hey!" Tess caught Carlos's eye. "That's a big guy there. What's his name?"

Glancing shyly over at them, Carlos continued stroking the horse's back with the brush.

Tess leaned against the fence. "The horse. What's his name?"

He nudged his hat brim back. "Sergeant."

Sergeant? Hmm. Did the horse like to give orders?

"Tess, lift me up!" Crystal attempted to climb up onto the first railing on the fence.

"Okay." Tess leaned over and lifted her to stand on the middle railing, her head still barely reaching the height of Tess's shoulder.

The afternoon sun danced across Sergeant's powerful flanks and rump. He switched his long black tail, swatting away a fly.

Crystal gazed imploringly up at Tess. "Can I pet him?"

"Maybe." As Carlos finished brushing Sergeant's rear legs, Tess called out, "Could you bring Sergeant over here so we can see him?"

Carlos angled his head her way. "I will bring him." Guiding the horse by his halter, Carlos maneuvered him around and led him toward the fence. Smartly stepping, Sergeant bobbed his large head.

"Say, he is a big one," Tess said, admiring the animal's size and agility.

Just as Sergeant neared them, he raised his dappled gray face and whinnied, as if in greeting. His black mane flared dramatically about his massive neck.

Impressed with the flamboyant gesture, Tess steadied Crystal so she could reach up and pet Sergeant's soft muzzle. But in that very moment, Crystal let out an ear-splitting shriek and jumped down from the fence railing, landing on unsteady feet. "What's wr— "

Crystal's small features contorted into an angry, fearful mask. "I don't like that horse. He's mean!"

Stunned at her sudden outcry, Tess tried to coax Crystal back into her former good mood. "Oh, honey, Sergeant's really friendly."

"No...no!" Spurting tears, Crystal stumbled backwards, then turned and bolted toward the cabin.

Her shoulders sagging in disappointment and empathy for Crystal's fragile emotions, Tess turned to Carlos. "I'm sorry. She was so excited to pet the horse..." Tess left him and hurried across the yard to give Crystal solace.

But Tess knew whatever she said probably wouldn't ease Crystal's fear. It went too deep. And what could she say to assure her that life wasn't full of frightful and mean things?

"Hey there!" a male voice hollered from the front yard.

At first glance, Tess couldn't be sure if the wiry built man wearing a plaid shirt and baggy pants held up by suspenders was who she thought it was.

"Is Grant at home?"

The raspy voice confirmed her recognition. Jud Pearl. The old coot himself.

And he wanted to see Grant—not her or Crystal.

"He's probably in his office," she called back then made a beeline toward the cabin's back door. She didn't have the time or inclination to talk to Jud anyway. She and Crystal had come all the way to Colorado to see him and he'd acted offended, disbelieving everything Tess had revealed to him about his daughter's disappearance and his granddaughter's existence.

Crystal hovered behind the screen door as Tess approached, her small face blotchy, her eyes red-rimmed. A lump as large as a boulder filled Tess's throat, but she drew on whatever reservoir of strength she had left and went inside the cabin to comfort her.

Chapter Seven

At sunset, Tess left the confining cabin walls and wandered over to the corral. Crystal was tucked in, sound asleep after a solemn supper. Tess had attempted to explain that horses had different ways of expressing themselves, sometimes loudly, but were still friendly animals. But a disinterested stare had come into Crystal's eyes and Tess might as well have been chattering to a mannequin. Crystal had gone back to play with Miss Tabby, a smaller less threatening critter.

Reaching the corral fence, Tess leaned against the top rail, its surface rough-hewn to the touch. Was Crystal sinking into some kind of clinical depression? Afraid of anything outside her immediate safe world? Nightmares. Outbursts of fear and anger. Weren't they telltale signs?

Even if Tess could afford one, where would she find a child psychologist in Sand Castle, Colorado?

Slashes of magenta and orange streaked the western sky, the sun a fireball melting into the San Juan Mountains. On a regular kind of day, the sight would inspire a Van Gogh or a Remington-conscious moment. The single awareness she felt was a ponderous weight descending upon her. The challenge of uniting Crystal with her grandfather only provoked anxiety. And second thoughts.

Why had she *ever* taken on this responsibility?

It would have been easier, probably for both Crystal and Tess, to turn the child over to a rescue authority. The state could have found her a caring foster home until the search for her mother was finished. Jud Pearl would have been contacted and eventually traveled to New Orleans or invited Crystal to stay with him here.

She squeezed her eyes shut, releasing a shuddering breath. Who was she kidding? In the frantic aftermath of

Katrina, the absolute chaos of missing and misplaced people, Crystal would have been shuttled off to some godforsaken holding area like a lost puppy. It had been everyone for himself. She swallowed hard. Even Crystal's cousin Winona, in her panic to save her own children first, had left Crystal behind. Tess tried not to blame her. Tragedies brought out the best and the worst in folks.

What road was there to take now? Unbidden tears pricked her eyelids and leaked from her eyes. Brushing them away did no good. The water behind the damn had been welling up for the past two weeks. A roiling ache rising in her chest. Tess leaned over the railing, buried her face in her hands, and released pent up sobs.

Seconds or minutes later, the sound of boot heels scuffing through dirt made her peek through her fingers.

Hat brim slanted over his rugged features, wide shoulders crowding out the space around him, Grant Wilder strode toward her from the barn.

She froze. The last person she wanted to see right now. Her new employer, a powerful man, a man who ran a straight-forward business. He would expect more from an employee than to discover a cry baby wimp.

Starkly embarrassed, she pulled back from the fence, sweeping her fingers over her wet cheeks. A complete weak sister. So this was what it felt like.

He came to a halt on the other side of the fence. "Hey, didn't know you got that sentimental over a sunset."

She dared look up through tear-spiked eyelashes. His expression held concern behind the attempt at levity. "Yeah. I didn't either."

He rested his hands on the top railing. Large, strong hands. Her knees weren't to be trusted beneath her. She was glad the fence separated them. Falling against that hard-muscled chest would only bring her further mortification.

He got right to the point. "You and Crystal okay?"

"Sure," she shot back. Then gave a swipe to her nose. "No."

"You two have been through a lot." He pulled out a rumpled handkerchief from his back pocket and offered it to her. "Want to talk about it?"

Tentatively she accepted the handkerchief, dabbed at a stray tear, blew her nose. She clung to the handkerchief, not wanting to return it soiled. "Oh, it's just that...the road's a little bumpier than I'd expected."

He nodded, understanding in his eyes. "Always is. Not that it can't get smoother – as you go along."

She glanced off toward the setting sun and back to him. "Right now, I don't know. When I decided to be Crystal's guardian, just till I could unite her with her grandfather, I thought he would be a lot more receptive. And she's not doing so well..."

"Did she catch something on the trip up here?"

"It's psychological. She's having nightmares. The other night, she was afraid a flood would come here, just like it did in New Orleans." Tess rubbed her forehead as if she could rub away the memory. "And today, even though she wanted to pet him, Crystal freaked out when your big Appaloosa whinnied at her."

"Sergeant? He is a big guy. Too big for a little gal like her."

Tess snuffled back another wave of emotion. "I'm afraid she'll want to stay in the cabin forever and never want to interact with the horses again."

Grant tilted his hat back above his dusky eyebrows. "Most kids are afraid of big animals, at first. That's something we can work on."

If only she could be so sure. "And Jud, that old goat. How can I work on him? He's the most stubborn man I've ever met."

"You know, Jud came by this afternoon."

"Yes, I saw him in the front yard."

"He wanted to tell me he called New Orleans, actually Baton Rouge, trying to find out any information about Carrie."

Tess sniffed, unimpressed. "At least he's acknowledged that she's missing. He wasn't so keen on recognizing Carrie's daughter in the photo yesterday."

Grant moved his hand a little closer to where hers rested on the fence rail. "I think ol' Jud is kind of overwhelmed at what's happened—he just needs some time to let everything sink in."

Doubting it, Tess shook her head. "Will he ever accept Crystal? Want a real relationship with her?"

"He probably will. Years ago, Carrie left the valley and Jud has never reconciled himself to it. He's still bitter."

"That's pretty obvious." Tess glanced back toward the cabin. "It just makes things more difficult—for Crystal."

The sound of unfamiliar bird calls pricked the descending twilight. Tess raised her gaze as a significant number of large birds circled widely over the valley floor. "Khrrrr, khrrrr!" came their throaty voices.

She watched in awe. "What are those?"

"Sandhill cranes...making their getaway south for the winter." He tilted his head back to get a better view. "Big fellas. Their wing spread is over six feet."

"Really? What do they do up here in the desert?"

Grant gave a low chuckle. "They've been busy nesting and raising their young in the low lying marshes.

Now they'll just fly on over the Arkansas River, through the mountains, to a warmer place."

Above them, the dark-winged birds spiraled higher, around and around, their strange calls becoming fainter. Running her fingers through her short hair, Tess sighed. "Hmm. Wish I was a sandhill crane."

Grant's voice was sympathetic. "I know what you mean. I felt the same way a few years ago."

Lowering her gaze, Tess concentrated on his strong, angular features. "But you didn't pick up and go."

He shook his head, a kind of private mask pulling down over his face. "I wanted to...for a while. Then I got over it."

When she didn't answer, he said, "Don't worry too much. Things will work out."

"Yeah," she responded in a low voice, unconvinced.

He touched his hat brim and stepped back. "Well, I've got an early day tomorrow. Goin' out on that weekend camping trip."

"Right." An early morning meant up before the rooster. "See you at breakfast."

"You can make it a light one," Grant called over his shoulder as he moved to the gate. We'll be having a big meal mid-day. I hired on a cook."

"Oh. Okay." A sense of relief filled her. She would have her hands full, playing receptionist, ranch sitting, and watching Crystal while he was gone. She waved, lingering at the corral fence for one long moment.

In the southern sky, the cranes had become tiny dots, their throaty cries barely audible.

* * *

After Grant and his camping party, a group from Illinois, left for the weekend, the ranch became a different place. Quieter. Still new and somewhat strange. Juan and Carlos hung around during the morning doing some chores, then drove off in their rusty truck for Alamosa. They wouldn't return until Monday morning. Roy Briggs, a retired rancher in the valley, would come by to feed the remaining horses on Saturday and Sunday morning.

Although Grant left a detailed list of instructions and phone numbers for her, Tess still felt like an interloper of sorts. He'd said she could drive the truck into town if she needed anything, but it was big and she didn't really like the idea of getting behind the wheel just yet.

Saturday morning, with renewed energy, Tess lit into the task of straightening Grant's office. From the window, she could watch Crystal playing in the yard with Miss Tabby, now a bit freer to explore her new territory. Tess pulled up a large waste basket and methodically went through every dusty stack of papers, tossing outdated brochures, advertisements, and filing miscellaneous correspondence. She dusted and polished the office furniture, avoiding a glance at the desk photo of Grant and his late wife. Why she avoided it, she wasn't sure. Maybe seeing the happiness in their faces would only make her uncomfortable. After vacuuming the carpet with a vengeance, she settled down to search Internet sites for the latest Hurricane Katrina survivor information.

Not surprised, she found sketchy data. The vast area was still in a state of chaos. Frantic pleas for assistance were posted in several New Orleans chat rooms. Loved ones and pets were missing. Neighborhoods still flooded with decaying debris. Citizens continued to be stranded in various outlying parishes. She came away frustrated and depressed.

To escape, she went to the kitchen and got out several cook books from the upper shelves. Food was a source of comfort. No one could deny that. By noon, Tess had book-marked breakfast and lunch recipes that tempted her taste buds and would hopefully satisfy the men's appetites.

She cooked a spaghetti and meatball dinner that evening, and even found a few used candles in a kitchen drawer to make the meal special. They made the kitchen a little cozier, in spite of the absence of its owner. Crystal perked up, too, setting the table for them.

The kitchen phone rang while they were cleaning up the dinner dishes. Tess wiped her hands quickly and answered. "Hello. Wilder residence."

"Hi. It's Grant." The mellow timbre of his voice came over the wire.

"Oh...hi."

"Just called to see if everything's okay."

"Everything's fine here."

"Good. Did Roy come by today?"

"Yeah, he did. He's kind of quiet, but he took care of the horses."

A pause hung in the space between them. She didn't think Grant was the kind of man who went in for small talk. "Oh, I cleaned your office this morning."

"Uh-oh." The smile in his voice was obvious. "Guess it was a boar's nest."

"Well, not too bad." *It was a boar's nest.* "Just didn't want you to think I'm taking it easy, watching the grass grow..." That was dumb. Why had she said that? "How's the camping trip going?"

"Great. Haven't heard too many complaints about saddle sores. We grilled some steaks for dinner. Gonna kick back by the fire for a while."

She envisioned the group, relaxing around a comforting fire after a hearty meal, sharing stories and probably a few jokes. "Sounds...nice."

"Well." She heard voices in the background calling Grant to join them. "Thanks for keepin' the place goin'. We'll get in later tomorrow afternoon."

"Sure. Have a good trip back." Tess placed the phone back in the receiver. From the window, she watched streaks of orange and purple glide across the evening sky. A discomforting wave of loneliness washed over her.

"Tess..." Crystal tugged on her jeans pant leg. "Can we have some ice cream?"

Glancing down at Crystal brought her to the moment. How could she have felt so alone?

She bent down and enfolded her in an impulsive bear hug. "Of course we can. Let's take a look in Mr. Grant's freezer and see what we can find."

They found a recently opened container of Rocky Road Supreme and Tess dished out large scoops into two bowls. Carrying their ice cream desert outside to the front porch, they sat in the swing and watched the evening shadows deepen.

The sound of Grant's mellow voice lingered in her memory. He was a good, reliable man. She felt gratitude toward him, the way he'd hired her on the spot. Whether she and Crystal came with a ton of emotional baggage didn't seem to bother him. He'd given her the benefit of the doubt, that she could handle the job. He'd trusted her to oversee the ranch while he was gone when she'd only been here a few days. He'd trusted her.

She took a bite of the decadent chocolate Rocky Road and let it melt slowly on her tongue. She listened for the sandhill cranes, thinking a few more might travel overhead again, but heard nothing of their throaty cries. What had Grant meant when he'd commiserated with her desire to fly away like one of them?

The deep grief he had suffered over his wife's death must have given him reason. They had something in common, both losing partners in a relationship they had thought would be permanent. The only difference, besides his wife's passing, was that Tess had been fooled.

A horse whinnied over by the barn and Crystal slid closer to Tess.

"Hey," Tess reassured, squeezing her small shoulder. "That's nothing to be frightened of. One of those fellas is just saying goodnight to us."

Chocolate ice cream rimming her mouth, Crystal darted a look up at her, then kicked her short legs against the underside of the swing.

* * *

From the edge of sleep, a male voice intruded. What was he saying? Who was he?

Lying beneath the light covers, Tess forced her heavy eyelids open and listened. The voice rambled on, drifting through the partially open bedroom window. It sure didn't sound familiar, couldn't belong to Juan or Carlos.

She slipped her legs over the edge of the mattress and got out of bed, careful not to wake Crystal sleeping beside her. Tiptoeing on bare feet to the window, she peered past the opening in the curtains. The sun lifted over the distant San Juan Mountains, tinting the sky with a rose pink glow. Inside the corral fence, the hired man Roy Briggs, carried on a one-sided conversation with at least six of the ranch horses.

Although she couldn't make out the words, from the tone of voice, it sounded like he was giving them instructions for the day. The stocky man brought out several feed bags from the barn and dropped them over the horses' heads.

From the bed, Crystal rolled over on her pillow and yawned, still half asleep. Lavender shadows arced beneath her eyes, mocha hair billowed around her small oval face. A displaced child floating between the past and present. At least there had been no nightmare last night.

"Hey, little girl." Tess patted her bottom through the blanket. "Get going, now. We don't want to waste this beautiful day."

After a light breakfast, Tess hurried Crystal out the cabin's back door. Holding her hand, she headed toward the corral. "We should meet Mr. Briggs and make sure he's doing his job for Mr. Grant."

Her hair pulled up in a springy ponytail, Crystal nodded. "When will Mr. Grant come back?"

"Later this afternoon."

At the corral fence, they stopped and watched the hired man check one of a mare's back hooves. "Hello," Tess called. "You must be Mr. Briggs."

The man she guessed to be in his late fifties turned toward them, ran a thumb over his bristly gray beard stubble. "They call me Roy." He sauntered over to the fence and extended a sturdy hand.

She shook it, admiring the strength of sinew and bone, the calloused palm. Roy was no slacker.

"I'm Tess Cameron and this is Crystal. We're watching the place for Grant...Mr. Wilder...while he's gone." She guessed that sounded rather obvious.

Roy glanced from her over to Crystal. He was probably curious as to her relationship to Crystal. "Nice to meet you," he said, then sauntered back across the corral.

Crystal leaned against a wooden railing, her eyes taking in the horses munching on their breakfasts.

"Ah, Roy..." Tess called after him. "Would it be all right if we came inside and got a closer look?"

He waved. "Sure. Just don't stand too close to their rear ends."

"Let's go see if we can talk to the horses," Tess encouraged as she slipped through the space between the middle railing. Crystal did the same but needed a little assistance to jump to the ground. Her legs were too short.

They watched while Roy removed the feed bags and the horses stepped away, a few wandering off to the side of the corral.

"Do you brush the horse's teeth?" Crystal asked Roy.

Roy gave a short snort of a laugh. "Nope. But maybe I should."

Tess guided Crystal over to a smaller brown mare with a docile face. "Hey, do you want to pet this girl?" Tess stroked the horse's wispy black mane.

Crystal studied the horse. "Is she friendly?"

"That's Sugar. She's real gentle," Roy commented from behind a larger pinto.

Tentatively, Crystal reached out her small hand toward the mare.

Crystal's intrigued expression sent a spark of hope through Tess. Horses were people animals, weren't they? Children loved horses, didn't they?

The child's fingers touched Sugar's front flank for a moment. Then she withdrew shyly.

"Here, I'll lift you up to pet her nose." Tess scooped Crystal up and held her close to the horse's face.

Crystal stared into wide-set large brown eyes.

"It's okay. Just touch her nose and feel how soft it is."

Her fingers reached out again, grazed the long muzzle. Sugar tossed her head slightly.

With all the energy of a jumpy four-year-old, Crystal struggled in Tess's arms. "Let me down. Let me down!"

Hopping to the ground, Crystal scurried over to the fence, and dived between the railings. A rigid frown and tight-lipped expression frosted her features when she glared from behind the fence.

The hopefulness inside Tess crumpled into an uncomfortable ball in her stomach. Coaxing her to return would be futile now. She gave Sugar an apologetic caress and went to rejoin Crystal.

Surprisingly, Crystal took her hand as they walked around to the back yard. "You know, Sugar would have been like a new friend, if you'd stayed a little longer."

The child's lip jutted out in a pout and she looked away.

In the distance came the sound of chiming bells. Church bells. To the east, the San Juan mountains were haloed in low-lying clouds. How long had it been since she'd been inside a church?

How many years ago had Tess walked hand-in-hand with her own mother to church on an Air Force base? In her mind she could still see the shiny black, patent-leather shoes on her feet. Recall the times when she would rub Vaseline into the leather to keep them shiny.

Crystal jerked her hand. "How long are we gonna stay here?"

Taken aback, Tess answered, "I don't know...just yet."

"Will we go back to New Orleans?"

"Well, there's no place to stay there, honey. Almost everyone's moved away."

Crystal pulled her hand from Tess's palm, held it fisted at her side.

Tess bent down and swiped a loose strand of hair from her forehead. "Don't you like it here?"

Amber eyes gazed downward. "It's okay."

What could she say to placate, to play for time? "Wouldn't you like to make some new friends? Maybe go to preschool in town?"

A sadness tinged Crystal's voice when she asked, "Will my mommy ever come back?"

The question was asked so unexpectedly, it hit Tess like a dart between the eyes.

After a deep breath, she said, "You remember all that rain? She was lost in the flood water. Now, people are looking for her."

"But will they ever *find* her?"

Inwardly Tess shuddered. Kneeling down on one knee in the high grass, she cupped Crystal's chin in her hand. "Many families lost their moms and dads, and children," she said softly, looking into Crystal's inquisitive face. "Many drowned...."

Words. The right words did not come easily. She had seen too much, witnessed too many painful scenes in the aftermath of Katrina.

Saucer eyes staring into hers brimmed with barely contained anguish.

Tess summoned her threadbare courage. "We can pray for your mom."

Crystal blinked. Two crocodile tears rolled over her cheeks to her chin. "Can Jesus help us?"

The child's remembrance of Tess's recent reference to Jesus and his status among the angels caused a jagged ache to lodge in her throat. She wasn't used to asking for favors. Hadn't prayed much herself until Katrina. "He can help us wait to find the answers. He can help us to be patient."

Short arms came up around her neck as Tess pulled Crystal close, inhaling the sweet, little girl fragrance in the crook of her neck. She snuffled into the tawny bare skin of her arms. "Will you help me do that?"

Her small body quivering with low sobs, Crystal bobbed her head, her ponytail brushing Tess's flushed cheek. "Okay."

* * *

The unanswerable question as to the whereabouts of Crystal's mother, Carrie Pearl, plagued Tess the rest of the day. It took all of her usually positive attitude to keep a bright demeanor through lunch and play time afterward in the back yard with Crystal and Miss Tabby. Thank goodness, the precocious cat had a companionable nature and curled up with Crystal under a tall cottonwood tree when afternoon shadows spread across the valley.

A preceding sound of clomping hooves interrupted their quiet setting. Tess turned to see the returning group of riders amble toward them on the ranch road.

Crystal pointed. "There's Mr. Grant."

Yes, there was Grant, sitting tall on a palomino, his western brimmed hat at a slant over his eyes. Surprised at the rising heartbeat at her throat, Tess got to her feet. Dust rose around the group as they approached.

She waited until Grant and his hired man had bid farewell to the camping party and taken care of the horses before walking with Crystal toward the house.

They met up with him in the side yard. He was dust-covered from head to toe and deeply tanned. "Hi, how was the trip?" she called.

"Hey!" He waved, a smile creasing his face. "It was great. How did things go here?"

"Just fine. Roy Briggs came both days and took good care of things." As Grant removed his hat and brushed off some of the dust, she added, "I thawed out a steak for you in the fridge and made a salad. Kind of thought you'd be hungry."

"That sounds great, but I hate to eat alone. I can take out another couple steaks and thaw 'em in the microwave. Then will you two join me?"

"Oh, Crystal's already eaten her supper..."

He shrugged. "I bet you're getting hungry. Won't take a minute to get 'em ready for the grill."

She hadn't had such a friendly invitation since... she couldn't recall. "Well," she glanced down at Crystal. "That's a very tempting offer, isn't it?'

93

A beaming response showed no argument from Crystal.

Grant opened the screen door. "Gotta jump in the shower first. Give me about twenty minutes."

Chapter Eight

Later, Grant grilled steaks on the wide deck. It was an older charcoal grill that spewed smoke skyward, the juices from the steaks filling the air with tempting aroma. A hint of hickory.

Tess's stomach rumbled as she laid out plates embellished at the centers with wild horses galloping over western plains. The way Grant hovered over the grill, an easy grace to his tanned physique, his hair slicked back in damp waves above a form-fitting navy T-shirt, solicited her attention. "Looks like you're no stranger when it comes to barbecuing," she observed.

He glanced over a broad shoulder. "It's not hard, once you get the hang of it. You like to cook out?"

She shrugged. "Haven't had the opportunity for a while. My ex-husband always burned whatever he tried to cook on the grill. Guess that's why he never liked to cook."

"Ah." He raised an eyebrow. "My wife was a great cook, but she let me do the messy stuff like this."

"Well." Why did his harmless comment make her feel about as useless as a one-armed fiddler? She shifted her attention to Crystal chasing Miss Tabby across the back yard.

"Say, Tess." Grant sent her a rebounding smile. "How about a cold beer? There's a few stashed in the fridge."

"I'll have a lemonade." She half turned, glad to have something else to do since the table was set with salad, condiments, and a huge loaf of sourdough bread.

Crystal came skipping toward the deck. "Can I have a cold beer, too?"

"No." Tess laughed at the child's spunk. "A lemonade would be your best bet."

"I'm big...almost as big as you," Crystal teased.

Giving Crystal's ponytail a little swat, Tess grinned. "You are big enough to help me bring out the drinks. Last one to the kitchen is a rotten egg."

Crystal's behind disappeared inside the back door in a whoosh. Moments like these reassured Tess that, although Crystal had traversed through unspeakable loss in recent weeks, she still possessed a buoyant spirit willing to participate in new experiences.

Tess and Grant sipped their drinks on comfortable chaises, waiting for the thick steaks to reach the "just right" stage. Grant tilted his can to his lips, draining half of it. He gazed at the distant San Juan range, a man physically tired after his working weekend but obviously satisfied with his life.

"Did your camping trip go well?" Tess asked, sitting forward on the chaise.

He nodded, took another pull from his beer. "Yeah. I think the big city folks enjoyed it. No complaints about saddle sores this time."

"The scenery must be even more beautiful in the mountains."

"It's peaceful up there most of the time. Next time, you should come along, try out some of your cooking skills..." He glanced over at her. "That is, if you plan on staying on a while."

She blanched slightly. If only she could say one way or the other. "I'd really like to stay on, now that my teaching job in New Orleans has disappeared. If Jud would cooperate, I could give a more definite answer." She sipped on her drink. "Sorry."

"Yeah, old crusty Jud. He needs a good boot to the britches."

Off the deck, Crystal looked up from chasing Miss Tabby and wrinkled her nose. "Is something burning?"

"Ah, the steaks." Grant leaped to his feet and strode over to the grill.

"I like mine well done," Tess called, in anticipation of the worst.

Grant forked the charcoaled slabs onto a serving platter. "Good thing." He let out a short laugh. "Cuz these critters are definitely crisp!"

Tess smothered a smile. At least Grant could make light of it. Howard would have cursed a blue streak, kicked the grill, and stomped off in a huff, leaving her to salvage the remains.

Crystal dived into her chair at the table as a barbecued steak was delivered to her plate. "I want lots of ketchup on mine,"

"Yes, ma'am!" Grant winked in her direction. "Hey, I've got a sweet little foal that would like to meet you, real soon."

"What's a foal?" countered Crystal, screwing up her face.

"Maybe we should keep it a secret," Tess suggested, "until tomorrow."

Crystal's amber gaze swayed from Tess to Grant and back. "Is this a game?"

"No, honey, it's not a game. It's...a surprise."

The expression in the wide eyes clouded. "Maybe I won't like a surprise."

And what if Crystal didn't? That would be one more roadblock.

As if sensing Tess's discomfort, Grant slid in to rescue. "You'll like this surprise. I guarantee it." He took a man-sized bite of his thick steak. "I'll tell you the other surprise soon as you eat your dinner."

Tess cut Crystal's meat into small pieces and buttered her bread. The child's appetite was not a problem. She came close to cleaning her plate while watching Grant quickly polish off his. Anyone could see the spark of obvious admiration firing up toward this new adult in her life.

Was it a good or dubious thing? Bonding too soon could be harmful to Crystal's fragile spirit. Especially if she and the child had to leave Sand Castle any time soon.

"I'm done!" Crystal announced. "What's the surprise?"

Grant observed with approval. "It's *ice cream bars*. You still have some room?"

Groaning, Crystal patted her small hand on her belly. "I think so."

After dinner, Tess cleaned up the kitchen. "I'll make scrambled eggs and pancakes for breakfast," she told Grant.

"Sounds great." He finished wiping off the counter, glanced over at her with an expression of gratitude. "It's good to have a woman on the ranch..." He glanced away as if feeling awkward with his words. "I really appreciate the job you've done."

She nodded, aware of the satisfied feeling she got doing domestic things for others. "I like working here."

The sun had slipped below the San Juan range, leaving a coral glow to the sky as Tess took Crystal's hand and strolled back to the cabin. Part of her relaxed in partial contentment. The evening had been well spent with good company and good food. Yet part of her wrestled with apprehension over tomorrow. A niggling fear that Crystal might not want anything to do with Grant's foal.

It was a distinct possibility.

* * *

The next morning, after breakfast, Tess found a toll-free number on the Internet for the Find Family National Call Center, a nationwide coordination center for persons seeking family members missing during Katrina. She jumped at the new chance to find Carrie, wanting to go make the call herself. But she thought of Jud, his need to find his daughter, or any information about her.

"Geez!" She gritted her teeth, detesting the nudge from her conscience to inform him. *The grizzled old coot!* Remembering the last encounter with Jud at his store didn't exactly endear him to her. But she had to do it. He had no computer knowledge that she was aware of and was stumbling around in the dark about expanding the search.

The phone rang eight times before he answered. Why didn't he own an answering machine? "Yeah?"a voice growled. Very businesslike, wasn't he?

"Mr. Pearl, this is Tess Cameron." She got right to the point. Gave him the center's number.

It took forever it seemed for him to take it down. "I'll call 'em," he mumbled. "Thanks."

Thanks. At least it was an attempt at civility.

Then boot steps clicked across the outer tile floor and she heard Grant's voice. "Tess, you in there?"

She answered, anticipating his towering appearance.

His tall frame filled the doorway. Tousled hair, western shirt open at the neck, well-fitting jeans. She cleared her throat, trying not to stare. He wasn't a handsome man, but, with his confident air and strong build, quite attractive.

He broke into a slight grin, like a kid eager to play a favorite sport. "Where's Crystal? That little foal I told her about is ready to get acquainted."

Tess hopped out of the swivel chair, unwanted apprehension nagging at her. "I'll go get her." She brushed past him then paused. "Grant, this is really a nice thing you're doing. Just...don't get your hopes up too much."

At the cabin, Tess found Crystal playing with Miss Tabby in the front room. "Mr. Grant says his baby horse wants to meet you, right away." After convincing Crystal that Miss Tabby would prefer to stay at home and wait for them, she hurried her out the door.

They bumped into Grant on their way over to the north barn where the new foal and her mother resided. "Can the baby horse talk yet?" Crystal asked as they neared the barn.

"No, horses can't talk like we do," Grant said. "But they have their own language that we need to learn."

From the expression on Crystal's face, Tess could see she was considering this new information.

In that instant, young Carlos came running toward them. His eyes flashed with dark fear. "Senor Wilder! The little horse–she hurt herself."

They all raced to the barn. Tess's heart banged against her ribs as she ran. Crystal's hand was like a hot ember against her palm. When they reached the open barn door, Crystal held back as Grant disappeared inside.

In a rear corner, Tess saw Juan hunkered down, treating one of the foal's front legs.

"What happened?" came the small voice beside her.

"It looks like she hurt her front leg," she said, hoping the damage was minimal.

She feared if the foal's injury was life-threatening, it could scare Crystal away. Falling back on some teacher's psychology, she added, "We can wait and see how they take care of her."

Grant sauntered back to the doorway a few minutes later. "Our girl's going to be okay. She just got a little too frisky and ran into some bailing wire out back. She cut her foreleg."

As if on cue, a wobbly, tan-colored foal peeked out from behind Grant's right leg. Above a narrow muzzle, liquid brown eyes framed by thick black lashes, observed the tall humans.

Stepping aside to give her room to come out in the yard, Grant announced, "This is Nina." Which sounded like *Neena.* "She's two-months-old."

"She's so short," Crystal marveled.

"Only about a head taller than you."

Nina limped outside then sniffed her obviously irritating bandage. Letting out a small snort, she hobbled ahead as if determined to see the world.

Tess admired the foal's slim but already muscular legs and alert expression. She turned to Grant. "What kind of horse is Nina? "

"An Azteca. Her lineage goes back to Mexico where they crossed the American Quarter horse and the Andalusian." He gestured in her direction. "Her breed makes very versatile horses. They have intelligence, spirit, and strength. When she gets older, maybe she'll learn to be more agile."

Noticing Nina's mother, a mare of a deeper tan color, watching from just inside the barn, Tess smiled. "She'll be a beauty, I bet."

Nina rambled toward them, letting out a light snort, yet still noticeably shy.

"Crystal," Grant called. "Go over and make friends."

Crystal frowned in a doubtful way and sprinted over to the corral fence opposite them.

Tess's jaw tightened. This is what she had expected. The child still harbored fears; maybe even the fear of an animal's rejection. Or was it simply a lack of self-confidence that another child from a sheltered, "safe" background might take for granted?

Climbing up on the next rung of the fence, Crystal leaned toward the foal. "Nina!"

Small ears perked up. Nina's narrow equine head swiveled to face Crystal. Foal and child studied each other.

"She has brown skin," Crystal observed. "Just like me. But her hair is straight."

Tess walked over to the fence indulging herself with sudden levity. "And she has four legs. And a tail."

Pure and spontaneous, a giggle escaped Crystal's lips. "I have a tail, too." She shook her ponytail.

It was the first time Tess had heard the child allow herself a humorous moment since leaving New Orleans.

Meanwhile the foal limped away toward the mare.

"Will Nina come to me?" Crystal questioned Grant.

"Hmm. Maybe not today. She doesn't stray far from her mom."

Crystal's expression sobered and she looked up into Tess's eyes. "We need to take care of her," she said earnestly.

"Yes," Tess agreed. "Mr. Grant will tell us how to do that."

Grant grinned as if in compliance. "Tell you what, Miss Crystal, let's give Nina a chance to give her leg a rest. Then tomorrow, you come back and we'll see how she's doing. Does that sound good?"

Crystal's small head bobbed in the affirmative. "Yeah."

The next morning, Tess and Crystal hurried to the barn after breakfast. Grant had called a vet to come out, and the man was bent over examining Nina's injury as they approached. Grant hovered off to the side.

"Who's that man?" Crystal asked.

Tess twitched her nose at the barn smells of fresh hay and dust. "He's the horse doctor."

From the open door, the two watched and waited. The vet carefully applied a new bandage to Nina's slim foreleg.

Crystal tugged on Tess's hand. "Is he fixing her?"

Before Tess could answer, Grant strode over to them. "Doc Whitney says Nina has a slight infection, nothing serious." He went down on one knee to talk to Crystal at her eye level. "He's going to give her some medicine that will make her leg heal better."

Crystal's bright cheeks lifted. She wiggled with enthusiasm. "Then, can she play with me?"

Grant tilted his hat brim back a ways. "She sure will. And you know what? I've got somethin' real special you can give her, soon as the doc's through with her."

He got to his feet and sent Tess a mischievous wink which set off a little tingle down her spine. Darn, if she knew how he could do that so easily.

Dancing on tip toe, Crystal squealed, "What is it?"

Tess slipped her hand over Crystal's shoulder. "Just a minute, wiggle worm."

The vet, silver-haired and stocky, ambled their way. "Well, I gave her an antibiotic. She should be good as new in a few days." He tipped his worn western hat and headed for an older model SUV parked in the driveway.

"Thanks, doc. Send me the bill." Grant turned back to Crystal, stuck his large hand in a back pocket of his jeans and pulled out something in his closed fist.

Crystal danced around his long legs, trying to reach Grant's secret treats. "What is it? What is it?"

He ruffled her tousled pony tail. "Come over here." Like a pied piper, Grant led Crystal and Tess, trailing close behind, to Nina's stall.

Crystal lingered at the stall door, watching Nina and her mother inside.

"You've got to come in here and stand by Nina," Grant directed Crystal.

Gingerly she did and stood next to him like a miniature shadow.

Grant took her small hand and held it palm up. He laid four brown sugar cubes inside it.

"Now, when you call Nina to you, you hold out your hand just like this. Maybe just give her two at a time."

Crystal's amber eyes grew luminous. She glanced up at Grant and then hesitantly at the foal and its mother.

"Go ahead. Call her over," Grant enthused. "LaDonna doesn't mind if you do."

In almost a whisper, Crystal called, "Nina." She walked ahead a few paces, her hand held out in offering. "Nina."

Tess watched the foal flick its long, black lashes and observe this new visitor. Smaller than the tall humans, she was used to. What was she thinking? Then, slowly, Nina limped toward Crystal. And Tess held her breath.

"That's a girl," Grant murmured.

Was he encouraging the child or the foal? Or both?

Morning's golden rays streamed from an overhead window, highlighting Crystal's mahogany crown and Nina's tan uplifted head and back. In the short space it took for the two to meet, Tess's heartbeat fluttered. With youthful equine curiosity, Nina sniffed at the small cubes then lowered her narrow head to Crystal's open palm.

Sudden wonder spread over the child's face as Nina's soft muzzle touched her hand for the first time. A giggle escaped from her upturned lips. "She likes those candies!"

As Nina munched on the sweet treats, Tess glanced at Grant across the stall from her and could swear he released the same sigh of relief as she. Thank goodness. A barrier had been broken, a fear dissolved. Crystal reached up and timidly stroked Nina's face.

Tess sent Grant a warm smile. "Say, do you have any more of those? I think LaDonna might like a taste, too."

* * *

Later, nearing bedtime, Tess tuned the battered radio on the bedroom bureau to a jazz station she'd stumbled onto. The voice of a bluesy songstress wafted out over the room. Billie Holliday? It reminded her of New Orleans...the French Quarter...and other songs.

Cuddled up in bed with Miss Tabby, Crystal gave out a sigh. "Mommy used to sing to me like that."

Tess slipped a nightshirt over her head and smiled at her. "She did? I guess your mom loved music, huh?"

Crystal gazed at Tess with a dreamy expression. "She does. Do you think Nina would like me to sing her asleep?"

"Hmm. I think Nina would like that." Tess found a pair of scissors in a bathroom drawer and decided to trim her hair. She couldn't recall the last time she'd been to a hair salon. The blues singer's lyrics floated on the night breeze jostling the curtains at the window. Tess stared into the mirror on the medicine chest and took a snip at her uneven bangs, dampened from her shower. "You can ask Mr. Grant tomorrow."

She trimmed around the edges of her dark mop, finger-combing it into natural waves. Not the style these days, but who would notice out here on the Colorado plains? Certainly not Grant. She knew she was too plain for him. Not nearly as pretty as his first wife. Tess studied her tomboyish face, the dimple in her right cheek. Maybe a swipe of black mascara on her lashes would emphasize the blue in her eyes.

She frowned at her reflection in the mirror. What was she thinking? She was on a mission here in Sand Castle. And it wasn't to snag a man.

Tess glanced around the bathroom door and saw Crystal, her arm protectively thrown over Miss Tabby. Both were fast asleep. A tender portrait.

Myriad emotions washed over her. This beautiful child, so dependent on her now, seemed to be slowly relaxing here. Her strained demeanor fading somewhat. And yet no answers were known about her mother's whereabouts, her grandfather still was in a quandary on whether to accept her as his own, and little was actually available on Crystal's vital statistics.

Where do I fit in here? She shook her head impatiently. *Heck, I can't even sing a lullaby.*

Another mournfully sweet cord from the radio played with her senses. Perhaps somewhere a woman with skin the color of toffee, warm and smooth, crooned to her lost child. Sang an old Creole song, with an aching heart. Listened to those mournful jazz notes limp along the humid, hazy days. Where had her little one gone? So many missing...

Swallowing over a ragged lump in her throat, Tess went to the radio and turned it off. Once she'd slipped under the bedcovers in the darkened room, she lay listening to Crystal's even breathing next to her. Felt the near warmth of her small body. Inhaled the clean scent of her pajamas.

What was she to Crystal?

A channel to safety.

A guardian.

A mentor.

A mother figure.

Lord, help me to be what this child needs.

Fighting back tears of frustration, Tess vowed to take Crystal back to New Orleans one day, to keep alive her memory of where she came from, and might wish to return. By then, the city would be up and humming again, rebuilt to its rightful zest and charm.

But could *she* ever really go back? No schools would open for some time to come. Perhaps she would simply have to move on after news of Carrie, her death or whereabouts, was revealed to them.

Where was poor Carrie Pearl? It all came back to Carrie. All of their future plans hinged on her fate.

* * *

Crystal ran ahead of Tess the following morning, racing to get to the corral. Near the barn, Carlos stood brushing LaDonna, her young foal meandering nearby.

Tess waved to Carlos. "How is Nina today?"

He nodded. "I think she is better."

Before Tess could stop Crystal at the fence, she had scrambled over the lower rail and skipped inside the corral. As she neared Nina, Grant swung around the front of the barn.

"Hey," he called to Crystal, "not so fast."

She skidded to a halt, a gleeful grin spreading across her face.

Grant held out his hand and walked her up to the horses. Tess followed. "Always let a horse know where you are," he said to Crystal. "Never run up behind them."

He lifted Crystal's hand to Nina's neck. "Pet her real easy. That's good."

As if wanting to catch a scent of this new, small human, Nina turned her head and nuzzled Crystal's cheek. Which caused Crystal to squeal and hop back a step. "Can I give her some more sugar cubes?" she asked Grant a second afterward.

From his back pocket, Grant pulled several brown cubes and gave them to Crystal. "You're gonna spoil her."

While Nina enjoyed her morning treat, Tess went over to LaDonna and stroked her forehead. "Beautiful lady. We don't mean to give your baby all the attention."

Grant glanced her way. "You want to ride her?"

Taken aback, Tess sized up the mare. "It's been awhile since I've ridden; but, yes, I'd love to."

"She's a gentle ride. We'll have to set up a time coming up soon."

Crystal headed over to Tess and LaDonna. "I want to ride, too. Can I ride Nina?"

"Oh, honey. Nina's too small right now."

At the mention of her name, Nina limped nimbly behind Crystal, following at her heels then sniffed at the back pocket of her jeans.

Grant and Tess laughed when Crystal whirled and stared the foal in the eyes, hands on her hips. "No more treats. You're gonna get spoiled!"

A repeated honking sound made Tess switch her gaze to the front road. Churning up clouds of dust, an old junker pickup rumbled toward the ranch. She couldn't see the driver for the dust, but she could make out the image of a large dog hanging out the front passenger window. Where had she seen that dog before?

Grant squinted in the truck's direction. "Looks like Jud Pearl's gonna make a visit."

Jud Pearl.

Tess's stomach twisted into a nervous knot. What news could bring him out to the ranch when a phone call would do? Only something big like a breakthrough about his daughter Carrie.

The pickup bounced up the drive, its brakes screeching to a stop. Grant waved. "Wonder what's caught his pants on fire?" he said, just loud enough for her to hear.

108

By the time the old codger had pushed open the door and climbed down, Grant was striding toward him, his boot heels kicking up a path of dirt.

Behind him, Tess slipped her fingers through Crystal's, unsure if she should bring the child out to meet Jud, or not.

"What does that man want?" Crystal implored, looking up at Tess.

Tess stared at Jud, shaking the dust off the brim of his hat. "I don't know yet."

What news did he bring with him was her question. Had he received that most fearful information about his loved one that everyone dreaded? A shudder skidded through her. How could she let a stranger deliver this sad message to Crystal?

She veered toward the cabin, not wanting to face Jud's crusty demeanor. Or whatever he had to say.

But Grant called to them, "Hey, come on over!"

She stopped in her tracks. Whatever Jud had to say, she wanted to hear it before Crystal did. She leaned down and said, "You go back and watch Nina, honey. I'll just be a minute."

With accelerating dread, Tess forced herself toward the front of the house where Jud Pearl stood fidgeting beside his run-down pickup.

Chapter Nine

Jud's yellow dog swaggered up to meet her, his head hanging, tongue lolling out of his mouth. Tess's mouth was dry, but sweat gathered under her arms and soaked her light cotton shirt. She purposely gazed away from Jud and Grant as she neared them, not wanting to show the fear that she felt. At about ten feet she stopped and squared Jud with a solemn stare.

Except for his mustache, he was clean shaven. Above baggy pants, nipped up by faded green suspenders, he held a battered hat. He bowed his shaggy gray head, she supposed in an effort to be polite. "Ms. Cameron."

"Jud." Tess set her jaw as she had so often when waiting for her dad, the sergeant, to mete out military penance. She anticipated the worst.

He cleared his throat. "I got a call today and I thought you'd want to hear about it in person."

Was there a lilt in his raspy voice? She focused in on an unmistakable light in the man's eyes.

"Winona called me from Houston."

Tess blanched in surprise. "Winona—Bingham?"

"Yep. My niece. Her husband found a job and she's livin' in Houston with her family. She's still feelin' guilty about leavin' you in New Orleans and hoped you'd brought Crystal up here."

A surge of resentment kept Tess's response mute, her expression tight-lipped. Yes, she'd brought Crystal here. What else could she have done? Leave her with strangers?

Jud's weathered cheeks colored. "Anyway, Winona wanted to apologize."

The memory of feelings of shock and abandonment surfaced, and the long trip here with a devastated child. The uncertainty of what they would find in Sand Castle. "I wish Winona could apologize to Crystal."

Jud scratched a sideburn. "I told her you was here and tried to talk some sense into me." He took a step forward, fishing a piece of paper from his shirt pocket. "Best thing, though, was the news she gave me about Crystal."

A frown tightened Tess's forehead. "News?"

Jud squinted at the crumpled paper. "Seems Crystal's birthday was June seventh. She's four years old. And Winona said she remembers that Crystal was born at New Orlean's General Hospital."

Surprise replaced anger. "Well, that *is* good news. Now Crystal will have a birthday to celebrate…like her classmates at school…when she goes to school." That was definitely something needing attention in the near future.

"Yep, she will." Jud shuffled over to his truck. "I got somethin' for her." He reached through the open window on the passenger side and pulled out a huggable female teddy bear wearing a floppy hat and calico dress. A lace collar and pearl necklace complimented her costume. He held the teddy awkwardly as if a child's toy was a foreign object.

Tess stared, taken aback by Jud's new change of heart. "That was…thoughtful."

Grant strode over to Tess and steered her back toward the barn. "Let's go find Crystal and see what she thinks about that bear."

"C'mon Henry, "Jud called to his old dog who then trailed beside him.

Crystal was nowhere to be found when they came to the corral fence.

"Bet she's inside the barn." Grant walked ahead across the yard, his broad shoulders disappearing inside the open barn door.

With some trepidation, Tess peered into the darkened interior. Smells of hay and horse entered her nostrils.

111

Inside the doorway, she blinked, seeing only silhouettes of stalls against backlit windows. "Crystal!" she called.

"They're over here."

Tess and Jud found Grant at a far stall, looking in on Nina and the mare and Crystal. The child was sitting cross-legged in the straw over in a corner. Nina had collapsed next to her, stilt legs folded beneath her slim, light brown frame. Crystal petted the foal's wispy dark mane.

Jud wagged his head, seemingly amazed. "Well, don't that take the cake?"

"Nina and me decided to be friends," Crystal said, grinning up at them

A satisfied expression swept over Grant's strong features. "Yes, you did."

Tess's earlier doubt that Crystal could bond with the horses faded. She'd found a companion more her size. Then she was aware of Jud standing near, fidgeting with his gift.

"Come here, Crystal. See what Mr. Pearl brought you."

The sound of a clearing throat at her side. "Just call me Jud."

At the sight of the teddy bear, Crystal hopped to her feet and came over to them. But she eyed Jud curiously. He was still a stranger.

"Got somethin' for you, little lady. " Jud handed her the plump bear.

She accepted the gift, her amber gaze settling on the dainty calico dress and pearl necklace.

"What do you say to Jud?" Tess asked.

With an awkward smile, Crystal managed a low "thank you."

"Well, I gotta get back to the store." Jud turned to leave. "Come on, Henry," he called to the dog.

"Jud, I'll walk with you to the truck," Tess offered, "if Grant will keep an eye on Crystal."

"Sure." Grant waved them away.

When Tess caught up with Jud outside the barn, she said, "I want to thank you for the gift. Crystal doesn't have many dolls…" It went without saying they had arrived in Sand Castle with barely the clothes on their backs.

Jud trudged ahead, his worn hat sloped down over his shaggy sideburns. "Hope she likes it."

"Your gift will help to open the door a little. You know, help her to get to know you." She wasn't good at this, communicating with this stand-offish man. "She needs to know she has family."

"No rush on that." He tugged at the brim of his hat." When her mama – when Carrie comes back, she can take care of those things."

When Carrie comes back?

More likely, what would he do if she never came back? Tess clamped her mouth shut to keep from expressing her doubts.

"Does Crystal remind you at all of Carrie?" she blurted suddenly.

He slanted a curious glance at her. "Nope. Can't say she does. Course, it's been about five years since I last seen her. She was bound she was gonna leave this little town and get her education. Didn't blame her for that."

Henry trotted up behind them, his ears drooping.

Tess remembered Carrie's classroom, filled with musical instruments. "Did she always love music?"

"Yep. She wanted to teach school." He looked ahead toward his truck. "I always thought she'd come back to Colorado. Plenty of good schools here. But she was stubborn like her ma. Made up her mind to work in New

Orleans. After my wife died, she didn't have a reason to come back. We didn't agree on much."

They reached the truck, squatting on its old tires. Jud opened the side door and the dog clambered onto the sagging seat cover. "Didn't guess she'd ever take up with a black man. Still hard to believe Crystal's my own kin," he said, a grudging tone in his voice.

An uncomfortable twinge twisted Tess's stomach. Prejudice was not an easy thing to tackle straight on, even if Jud believed his feelings were justified. He had a right to his beliefs, even though they didn't sit well with her. "Carrie must have known how you'd feel about her after she had Crystal. It's hard not to see the brightness in Crystal. Many would say that she's a beautiful child."

She could swear she saw a glimmer of emotion in the old coot's eyes.

He gave an abrupt nod. "Yep. She is kinda pretty." The door creaked as he opened it and climbed onto the front seat. "Hope you'll keep lookin' for word of Carrie, Ms. Cameron."

"I'll get on the Internet this afternoon, Jud. And you can call me Tess."

The truck lumbered down the road, its worn tires spinning up gravel. Henry hung his head out the side window, tongue lolling, and swung a doleful look toward her through the rising dust.

* * *

Walking back to the cabin, holding Tess's hand and clutching her new teddy bear, Crystal was in a somber mood. She cocked one small brow and fixed Tess with a questioning gaze. "Was that man my grandpa?"

Tess could only imagine Crystal's confusion. Until a few short weeks ago, Jud had been a total stranger. Now he was coming around bringing her gifts, when at first he would have nothing to do with her. She decided to just be straight forward with the child's question. "Yes, honey, he is your grandpa. You can call him Grandpa, if you want to."

Crystal's lower lip jutted in a pout as they continued walking. "Then…why didn't he come to see me?"

The kid knew how to throw a curve ball. "You know," Tess improvised, "Jud lives a long way from New Orleans and he had to be here to run his store."

"Does he want to find my mommy?"

"He wants to—very much."

As they approached the cabin, a piece of gray fluff lay ahead in the dry grass. Tess nudged it with the toe of her shoe.

Crystal bent over to have a closer look. "What's that?"

"Don't know." Tess pushed the furry ball again and saw the white fur underside.

"It's a bunny tail!" Crystal exclaimed.

An uneasy feeling gathered at the base of her rib cage. Tess gazed from the white fluff several feet away to the nearby tool shed. A family of cotton-tails lived beneath it. A hole near the corner of the shed was their entrance.

"Where's the bunny now?" Crystal whined.

Tess thought of the mottled black cat she'd seen prowling near the barn a few days ago and recalled Grant mentioning the occasional fox and coyote trespassers on the ranch. From the corner of her eye, she glimpsed other bits of gray fur scattered near the path. She sighed. "The barn cat might have chased her away…"

Or had her for dinner.

The child's lower lip trembled. "He bit her tail off. He *hurt* the bunny!"

"Maybe the bunny ran so fast and jumped back down her hole." Tess led Crystal over to the shed.

They peered down into the dark hole. Tess's optimism waned.

"I hate the barn cat!" Tears glistened in Crystal's eyes as she pulled back and dashed to the cabin's back door.

Life and death on a ranch. Neither believed the bunny was still alive. Tess in her cynical adult's mind. Crystal in her still fragile state of confusion over the disappearance of her own mother.

In the middle of the night, Tess awoke to the sound of muffled sobs. Rolling over in bed, she turned to Crystal, a narrow shaft of moonlight streaming across her face from the bedroom window. She still clung to her teddy bear. Her pillow case was damp with spilled tears.

Tess cradled her. "What's the matter?" She knew without asking.

"The cat killed our bunny." She moaned softly.

"We don't know that for sure." She stroked Crystal's thick disheveled curls away from her forehead.

"She's never coming back."

A sudden sharp ache rent Tess's heart. Neither Crystal's mother nor the bunny were probably ever coming back. "We'll say a little prayer that the bunny's safely back under the shed with her brothers and sisters," she whispered.

A silence hovered in the space between them. Then Crystal touched her small warm hand to Tess's cheek and sighed.

Long after Crystal faded off to sleep, Tess lay staring up at the beamed ceiling. Another fruitless search of the Internet sites today and still no leads to missing persons. *Where are the answers, Lord? Help us to find the right answers.*

It seemed forever before she fell into a fitful sleep.

Journey to Sand Castle

She was under water. Floating. No, trying to swim through dark, murky water. Lost. Clumps of iridescent seaweed surrounded her, impeding her momentum. Strange fish, long and bloated, with red eyes, gaping mouths, and tiny sharp teeth undulated by. She had no oxygen mask--how long could she stay at this depth until forced to resurface? Her arms and feet flailed in slow motion. How had she gotten here?

Ahead, a body...a woman. Hands reaching out to her. Hair haloed in purple wiggly strands about her head. Tess swam to her.

Must tell her to swim up. Save herself.

No words came. Only the watery silence. The woman's face was so pale, like white marble. Her eyes...open...the color of the sea. A school of small fish, shimmery coral, skimmed through the water above. They wound round the woman's bare outstretched alabaster arms like sparkling bracelets. Some shimmied through her wiggly purple hair and swam out her eyes!

A silent cry. Gulping for air, shaking in a cold sweat, Tess awoke. Perspiration drenched her night shirt. She sat up on the edge of the bed, dazed. In the semi-dark room, she padded over to the closet. Groping inside, she found another night shirt hanging on a hook. She yanked off the wet sleep shirt and let it fall in a heap at her feet then pulled the dry one over her head. It came to her knees.

She couldn't breathe. She had to get out of this room. In the rumpled bed, Crystal snored lightly. In the shaft of light, Tess saw Miss Tabby curled at Crystal's feet.

Pulling on a flannel jacket and her furry slippers, Tess emerged from the cabin. *Get some air. Shake off the nightmare.*

It was nearing dawn, the sky hazy over the San Juan Mountains. She navigated over the stubby grass to the corral, taking the chill morning air into her lungs. Once she reached the rough-hewn corral fence, she grabbed onto it like a lifeline. She had to anchor herself…get a grip!

Tess arched her back, raising her hands to knead the kinks from the back of her neck.

From the barn a horse gave a loud waking snort. Smells of hay filled her nostrils. She hugged herself and gazed off to the mountain peaks, trying to make sense of the eerie dream, attempting to push away her fear of Carrie's probable death.

A familiar deep voice came from behind her. "You're up early, Miss Cameron." A large hand wrapped around her upper arm.

She jerked and looked up into friendly hazel eyes. "Whew…you scared me." She forced a smile.

"Sorry. You okay?" He released her arm.

Of course, she wasn't okay. She was miserable. All she could do was nod her head in the affirmative and continue to look up at Grant. His hair was ruffled like he'd just finger-combed it, beard stubble grazed his jaw. His eyes, in the gradual light, drew her in. Strangely, she felt an overwhelming pull to just step into that broad, welcoming physique, bury her weary head against his strong shoulder. "I couldn't sleep," she confessed, regretting the release of his hand from her arm.

He let go of a slow sigh. "Me neither."

Before she could mumble a response, he said, "Hey, I'm gonna check on the horses. Want to come with me?"

"Sure." She'd gladly go with him. First, she swung a glance back at the cabin. "Crystal's sleeping…"

"Then let her sleep," he said, a smile in his voice. "She'll let you know if she wakes up."

"You've got that right." She laughed to herself and let Grant lead the way into the barn.

They made small talk as Grant checked the horses in their stalls. He gave each horse a special greeting, like they were all old friends. A man who loved animals had to be a good man, she thought. Then she blurted out how she'd had this frightening nightmare. "I know it's because I'm worried about Carrie."

"Yeah. I can understand that. We all are." He looked out toward the first light rising over the Sangres. "I have bad dreams too, sometimes."

She wondered what his bad dreams were about. Grant was such a private man. She wished she could make a pot of coffee and sit down and share their bad dreams. Just the two of them. Making breakfast every morning for everyone was always a busy, noisy time with the others in the kitchen. Although she had come to enjoy it. But then, Grant was her boss. She shouldn't forget that.

"Guess I better get Crystal up and ready for breakfast," she said, aware of the early morning breeze chilling her legs and other naked parts.

"Sounds like a good idea. I'm starving." He sent her a grin before turning back to his chores.

* * *

After breakfast, Tess walked with Crystal across the back yard thinking that she should try to find a preschool in town for her. When Grant drove her to town to grocery shop this afternoon, she would mention it to him. It was time Crystal got into an organized group and prepared for kindergarten. The school system in this area was an unknown phenomenon, but it couldn't be farther behind than the conditions she'd found in New Orleans. Katrina had only made things worse for their public schools.

Over in the side yard, she caught sight of a medium-size bunny, its back turned their way, nibbling in a patch of grass near the shed. She wondered if it might be a female.

Running ahead, pigtails flying, Crystal chased Miss Tabby.

The bunny hopped a few feet forward. That's when Tess spied its rear end and almost laughed out loud. "Look, Crystal. Quick!"

Crystal whirled and peered curiously.

Tess pointed with glee. "See, the bunny has no tail!"

Surprise rounded Crystal's eyes as she saw the smooth rump for herself. She ran over to Tess, mimicking in an excited voice, "The bunny has no tail!" When the animal hopped ahead again, Crystal jumped up and down like her short legs were on springs. "She's okay. She's okay!"

Tess squeezed Crystal's small shoulder. "She didn't need that tail anyway."

The child giggled as they watched the bunny preen itself near some scrub bushes.

A meow interrupted their reverie. Miss Tabby loped in her lopsided way across the grass toward them. "Miss Tabby only has three legs, but she can still play." In a flash, she romped off toward the cat.

A soft autumn wind rustled the cottonwood leaves on the edge of the property. Tess smiled to herself. A tail. A leg. A piece of one's life gone. Just pick yourself up and keep going. As long as you could find a place, set out on a new path, everything would work itself out. Right?

Hearing the approaching human sounds, the bunny flattened, pointy ears slicked back, camouflaging itself into the stubbled grass. Alert brown eyes focused forward.

When Crystal and the cat ventured closer, the bunny zigzagged back to its refuge, down the hole next to the shed.

"Is she afraid of us?" Crystal wanted to know.

Tess stood with hands on her hips, her head cocked. "Who? Mrs. Stumpy-rump? She's not afraid of anything."

Crystal grinned, a sparkle lighting her eyes. "She's not afraid of *anything*!" she announced then chased Miss Tabby over to the corral fence.

~**Tess**~

Chapter Ten

"Where are we goin'?" Crystal asked for the sixth time.

Tess turned the pickup truck off Main Street onto West View Avenue. Grant had let her borrow it for the morning to run errands in town and visit the new school. "I told you, honey. We're going to stop by a preschool for kids."

At the end of the block, she saw the bright yellow and red sign in a front yard. Little Red School House. A square-shaped, two-story frame house painted barn-red stood behind it.

"What's a pru-e-school?"

Pulling up in front of the chain link fence, Tess came to a stop and switched off the ignition. "Here it is." She pointed. "A little red school house, where you can play with other kids and learn new things."

Crystal's left eyebrow rose a fraction behind her new pink-framed sunglasses as she observed the unfamiliar dwelling, the small front porch complete with porch swing. A lone ponderosa pine anchored a corner of the yard, patches of dry grass surrounding it. "Will I like them?"

With a shrug, Tess smiled. "Guess you won't know until you go inside." From the side door, Tess unclasped the belt on Crystal's booster seat and helped her jump to the ground. She slid Crystal's sunglasses into her shoulder bag. "C'mon, let's go." They entered through the front gate. As they walked over the bumpy cement sidewalk to the porch and up to the screen door, she held her hand. It was warm and clammy, no doubt from some anxiety.

"Hi!" A thirty-something woman popped up behind the screen soon after Tess knocked. She opened the door. "You must be Crystal," she said brightly and invited them into the small front room. "I'm Jenny Stotter." She coaxed a strand of reddish brown hair back into a loose ponytail. "You can call me Jenny," she directed at Tess.

Her lips set in a contemplative straight line, Crystal stared up at the woman.

Tess placed a hand on her shoulder. "Say hello to Miss Jenny."

"Hello," Crystal said then stepped behind Tess, as if for protection.

Sounds of children's voices carried from the next room, and the aroma of popcorn.

"Hey, we just made some snacks." Jenny grinned. "Bet you'd like some, huh?" She whirled in her over-sized orange T-shirt with Bronco logo and faded blue jeans, and led them back to a noisy kitchen.

Three girls and one boy sat at an oblong table in the center of the room, stuffing their faces with popcorn from a large ceramic bowl. What looked like red Kool-aid filled their paper cups. Jenny found a chair for Crystal and introduced her to the group. "The boy's mine. Sam, say hi."

Sam, a stocky urchin with static hair, screwed up his face, his mouth as red as a clown's. Jenny shook her head at his boyish animation. Crystal sat in the chair but made no move toward the popcorn.

"Never know how many kids are going to show up from week to week," Jenny offered to Tess. "Their folks are ranchers and some are transient…it depends on whether they can get away from their work to bring them in."

Tess nodded. "Well, a smaller amount means more attention. I breathed a little easier when my classroom wasn't so full. In New Orleans."

You've been through a lot," Jenny commiserated. She beckoned for Tess to follow her around the door frame to a play room where they could talk away from the children's chatter. "Have you heard any more about Crystal's mom?"

Tess sighed and glanced around the comfortable play area with its toys, dolls, and shelves holding painting materials. "Not yet. We are in touch with the State Rescue services... I've contacted the hospital where Crystal was born, and they've located her birth certificate. So, they should be sending a copy of it to Jud soon."

"Gosh, I couldn't believe it when you said Jud Pearl was her granddad. That old crank-butt." Her eyes, the shade of nutmeg, crinkled at the corners. "Sorry. It's just that he isn't the friendliest man in town—or the most open-minded."

Tess had mentioned to Jenny that Jud was Crystal's grandparent and was cooperating in the search for further information. "I have to admit, he didn't do cartwheels when he first met her." Hesitant to reveal more of Jud's cynical attitude of disbelief, she gazed out a dusty window to the fenced backyard just large enough to include a swing set, sand box, and several tricycles.

After all, Jud was finally starting to show some interest in Crystal.

"Hey, come on outside and I'll show you the kid's playground. It's not Disney World, but they have fun out here." Jenny bounced out the back door her pony tail swinging side-to-side.

Tess glanced around the fenced yard. It was sparse with only a stumpy cottonwood providing a patch of shade. The leaves now turning brown would soon be on the ground. But the yard was free of litter or objects that might be a danger to curious small ones, such as a lawn mower or sharp gardening tools. "Crystal needs a place like this. After all she's been through, making new friends in a comfortable setting will give her some feeling of security."

Jenny observed her with a compassionate gaze. "You must care a lot about Crystal—and her mom—to bring her all the way from New Orleans."

Jenny's comment triggered a flashback and an ironic smile from Tess. Only weeks ago, she'd been a free spirit, never dreaming of being responsible for a four-year-old. "I do care very much about Crystal. But to be honest with you, she was dropped in my lap. I hadn't ever seen her before. And Carrie and I hardly knew each other. Her classroom was upstairs and mine was on the first floor. She was a single mom."

"And her dad?"

"No one seems to know much about Crystal's dad."

Jenny's eyes grew thoughtful. "I can't imagine how tough it's been for Crystal. You can be sure, though, she'll make some new friends here."

"I would like to bring her a couple days a week. My finances are in limbo right now, but I think Jud will kick in. And maybe I could assist you with the kids, teach them some developmental skills, to help offset the cost?"

Crystal's small frame appeared behind the screen door. "Are we going now?"

Somewhat deflated, Tess nodded. "Okay, honey. Just a minute." She'd hoped Crystal would fall naturally into play with the others and want to stay a while. Adapting to new people and places would clearly take time.

As they left, Jenny sent Crystal away with a homemade snicker doodle cookie. "Let me know when you'd like her to start," she said to Tess. I'm sure we can work out the details later."

Sam dashed up beside Jenny and hollered to them. "If she comes back, she can play with my new truck."

* * *

"Grant," Tess called that afternoon as she stepped from the office into the hallway. "Where are you?"

"I'm up here."

She followed the sound of his deep voice to the living room and saw him leaning over the upstairs' loft railing. The back light emphasized his broad shoulders and tall, casual stance. She licked dry lips, wondering why she hadn't applied lip gloss earlier. "I have a phone message for you about a construction job."

He smiled. "Good. Come on up."

Clutching the telephone message, she dashed up the stairs to the loft that Grant used for a study, furnished with a couple of easy chairs, roll-top desk, library shelves, and file cabinets. The room enveloped her with the feel of comfort and disorder. A man's sanctuary. A collection of western titled books, non-fiction and men's fiction, occupied several library shelves. Grant was bent over a top file drawer in the corner, his plaid shirt haphazardly tucked into snug-fitting jeans

"I'm tryin' to locate an old file. Shouldn't take me a minute," he said over his shoulder.

"I'll set the message on your desk." She noticed his sandy-brown hair was uncombed and reached nearly to his shirt collar. He needed a haircut. She ran her fingers through her own hair, thinking she did a fair job of cutting it. Maybe she could offer Grant a trim.

His gaze swung from the files to her. Dusky beard stubble grazed his tanned lower jaw. Tess had grown up surrounded by clean-shaven men, military clean, but

127

Grant's light beard only made him look more appealing. "How'd it go today with the preschool?"

Disarmed, she cleared her throat. "Oh, yes. It was…it was okay. There were about four kids, and I liked Jenny Stotter, the owner. She has a nice, easy way about her. There's a play area in the back of the house that looked like it could be fun."

"How about Crystal? Did she like it?"

Tess looked out the window behind Grant to the sand dunes flowing in the distance beneath the mountain range. "Well, I think she will. You know, things are up in the air for her right now. I want to talk to Jud about helping out with the tuition for a couple days a week…if I can also work out borrowing the truck from you to go into town."

"Sure, we can come up with a plan." Grant continued rifling the files, searching. "Ah, here's that dang thing." He gave a yank and pulled out a file. A photo dropped from its contents to the floor.

Both of them stooped to retrieve it, their heads almost touching. Tess peeled it up quickly. Glancing down at the photo in her hand, she saw the familiar image of Grant's deceased wife standing by a roan horse, her blonde hair lifted free in a morning breeze. "Oh," Tess murmured, a strange knot forming in her stomach, "it looks like…Laura." The name sounded awkward on her tongue.

Grant's fingers brushed hers as he took the photo and stared at it. His half-buttoned shirt revealed his upper chest covered with crisp brown hair. Suddenly the room around them seemed to shrink. "We were getting the horses ready to go out on a camping trip. Don't know how this got lost in that file."

Laura was wearing jodhpurs and high boots accenting her slim shapely legs. Tess gulped, picturing herself trying to mount a horse. She hadn't ridden a four-legged animal since she was a kid. "So, Laura was a horse woman?"

Grant's eyes caressed the photo then glazed with moisture. "She could sit a horse pretty well." His pain was palpable between them, and he turned away.

Through the window, the sand dunes stretched out against the Sangre de Cristo range. Attempting to shift the uncomfortable conversation, Tess asked, "Do you ever go to see the dunes? I mean see them close up?"

He straightened to his full height, inches above her. The photo disappeared somewhere behind him on the cluttered desk. "Not lately. Dad used to take my sister Sarah and me over there a lot when we were young. We'd scramble up those hills like a couple of mountain goats."

"They look like they've been there a long time," she observed, relieved to take his mind off of Laura for a few minutes.

"They have. Over ten thousand years. They're wild—always moving with the wind."

She moved closer to the window. "What keeps them from just blowing away?"

He stepped up beside her. "Well, the snowmelt from the mountains, the groundwater, and, I guess, Medano Creek keep them stable at their base."

His closeness made her slightly uncomfortable. He smelled like the outdoors and wood after it's been freshly cut. She realized he'd asked her something and she didn't have a clue what it was. "Excuse me?"

He cocked his head, a curious expression on his face. "I said would you like to go there some time? The tourists are pretty much gone now and I could take you and Crystal one of these days."

"Sure." He was looking at her so intently. For some odd reason, her cheeks flushed with heat. "I know Crystal would love to see them…up close." The space between them suddenly became too close, the air around her limited. She stepped away a few feet. "Thanks,

I'll…we'll take you up on it…one of these days." She left Grant to his file and slipped back down the loft stairs.

What was wrong with her? She felt almost feverish. She made her way to the kitchen and found an old cookbook on a lower shelf. Breakfast menus. That's what she needed. Some fresh ideas for tomorrow's breakfast would be a welcome diversion.

Back in the cabin, Tess made an early chili supper for her and Crystal then dived into the cookbook. Now that the mornings were cooler, her thoughts turned to heartier breads than toast. The middle section of the book was devoted to muffins and fruit breads.

Crystal leaned over her shoulder while she sat at the small kitchen table. "What ya lookin' at?"

"Muffins—for breakfast," Tess answered, observing various recipes.

"I like chocolate chip muffins." Crystal picked up Miss Tabby and propped her up on her shoulder. "We both do." She chuckled.

"You like anything with chocolate chips." An idea struck. Pumpkin muffins. *Pumpkin muffins?* No! Too sissy for men. She could hear Juan and Carlos tease her about that "little girl food" the rest of the week. She continued to flip through the bread section.

"What are ya gonna make?"

Tess sat back in her lattice-backed chair. "Pumpkin bread. That sounds good, don't you think?" The men should definitely favor that. "Mr. Grant should like it."

Wrinkling up her nose, Crystal plunked Miss Tabby on Tess's lap. "Pumpkin bread sounds yucky."

"Oh, go get ready for bed, little Miss Pumpkin." She gave Crystal a light swat on the rump and she scampered off to the bedroom, giggling.

A horse's whinny made Tess glance out the side window toward the corral. Grant was mounting his palomino. He sat tall in the saddle, reminding her of a cavalry soldier preparing to lead a field brigade. Where was he going at this time of night?

Through a stand of cottonwood trees, their leaves fluttering golden in the early evening sun, she watched him ride over to the road. It was a perfect autumn night. The shadows soft across the side yard. A wave of yearning washed over her. If circumstances were different and she knew how to ride, maybe Grant would have asked her to join him. She imagined the two of them riding up along the mountain range, taking in the vast, vivid sunset across the valley.

"Tess, please read me a story," Crystal called from the bedroom.

Releasing a sigh more weary than intended, Tess turned away from the window. She had tried to read to Crystal in the evenings before bedtime, even though their supply of children's books consisted of only a few she'd found at the town drugstore. "Find one you like. I'm coming."

A few hours later, too awake to think of sleep, she sat in her robe curled up on the frayed easy chair by the front door. From the former resident's ancient radio, a song by Thelonius Monk crackled into the room. She leaned her head back against the chair and closed her eyes. Somehow, listening to the strains of jazz gave her a modicum of peace, reminded her of the good days in New Orleans. Before Katrina. When her life was a whole lot simpler.

The front door set ajar slightly, letting in a fresh breeze. Crickets chirped in their secret hideaways. Horse's hooves clopped up the dirt road.

Alighting from her lumpy chair, Tess padded to the door and looked outside. In the twilight shadows, Grant trotted up to the corral fence and dismounted. Where had he been all this time? He took his horse inside the barn and emerged a few minutes later. She lingered on the threshold behind the screen door.

The sound of his boots crunched on gravel. Her heartbeat lifted a notch. Maybe he'd stop and say goodnight. She tugged the sash on her robe a little snugger. With a deliberate stride, Grant walked right past the cabin and over into his back yard. His hat sloped down over his forehead, his somber silhouette moved against the night sky. Surely the light in her front window must have caught his eye. But he gave not so much as a glance or a wave.

She fought a sinking feeling in her gut. Stepping back, she closed the front door and locked it. Where had he gone? *Not your business, girl.*

A stubborn streak still made her wonder. Where would Laura be buried? There was a small cemetery on the outskirts of town, but that was too far to ride a horse. She scrunched up her shoulders and turned her head from side to side. Her back was tight as a drum.

A bluesy tune from the radio added to her discomfort. No use trying to figure out her employer's comings and goings. One thing was sure, Grant Wilder was a mysterious man…carrying emotional scars. His still tender grief over the loss of his wife had been very evident this afternoon.

She snapped the radio off and turned off the dim front room light. Surrounded by the darkness, she realized that all three of them—Grant, Crystal, and her— had their share of scars.

And there was nothing much she could do about it.

* * *

"I've got a tummy ache."

Tess looked down into Crystal's somber eyes, the slight frown creasing her almond-hued forehead, and gave the child's hand a squeeze. "You're my big girl today."

They were heading up the front walk to The Little Red School House, Crystal's first official day at preschool. After a bit of arm-twisting, Grandpa Jud had agreed to contribute the funds for a twice-weekly visit. Tess was cautiously hopeful this would be a constructive experience for her charge. One step at a time. Right?

"They're here!" a boy called from behind the screen door. He bounced from one leg to the other, an eager expression on his urchin face.

"There's Sam."

Quickly as he had materialized, Sam disappeared.

Beginning to chew on her lower lip, Crystal stared straight ahead as Tess coaxed her forward.

Once inside, the combined voices of five energetic preschoolers greeted their ears from the next room. Jenny emerged with three little girls hovering behind her. Two were dark-haired, wearing beautiful smiles and small gold earrings in their pierced ears. The third, in need of a comb to her thin blond locks, regarded Tess and Crystal with concerned, light blue eyes.

Jenny brought them together. "The sisters are Teresa and Anna Robles. And Erleen Stoltz." She smiled at Crystal, hanging back beside Tess. "This is Crystal."

The taller sister giggled. The shorter sister managed a shy smile.

Blond Erleen stared at Crystal, then said "Hi. How old are you?"

Crystal lifted her chin. "Four. I came from New Orleans."

"I'll only stay a minute," Tess whispered to Jenny. "I've got some errands to run."

"That's fine. Come into the playroom with us." Jenny maneuvered the girls into the adjacent, sun-filled room and Tess followed. Sam and a larger, red-haired boy huddled in the corner making loud motor sounds over a toy truck and miniature cars.

"That's Butch," Jenny said. "Hey Butch, can you say hi to our new friend, Crystal?"

Head bent, Butch continued his focus on the cars.

Jenny shrugged good-naturedly. "Boys are no fun. Come on over here and let's look at the doll house." She led the girls over to a three-foot high doll house on a side shelf furnished with plastic furniture.

As the girls took notice of the doll house, Butch jumped up from the floor and came up behind Crystal. "I'm six," he announced.

She ignored him.

He reached up and yanked her ponytail.

"Ouch!" She whirled and glared at him.

On the sidelines, Tess cringed, yet she didn't think it was her place to intervene.

"No hair pulling, Butch," Jenny admonished.

Butch's eyes squinted up making him look like an ornery little pig. "Her hair is fuzzy."

With a disheartened glance toward Tess, Jenny said, "Crystal has nice hair."

"Is she a nigger?"

Tess recoiled as if she'd been punched in the gut.

"Young man, I *never* want to hear you use that word again!" Jenny placed her hands on Butch's shoulders and forced him to face Crystal whose eyes had grown wide in confusion. "Now say you're sorry."

Butch clamped his lips together, his pudgy cheeks flaring.

"Say it." Jenny's eyes meant business.

"Sorry," Butch muttered.

Tess exhaled a ragged breath. So this would be Crystal's first brush with prejudice. She hovered on the brink of wanting to grab the child's hand and flee this place—or let her stay.

Without missing a beat, Jenny brightened. "Who wants to make hot chocolate?"

All small hands shot up. "Me!" voices chorused.

As she herded the group toward the kitchen, Sam pointed a finger at Butch. "He farted."

Color tinted Butch's pugnacious features. "Did not!"

"Did too. It smells bad," Sam retorted, screwing up his nose.

Tess escaped out the front door, leaving Jenny to resolve the hijinks. A combination of relief and angst rode on her shoulders all the way to the hardware store at the other end of town. Relief that Jenny squelched what could have escalated into a hurtful episode for Crystal. She doubted Crystal had ever been called the "N" word before or could understand its meaning.

Her concern was how Crystal would react to being in a new environment with kids from a completely different part of the country with a new set of prejudices.

* * *

"I don't want to go back there," Crystal said later, her lips in a pout, as Tess buckled her into the booster seat that Grant had rigged together with cushions and wide leather straps.

"Where do you mean?" As if Tess didn't know. Even though Jenny had painted a more congenial picture of the morning's activities at the preschool, Crystal's displeasure had been obvious. Scuffling over the sidewalk to the truck, she'd hung her head without saying a word.

"The school house," she replied now, pointing back toward the offending red building.

Tess switched on the truck engine, her thoughts jumbled and disappointed. "Gosh, you can't mean you won't give it another try?"

Crystal swung her head from side to side, her eyes unreadable behind her pink sunglasses. "I don't like those kids."

Tess turned off the residential area onto the road out of town. "Most of them seem very nice. And Jenny is really super, huh? Didn't she make you guys hot chocolate?"

A pause from the back of the cab. Then, "yes."

Tess looked into the rear view mirror at Crystal. "You like Jenny, don't you?"

"Mm, kinda." Crystal's lower lip pulled into a straight line. "What is a nigger?"

Tess's hands gripped the steering wheel. There it was again—that discomforting name—always raising its prickly head where it wasn't welcome. She blew out a sigh. "Honey, it's a mean word to call someone who has brown skin like yours-"

"Butch is mean," Crystal spurted out before Tess could expand.

"Butch doesn't know you yet, Pumpkin. He'll soon find out how beautiful you really are."

Crystal wrinkled her nose, the corners of her mouth turning upward. "I like Sam. He said I could play with his new red truck."

"I like Sam, too," Tess answered, relieved that Crystal had made a friend, as well as a foe.

The sand dunes glowed in the distance beneath a blue sky filled with lazy, cream colored clouds. The Sangre de Cristos rose behind them, inviting. She slapped the steering wheel. "Hey, you want to go to the Dunes?"

"Where?"

"The sand dunes!" She angled her head. "Over there."

Instant excitement. Crystal bounced in her cushioned seat. "Yes! Yes! Let's go over there. Can I play on them?"

"If we can get close enough." Tess sat up straighter, pressed the accelerator to pick up a little speed, and they sailed down the main road.

At the Visitor Center, Tess paid the entrance fee then called Grant on his cell phone to let him know where they were. When he didn't answer, she left a message. Her sudden decision probably sounded a little crazy, and she hoped he wouldn't be offended that she'd jumped the gun to take Crystal when he'd offered to take them all one day soon. Oh well. Serendipity came quickly sometimes, without warning.

The Dune Field snuck up on them as they drove nearer. Rising and falling, arching higher towards the clouds, in a crystalline brilliance. Sun and shadow. Hardly any cars on the road now that tourists had gone home. A treasure of wide open space. Medano Creek meandered alongside the rambling dunes; leafy trees on a small island nearby rustled in a bright orange blur.

Crystal leaned forward. "Can I make a sand castle?"

Tess laughed. "We'll see. There's certainly enough sand."

She entered the parking lot and parked the truck. Wind whistled around them. She made sure that Crystal put on her visor and sunglasses, and she did the same. After slathering sunscreen on both of them, she helped Crystal out of the pickup. Holding Crystal's warm hand, they headed toward the ancient dunes.

Like flowing giant waves crashing against the mountain's shore. Relentless. Roaring in her ears. Like

Katrina. Tess's mouth went dry. Her stomach rolled in a wave of nausea.

Crystal broke free, running ahead onto the muddy creek bed. Running toward those giant waves.

Tess halted on the rough path, wrapped her arms around herself, roiling inside. Panic snuck her breath away. "Crystal," she called against the wind. "Come back!"

But the child skittered here and there, unhindered by tethers real or surreal.

Gulping in air, closing her eyes against the unbidden fear, Tess mentally talked herself back to a place of calmness. Her racing heartbeat slowed. *You're in Paradise, foolish woman. Not hell.*

She focused on her surroundings: the vast yellow-ochre scrub brush and forest green ponderosa scattered on either side, the scrunch of sand giving way beneath her Nikes with each step forward.

When they reached the creek's edge, the dunes, like a vast sand box, stretched out forever. Crystal squatted down, swirling her short brown fingers in the sand. She grinned broadly. "This is fun!" Her arms flung upward towards the cottony clouds. "I can make a sand castle as big as the whole world!"

"Yes, you can." Tess ventured a ways just to get the feel of being there, amazed at the deep grooves her shoes made in the slithery stuff. She returned to Crystal and helped her build a lumpy sand castle. The afternoon breeze, the sand crystals tingling their faces, the near silence, except for the occasional cry of perhaps finch or prairie grouse, eased her earlier discomfort. She looked over at Crystal intently adding another turret to her creation. "Do you think you would like to live here? You know, after you get to know your grandpa better and make some new friends?"

Crystal lifted her head from her work and gazed back at Tess through her pink heart-shaped sunglasses. "Will my mommy ever come here?"

Another knock-out punch in one day. Tess's breath caught in her throat as her mind flashed back to the recent dark dream of Carrie drowning in a sea of shiny little fish.

"Is Mommy dead?"

Miserable inside, Tess grappled for an answer to satisfy. "We don't know. Your grandpa Jud has been calling New Orleans. People are still looking for her every day. They will let him know if they find her."

The corners of her mouth turning down, Crystal continued patting the sides of her castle. How fragile it looked, ready for the next strong wind to blow it back across the dunes.

"Let's walk down the beach. I think I see some little deer." Tess pulled Crystal to her feet and she reluctantly bid her creative dwelling goodbye.

Late afternoon sunlight filtered through golden cottonwoods along the creek bank ahead. Tess wished Crystal's questions would blow away on the breeze. There simply were no answers right now. But Crystal was persistent

"Will we ever go back to New Orleans?" she asked, her tone wistful.

"Maybe someday you will." Returning any time soon was impossible. She had no money, no place to stay, and definitely no inclination to face the ongoing chaos and misery still existing there. She hurried her pace alongside the zig-zagging creek. "Hey, we can pretend we're near New Orleans right now. Look at this sandy beach—our own beach by the sea."

Crystal shed her small sandals and dashed over the wet sand. Tess also removed her shoes and gave chase. "Wait for me!"

Yards ahead, Crystal leaped and jogged, leaving a trail of giggles behind her. A bird flew over them toward the clustered cottonwoods on the other side of the creek bed. Spreading her arms wide, Crystal teetered on tip toe then swirled in circles. "I'm a bird too. I can fly!"

Tess followed, laughing at the child's eager imagination, the ease with which she could blend wistful into carefree. Oh, to be a child again…lost in the moment. Free to become the bird, the wind gusting over the shimmering dunes, or the water skimming the edge of the valley.

Tess caught up and gently coaxed her back along the beach. She paused, her gaze catching a trio of small brown-and-white deer, observing them from a clump of brush across the creek.

"Look," she whispered. "Those deer."

Crystal stared. "Oooh. I want to play with them."

The deer twitched their white-tipped, pointy ears and retreated into a stand of cottonwood.

"Not today." They headed back to get their shoes, the damp sand squishing between their toes. All in all, this had been a successful adventure, serendipity at its best.

"I want Mommy to come live with us on the ranch," Crystal announced, looking fondly up at Tess. "Then she can play with us on the beach—and we can show her the deer."

Reverie sunk to the pit of Tess's stomach. She knelt down next to Crystal. Wrapping her arms around her narrow shoulders, she pressed a kiss on her warm, smooth cheek, a salty-tasting kiss from her own tear. "I know you miss your mommy. I want her to come back too."

What more could she say?

Tess gazed out over the high-rolling dunes, wondering what the odds were that Carrie Pearl would ever come back into their lives? She might as well bet on the state lottery.

Chapter Eleven

"We're havin' a party, Nina," Crystal confided as she reached up and brushed the fly-away mane from the foal's long neck. "You have to look your best."

From across the stall, Tess observed the two: animal and human companions. Nina, already almost a foot taller than Crystal, permitted the grooming for a moment longer then bolted on her stick-thin legs. She romped toward the open barn door, her earlier injury almost invisible, with Crystal chasing right behind, her pig tails bobbing. Inseparable. And both unpredictable.

In the next stall, Roy, the hired hand, finished putting on Sugar's halter. "Those kids are gonna have some fun today." He led the docile brown mare out to the corral.

"I hope you're right, Roy." Tess glanced at her watch—almost nine o'clock. Where were they? Jenny had said she'd bring the preschool kids out to the ranch by eight thirty for a morning of touring and horse rides. Kind of a get-acquainted, make friends party for Crystal.

Tess had come up with the idea after Crystal's reluctance to go back to the Little Red School House. She feared the child would continue to feel out of place there. If Crystal could make friends in this unfamiliar environment, she'd be more likely to ease into a new life here.

Hesitant to ask Grant the huge favor of allowing her to host such an event, especially after his disappointment at not being included in the girls' jaunt to the dunes, Tess had baked a batch of chocolate chip, cowboy-size cookies before approaching him.

Lucky for her and Crystal, Grant had agreed, even liked the idea. Of course, he'd said he wanted to supervise the riding. Put kids and horses together and there was always room for accidents. Then a slight cloud of concern had lifted from his eyes and he'd winked, the beginning of a smile lifting the corners of his mouth. That smile had instantly warmed her from across the kitchen table as they shared the chocolate chip cookies, still fragrant from the oven.

Now Grant rode up from the east pasture where he and Juan had taken some of the horses to graze right after he'd finished an early breakfast. He dismounted with ease from his palomino, the brim of his hat set at an angle over his forehead.

Morning light reflected in his hazel eyes—eyes that showed assuredness and an independence of spirit. "Where are those little buckaroos? Thought they'd be here by now."

She shrugged. "I did too. They should be arriving any time."

He handed the reins over to Roy who led the horse into the barn.

Crystal left Nina's side and sprinted up to Grant. "Hi. Are you gonna stay and play with us?" she asked, gazing up at him as she would a tall tree.

"Sure, honey." He knelt down and, almost knocking his hat off, hoisted her onto his shoulders. "Come on. Help me keep a look out."

Responding with surprised giggles, Crystal held fast to his large hands, her short legs dangling around his neck. Grant nodded at Tess then strode over to the other side of the corral nearest the road.

She smiled to herself. If anyone could win Crystal's heart, it would definitely be Mr. Grant.

"Here they come!" Crystal shouted, her small body vibrating with anticipation.

Beyond them, a cloud of dust billowed up from the dirt road and a horn blared.

An older model SUV, mud-encrusted along its sides, rambled up to the front yard, then slowed to a stop several yards closer to the corral. Jenny Stotter poked her head out of the driver's side window. "Sorry we're late! We saw some buffalo on the way and the kids made me stop. I brought their helmets like you suggested; they're in the back."

Then doors swung open and a gang of kids leaped from the vehicle, all talking at once.

"I brought their helmets like you suggested," Jenny said. "They're in the back."

"Where's the horses?" Sam Stotter called, his hair electric dandelion fuzz above a red checkered western shirt, jeans and western boots.

Butch, a half head taller, face flushed, ran beside him, his short, stocky legs pumping faster. "I wanna ride a big one!"

The two Robles sisters quickly flanked Jenny, each holding one of her hands, their dark eyes shining, their long black hair braided in pigtails.

Only Erleen lingered inside the vehicle, her light hair framing big, frightened azure eyes staring out from a rear window.

Next to Tess, Crystal squirmed on top of Grant's broad shoulders. "Let me down!"

As Grant set Crystal onto the ground, Tess whispered in her ear. "Let's go say hi to Erleen."

Crystal paused a moment then nodded, and off she bolted. She came to a halt at the open side door. "Erleen—are you gonna come out of the car and play with us?"

Erleen was shaking her head *no* as Tess approached. So much for unanimous enthusiasm. Tess put on a hopeful smile. "It should be fun. You'll get to see the horses and then we'll have a picnic."

Crystal hopped from one foot to the other. "And you can pet my new pony, Nina."

Now that should have been an offer no child could refuse, Tess thought.

Erleen's expression softened, but she made no move to join them.

A whistle split the air behind them. "Okay, who's ready to come watch the horses eat their breakfast?"

Crystal's eyes widened and her voice echoed the other's in a loud "me!"

Still no movement from the child inside the SUV.

"You better come with us, Erleen," Crystal commanded, her small hands on her hips.

There were other ways of persuasion. "Come on, honey. We'll let Erleen catch up with us later," Tess said, taking Crystal's warm hand in hers. "You can come see the horses whenever you're ready, Erleen." She led Crystal toward the corral and the gyrating pre-schoolers.

"Jenny, I'll take the kids on the barn tour if you'll keep an eye on Erleen. She's a little hesitant right now."

Jenny swung a look back at Erleen still watching from the rear window. "Sure thing. Here, Teresa and Anna can go with you." She released the dark-haired sisters to Tess.

"Yahoo!" Butch hollered, Sam at his heels, as they bounded for the barn door.

"Hey! Stop right here." A pillar of authority, Grant stood in front of them, his man-size boots planted in the dirt. "The horses don't like a lot of shoutin' when they eat. So, zip your lips, cowboys."

The boys looked up at him, glanced sideways at each other, and back to his no-nonsense expression, their demeanor immediately showing respect. Sam stuck his hands in his back pockets, barely able to contain his enthusiasm.

"Okay, come on in." Grant led the way inside the barn.

Holding the Robles sisters' hands, Tess followed with Crystal. "Do you girls have horses at home?"

Both girls bobbed their heads. "We like to ride sometimes," the older girl Teresa said.

Younger Anna smiled. "Daddy lets us ride Ginger."

"That's great! I wish I knew how to ride," Tess said wistfully. Maybe she'd learn a few tips today.

The interior of the barn smelled of fresh hay and horse. She was beginning to like the earthy aroma, welcome entering this man and animal world: see the horses' heads above the stalls, their liquid brown eyes greet her, touch the large rounded backsides and sweep her fingers through their swishy manes. Some of them were becoming more familiar to her, like new friends.

Crystal found Nina back in her stall and coaxed Teresa and Anna to join her. Squeals of delight echoed from the sisters when they first saw the prancing little foal. They both wanted to pet Nina at the same time. "Too bad we can't ride Nina yet. She has to grow up first," Crystal explained.

"She's kinda scrawny," Butch remarked as he and Sam passed by with Grant to see the other horses.

"Nina is a princess!" Crystal called back, an indignant frown on her small brow.

"You stepped in some horse poop," Sam said to Butch.

"Did not. You did," Butch muttered.

Tess sighed, hoping she wouldn't live to regret this day.

To her surprise, Erleen's small blonde head poked around the barn door frame. She gazed inside the darkened interior. "Come with me to see the new foal," Tess offered, moving toward her and extending her hand.

Tentatively, Erleen slipped her fingers across Tess's open palm. They were reed-thin and dry to the touch. In fact, Erleen reminded Tess of a pale dandelion, ready to blow away in the wind. She smiled down into the child's upturned face. "You'll like Nina."

At Nina's stall, Crystal and the sisters chattered away as she charmed them by nuzzling their necks then coyly stepping back when they reached out to pet her dark mane.

Erleen's expression changed from hesitant to awestruck.

"Would you like to pet Nina?" Tess asked.

Erleen nodded slowly.

Leading Erleen over to the girls, Tess caught Crystal's eye. "Crystal can show you what makes Nina happy." She pulled a handful of sugar cubes from her shirt pocket.

Instant attention. Suddenly everyone wanted to feed Nina. Crystal enthusiastically provided instructions to Erleen on the best way to hold her sugar cube in her open hand so that Nina could nip up the sweet treat.

"Oooh, her nose is soft—and tickly!" Erleen exclaimed, breaking out of her solemn shell.

"That's her muzzle," Crystal corrected.

While Teresa and Anna took turns petting and feeding Nina their sugar cubes, Grant strode by leading a bay quarter horse. Roy followed with a smaller pinto, Butch and Sam not far behind. "We're bringing Scout and Bessie for the boys," Grant said over his shoulder. "Bring the girls outside when they're ready."

"We want to ride, too," Crystal called.

Tess winked at her, impressed at how much more emboldened Crystal was becoming. "You will. Let's go watch them." She took the four girls out behind the corral fence where they could view the boys ride from a safe distance.

147

Inside the corral, Jenny was adjusting Butch's helmet strap under his chin. He screwed up his eyes disagreeably. "I don't want to wear a helmet—I want a cowboy hat!"

Grant tapped the top of his helmet. "The helmet's good for now. You can wear a cowboy hat when you grow into one, pardner." With a low chuckle, he scooped up the chubby rider and hoisted him onto the bay.

From a much higher viewpoint, Butch's cranky expression shifted to amazement. "Wow! I can see clear over the fence."

"This is Scout," Grant said, handing Butch the reins. "He's a good ol' boy. You be good to Scout and he'll be good to you."

Butch grasped the reins in both hands. "Yeah. He's big."

Roy already had lifted Sam onto the smaller pinto, Bessie. After telling the boys how to hold the reins and "sit up straight," they started the horses walking around the circular corral. Grant stayed alongside Scout and Roy ambled next to Bessie.

Tess imagined this was the first time either young cowboy had sat a horse.

The look on Sam's face was priceless. His pint-sized boots hugged the pinto's round back. "Go, Bessie," he commanded softly as they went by. It was obviously love at first sight.

After the first round, Butch snapped the reins on Scout's neck and bounced anxiously. "Come on, Scout. Let's go!"

"Not so fast, dude." Grant clamped a hand over Butch's shoulder. "Let him get to know you a little bit first."

The next go around, Grant stopped in front of the fence near Tess and the girls. "We'll see how he does on his own," he confided to her, referring to Butch.

148

"They're doing well," Tess offered, and Jenny nodded, a proud mom look on her face as she watched Sam go by on Bessie.

Crystal stuck her head between the fence railings. "Can we go next?"

"Pretty soon, cowgirl," Grant said.

As the horses swung round on the far side of the corral, Butch bounced again, his features flushed with impatience. He slapped the ends of the reins across Scout's ears as he dug his sneakers into the horse's upper rib cage.

"Butch, stop!" Grant called out and moved toward them.

Ignoring Grant, Butch continued snapping the reins about Scout's neck and ears. The horse shook his head, his eyes showing agitation. In a deliberate motion, Scout sidled over to the corral fence and began rubbing up against it as he walked.

"Ow—ouch!" Butch hollered while attempting to free his foot from scraping against the top railing. A scarlet flush burned Butch's face beneath his helmet. He yanked the reins back to his chest, the action prompting Scout to jerk suddenly, throwing the boy off balance.

Tess flinched, imagining the pain in Butch's foot and the horse's painful mouth beneath the metal bit. Would the disgruntled animal try to toss Butch off his back?

In that moment, Grant dashed across the corral and ejected Butch unceremoniously from the horse. Wresting the reins from Butch, he set him awkwardly on the ground.

Tess had never seen Grant lose his temper, but from the way his jaw was set, she could tell anger bubbled beneath his usually calm exterior.

"Young man, don't ever treat a horse like that or you won't ride one here again," Grant said in a stern voice.

Butch's features showed rebellion. "He…he tried to push me against the fence. He hurt my foot."

"We'll take a look at your foot. But I want you to remember what I told you. Be good to a horse and he'll be good to you." He knelt down and removed Butch's helmet. "Can you promise me you'll remember that?"

Butch lowered his eyes to the patch of ground in front of him. "…yeah."

Behind them, Roy had brought Bessie to a halt and lifted Sam off of her. "Mom, I rode a horse!" he announced with boyish bravado and raced to Jenny who was entering the corral.

Jenny patted Sam's shoulder in approval, but didn't stop until she reached Grant and Butch. "Butch, you need to apologize to Mr. Wilder for the way you treated Scout."

Suddenly Butch grabbed the front of his jeans. "I gotta pee."

Grant shook his head, half-smiling. "Roy, would you take this little dude to the john?" And check his foot while you're at it?"

"Sure thing." Roy whisked Butch off toward the main house.

"That boy needs more discipline," Jenny muttered. His dad drives a truck for the same company as my husband, and he's not home much."

Grant shrugged his shoulders. "Maybe not so much the discipline, just more of his dad's attention." He picked up Scout's reins and started to lead him back to the barn. "Don't worry, being around animals usually brings out the best in kids. You did very well, Sam."

Sam grinned. "Can I ride Bessie again?"

"Sure, next time. But the girls are waiting their turn. Tess," Grant called, "you can tell the cowgirls their rides will be next." She gave a wave and the little gals gathered around, jumping with excitement. Having children around her suited Tess; they helped bring out a sunnier personality than when she'd first come to the ranch. It made him feel better seeing her smile, getting her mind away from the troubles she'd left behind in New Orleans.

When Roy returned a few minutes later with Butch, Grant had led an older male gelding into the ring. "Here's Dusty," he called to the girls. "He's a gentle old boy. Who wants to ride him?"

The Robles sisters raised their hands. Grant feigned a look of surprise. "You both want to ride him?"

Holding Anna's hand, Teresa stepped forward. "She's only four, so we should ride together."

"That's fine with Dusty. Come on over and I'll introduce you." They scrambled over and Grant lifted them up onto the saddle blanket, the older sister Teresa behind. He volunteered Roy to walk beside them.

Crystal and Erleen watched from Tess's side: Crystal eager, Erleen still shy.

"Well, I've got sweet Sugar here," Grant said referring to the brown mare, "and Bessie's ready to go again."

Skittering up to him on tiptoe, Crystal exclaimed, "I want Bessie!"

Grant looked at Erleen, a glow of interest in her blue eyes. "Let's let Erleen choose. She's our guest today."

Tess patted Erleen's shoulder. "Which horse would you like?" Wide-eyed, Erleen chewed on her lower lip for a second. "I like Sugar," she answered softly.

Grant sent her a wink. "Good choice. She's waitin' to give you a mighty fine ride." When Tess brought her over, Grant easily set Erleen on top of Sugar's warm back. He held his hand on her arm for a moment to give a show of reassurance before easing the reins into her small hands. Erleen accepted the reins tentatively. "I'll walk beside you just to be sure Sugar is paying attention."

"Now me, please," Crystal implored, gazing up at him expectantly. She had a way of melting him, no question about that.

"Up you go, babe." Grant lifted her onto the little pinto while Tess held the reins. "Tess said she'd be your escort today, okay?"

Crystal nodded, a beaming grin on her face. "This feels fun!"

He turned to Tess and gave her a slight cuff on the shoulder. "Maybe Tess would like a turn…afterward."

Her smile dimpled and she cocked her head that certain way she had of engaging him. "Sounds like a plan, cowboy."

He made a mental note to follow up with a riding lesson. Every woman on a ranch should know how to ride.

When Grant started up the caravan, Tess fell in behind, walking with Crystal and Bessie. Roy came up behind them, the Robles sisters atop Dusty. Striding ahead, his tan western hat slanted at a jaunty angle above broad shoulders, Grant set an imposing image. He had intimated that her turn might come next. She wondered what horse she would ride. Not today, but a riding lesson intrigued her. Grant would be a patient teacher. She saw how helpful and attentive he was to Erleen, bringing out a bit of self confidence in the way her back straightened and she held the reins.

Tess imagined how he would have to boost her up onto the saddle. Gad, she hoped she wouldn't make a total fool of herself, like miss getting her foot into the stirrup and fall off the other side. But the reward of being on a horse, no matter how clumsy she'd be at first, would be worth it. They could follow a trail looking over at Blanca Peak after the first snowfall.

If she was still here on the ranch…then.

Next to her, Crystal exclaimed, "Can I get some cowboy boots? I can't be a cowgirl until I get boots."

"We'll see, honey." Tess thought she'd like a pair, too. But new boots cost money—something in short supply right now.

After about fifteen minutes, the girls had all become enamored with their horses. Even Erleen seemed to be more relaxed and talkative with Grant walking beside her and Sugar.

The boys, however, were going bananas without a diversion and, despite Jenny's efforts to curtail them, scampered like monkeys outside the corral, climbing up on the rungs, and making silly noises as each girl rode past.

"Time for lunch," Grant called out. "Anybody like goat's tongue?"

Butch peered through the fence rungs, his eyes pinched up. "What?"

"Well, how about mouse burgers?"

A few feet away, Sam hung upside down, his legs clamped over the top rung. "Yuck!" he spat out.

Grant brought Sugar to a halt, signaling to the others that the rides were over. "Aren't you boys hungry?"

Butch's expression was dubious. "I don't want no goat's tongue!"

His unabashed candor made Tess laugh. "It's a surprise. Only the cooks know."

* * *

After the group was rounded up, they made their way to the deck behind the main house. While the children washed up, Tess and Jenny got busy in the kitchen setting out lemonade and soft drinks, jumbo franks and buns, pretzels and chips.

"Gosh, this is a super kitchen," Jenny observed. "Bet you enjoy cooking in it."

Tess took a tray of ice and a large lemonade pitcher out of the refrigerator, and set them on the center granite island. "You know, I only used to spend enough time in my kitchen to pop a frozen dinner into the oven." She glanced up at the collection of cookbooks on a top shelf. "Now, I-I actually find it rewarding to make meals from scratch."

Jenny gazed at her with a knowing smile. "Guess it depends on who you're cooking for."

The back door slammed shut and boot heels clicked across the hall tile. Tess automatically raised her head and looked toward the kitchen doorway.

"Need any help, ladies?" Grant asked as he rounded the far kitchen counter, his shirt sleeves rolled up over strong forearms.

"Well, you could carry this lemonade and ice outside to the deck. The glasses are already out there," Tess said, gazing into his inviting smile.

He whisked the tray and pitcher out of the kitchen. "The grill is ready. I'll be back for the franks and buns," he called over his shoulder.

Jenny looked after Grant. "Now, there's a reason for being in the kitchen every morning." She swung back to Tess, an eyebrow lifting in conspiracy.

Heat rushed up Tess's neck to her face. "Jenny—he's my *boss*."

Jenny's features expressed mock surprise. "Oh, is he? Well, Grant Wilder is also a very attractive man—in case you haven't noticed—an attractive, *available* man."

"Don't be ridiculous," Tess sputtered. "I'm working here strictly as Crystal's guardian, until…" Until what? Until Carrie Pearl turned up alive—or not?

"Sure." Jenny pressed her lips together as if not wanting to make the conversation more awkward.

They carried the rest of the food outside to a hungry crowd. Grateful to drop the subject of Grant, Tess nevertheless wondered why her reaction to Jenny's comment had been quite so defensive. She was relieved to keep busy dishing up plates and pouring drinks.

"We looked for Mrs. Stumpy Rump but we couldn't find her," Crystal confided to Tess when they were finishing their hot dogs. "I told Erleen how the barn cat got her tail, but she escaped down the bunny hole." Erleen's eyes lit up at the latter part of the story.

"Well, we'll look for Mrs. Stumpy Rump after lunch," Tess reassured.

Grant emerged from the back door, carrying a huge tray loaded with ice cream, multiple toppings and colorful plastic bowls. "Hey, who wants an ice cream sundae?"

Everyone raised their hand and Grant was surrounded before he could set the tray down on a table. Butch and Sam grabbed up ice cream scoops and were about to dive into the huge gallon containers.

"Not so fast, guys." Grant held them back with large hands. "Ladies first." The boys grumbled loudly. Grant's wink at Tess held mischief. "Better hurry up, gals, before it disappears."

The girls didn't have to be asked twice. Soon everyone was elbow-deep in vanilla and Rocky Road ice cream, and building giant hills of mixed toppings.

"Miss Tabby likes ice cream too." Crystal said, midway through her sundae. She darted an imploring look at Tess. "I'm gonna go get her, okay?"

"Sure—if she wants to join the party."

Crystal jumped up from the picnic table bench. "C'mon, Erleen. Let's go get Miss Tabby." She grabbed Erleen's hand and off they scampered to the cabin.

Tess watched, encouraged to see a renewed enthusiasm in both the girls. But a few minutes later, when they returned, Crystal carrying the squirming cat, she wondered if this was such a good idea.

Butch and Sam looked up from their second helpings. "Wow, a three-legged cat!" Butch announced and ran over to the edge of the deck to get a closer look.

His mouth smeared with Rocky Road ice cream, Sam asked, "What happened to his other leg?"

Crystal sent him a disbelieving glance. "It's a *her*. She's Miss Tabby."

Butch peered at Miss Tabby's lower parts. "Did a car run over it?"

Brushing past him, Crystal answered, "Yes…in New Orleans. But it doesn't bother her. She runs just fine without it." She carried the objecting cat up to the ice cream table. The Robles sisters came over. Teresa petted the top of Miss Tabby's head.

Tess joined the group. "So, you think Miss Tabby would like some vanilla ice cream?"

The girls' heads bobbed vehemently.

"We'll start with a small scoop." Tess set a paper plate with the ice cream under the table. As Crystal set her down, Miss Tabby responded quickly with a meow and a furtive glance around the deck at the towering humans. Apparently no ice cream lover, she dashed under a chair and loped away into the side yard.

Frustration furrowed Crystal's small forehead. "Come back!" In a blur, she chased after the escaping feline, the others stampeding behind her.

Tess ran a hand through her hair and looked over at Grant's amused expression. "Guess the party's over."

* * *

Later in the kitchen, after everyone had been herded together into Jenny's SUV and traded their thanks for an "awesome" party, Grant helped Tess clean up the mess.

She finished rinsing soap suds off the large lemonade pitcher and set it on the counter next to the sink.

Grant picked up the pitcher and dried it with a dish towel. "Well, the kids had a good time. Don't you think?"

"Yes, it was definitely a success." She turned to watch Crystal playing with Miss Tabby across the tile floor. "Did you have fun, honey?"

"Uh-huh." Crystal teased the cat with a floppy-eared mouse on a string. "Erleen's my new friend."

"I'm glad to hear that." Tess removed her half apron and hung it on a bar beneath the sink. "Did you thank Mr.Grant for letting us have the party?"

Crystal's amber eyes took on a glow. "Thank you, Mr. Grant."

He strode over to her and playfully tugged one of her pigtails. "You're welcome."

"I liked the horses best."

Tess smiled up at him. "Me too."

"We'll do it again some time," he said. "Maybe in the spring."

A strange feeling passed through her. As if she'd somehow lost her balance, didn't know how to react. Actually she didn't know if she'd even be here come spring. It all depended on...

A flicker of unease surfaced in Grant's eyes as if he knew he'd spoken too soon.

She cleared her throat, not sure of how to continue without making the conversation awkward.

Thankfully, Crystal gave her a cue by suddenly yawning. "Hey, I think it's time the cowgirl took a little catnap."

Crystal screwed up her nose. "Catnap?"

"A nap with Miss Tabby."

"Okay," Crystal drawled out the word. "Miss Tabby is kinda tired."

When Tess followed Crystal and the cat out the back door, she turned to Grant and put her hand on his shirt sleeve, and felt rock hard muscle beneath. Although the gesture seemed a natural thing to do, the sheer strength of him made her slightly uncomfortable. "Thanks again, Grant. Or should I say, boss?"

"It's Grant," he said, his eyes holding hers captive for a second longer than he could have. Or should have. Long enough to cause a catch in her throat.

"I'll come back to the office after I tuck her in, and check the phone messages."

"Fine, I'll be working out around the barn."

An hour later, after checking the messages, Tess went to find Grant. A call had come in about a possible construction job. She knew he needed the extra work now that the tourist season was coming to an end.

Her thoughts bounced back to the day, the satisfaction that the party had been a success—a step forward for Crystal. She'd made new friends. Now, going to preschool could be looked upon with eagerness instead of dread.

The vision of Grant—assured, mentoring, entertaining—came to mind. He had even helped her afterwards clean up the kitchen. It'd been fun having a willing partner to help with the dishes.

No such pleasant memories of Howard. The Alpha man. What? Share the work in the kitchen? Rarely. Other than make himself a sandwich or run the dishwasher, he never stepped foot into the "woman's quarters". Mostly what Tess remembered about Howard were the arguments.

Late afternoon shadows fanned out beyond the barn, lavender-hued across the yard. Golden leaves fluttered in the cottonwoods. Tess entered the corral. It seemed so quiet after this morning's chattering voices and the clop of horses' hooves in the dirt.

Not seeing Grant anywhere, she went to the open barn door and moved inside. Roy had evidently left for the day as well as the other hands. A horse neighed in one of the stalls. The smell of harness and hay and tamped down earth filtered through her nostrils. Smells becoming more familiar to her.

A faint sound drew her toward the rear of the barn. In a far corner, she saw Grant bent over a work table in his small workshop. She'd never been back to this area, and the sight of him so intent on some project intrigued her.

As she quietly approached, she saw that he was sandpapering a miniature cradle. His large hands carefully smoothed the sides in deliberate, precise motions. About three feet long, the cradle was in the design of an old fashioned rocking cradle. But was it meant for a baby or a doll?

So absorbed was he in his work that he hadn't heard her approach. Sunlight streaked his light brown hair, casting a soft glow over his strong shoulders and bent head.

Tess stood stock still, not wanting to disturb him, almost wishing she could capture this image on film, for it seemed an important task he had set for himself.

And then, without warning, something triggered a change in his motions. His face flushed a bright red and he slumped forward slightly; the sandpaper slipped from his hand.

A tear slid downward over his cheekbone to his jaw, and then another. Quickly he brushed them away on his sleeve. A long sigh escaped his lips, an audible sadness drifting over the small cradle.

Tess froze. A naked realization that she had witnessed something intensely private jolted through her.

159

A fierce desire to whirl and run enveloped her. Yet another impulse within made her yearn to enclose Grant in her arms. Offer comfort for the unknown pain that possessed him.

Barely breathing, she hovered in the shadows. After an agonizing moment, Grant closed his eyes then opened them, took up the sandpaper and resumed his meticulous polishing of the cradle.

Silently, Tess backed away along the row of stalls. Now was not the time to approach him about the telephone message. She would leave it on his desk and tell him in the morning.

Why was he making this cradle? Not for anyone's baby that she knew of. For a doll? For Crystal's dolls? Perhaps.

Yet such a task would seem a joyful thing to do. Not one that would evoke pain.

Dare she ask him about it? Was it her business? No. No, she dared not probe into his private thoughts. It would be completely up to Grant, if he ever chose to reveal them.

Chapter Twelve

By midmorning the following day, Tess was quaking in her boots. Well, more likely in her Nikes. She didn't own a pair of western boots. All the more reason to turn down Grant's offer to go for a ride.

She had just pulled the pickup into the front drive after dropping Crystal off at preschool. Grant had sauntered up to her as she stepped down from behind the wheel. "Hey, did I hear you say you wanted to try out one of these horses?" His hat brim had partially shaded his eyes, but she thought she'd detected a hint of humor in them.

That was her first opportunity to just pass. Truthfully, she hadn't straddled a horse since maybe her teen years. And she hadn't expected he'd take her up on it so soon. "Well, I..." she'd hesitated, gazing out over the side yard to the cottonwoods shimmering in the autumn light.

"I'm riding out to the south pasture to check on the horses. You can ride along if you'd like."

That was the moment her knees had started knocking just a little. What had seemed like such a fun idea yesterday, now gave her the willies. If she could have thought it over for a day or two....

"Good," he'd decided for her. "I'll see you over at the barn in about ten minutes." He had strode off in that self confident way like Robert Redford in the *Horse Whisperer.*

Now she approached the barn with the distinct irrational fear of a tourist at a dude ranch. Her palms were clammy and her insides quivered like jelly. This was ridiculous! A grown woman afraid to get on a horse? Heavens, if little Crystal could do it, and enjoy it, so could she.

Grant stood waiting beside a medium size roan. The masculine image he projected in his cocked hat, broad shoulders, and well-fitting jeans made Tess ask herself if the reason she had these unwitting jitters was because of the prospect of being with Grant as well as being on a horse?

She took a deep breath and smiled, attempting to hide her nervousness.

"This is Rosy. She's a gentle gal," he said, not wasting any time.

"She is a pretty one," Tess managed, barely having time to give Rosy's auburn mane a quick stroke before Grant plopped a worn western hat on her head.

"You'll appreciate this when we get out under that sun."

Fortunately the hat had an attached cord she could tighten under her chin. Could it have belonged to his wife Laura? No time to think about that; Grant held the stirrup ready.

She grabbed his shoulder for support, stuck her left foot inside the stirrup, and hopped. Somehow, her right leg wouldn't cooperate. A cheerleader's lunge would have gotten her over the saddle. No such thing happened. Instead, she crumpled backward and luckily Grant caught her in his strong arms.

"It's been awhile," she blurted, a wave of embarrassment flooding through her. *What a klutz!* he must be thinking.

With the next leap upward, Grant assisted with a firm boost to her behind.

Her pride as well as her cheeks burned as she made contact with the hard leather saddle. "Whew! Sure glad Rosy's not in a hurry," she joked, taking the reins.

The corners of his mouth curved upwards. "She's used to city gals."

That had been twenty minutes ago, and, after a brief lesson on how to hold the reins, give direction, and stand in the saddle when trotting, Tess's fear had slightly eased. The glorious, rugged Sangre de Cristo range stretched out alongside them, Mount Blanca rising to the east, its summit already dusted with snow. Across the broad San Luis Valley, the San Juans ran parallel, a parade of gauzy clouds gliding above them.

"How beautiful this is," Tess enthused, "like no other place I've ever been."

Riding next to her, Grant eased forward in his saddle. "You've traveled a lot?"

"Well, my dad was an officer in the Air Force and we were transferred around, mostly overseas."

"Your folks live in the States now?"

"No. My dad passed away several years ago and Mom remarried. After being uprooted so long, I thought she'd want to settle here, but she's living in Germany with her retired husband. Another Air Force man."

He glanced over at her with a smile. "That leaves you pretty much on your own."

She shrugged good-naturedly. "I've been on my own since college, except for a marriage that didn't work out." She bit down on her lip, not wanting to bother him with her life story.

The comment about her failed marriage didn't seem to affect Grant one way or the other. He was obviously a quiet man, given to his own thoughts and memories. The image of him bent over his woodworking yesterday surfaced in her mind, and a twinge of empathy.

He pointed to an outcropping of scrub trees about twenty yards away. "Look over there."

A clan of short, paddle-eared deer grazed, observing the two riders. Catching their human scent on the wind, they scampered off into the ochre brush. "Those deer are the same kind that Crystal and I saw at Medano Creek the other day."

"Mule deer. They're wintering early this year—down from the mountains."

"Crystal wanted to play with them."

"She's starting to like it around here."

Tess glanced over at him, her tone turning wistful. "I think she is. She said she wanted her mom to come here and live on the ranch."

Beneath his shaded brim, Grant's eyes grew somber. "And what did you tell her?"

"That I wished she could. It's so hard to know what to tell her…"

Grant nodded in agreement. "Yeah. Have you talked to Jud—has he heard anything new from New Orleans?"

"Not yet. I check the websites every day, hoping to find something. So many still lost and so much confusion. I'm just trying to be here for her."

Grant reined his palomino in closer to Rosy so that his stirrup nearly touched Tess's. "You know, my mom told me a story once about when she was a girl on the ranch and this mother hen and her chicks. A dust storm blew in one day—a bad one. It covered everything. When it ended, the hen looked like a clump of dirt. After they literally shook the dust off of her, they found she had spread her wings to protect her chicks."

"Did the chicks come out okay?"

He grinned with amusement. "Yep. That little hen was just buried in dirt, but her chicks all lived."

Despite the crisp coolness of the morning, a warmth spread through Tess, not unlike the reaction she'd have if a friend presented her with an unexpected gift. "Nature sure can surprise you."

Grant cleared his throat. "Anyway, I wanted to say...Crystal's a darn lucky little girl, having you to look out for her."

The admiration in his voice brought moisture to her eyes, touching a part of her that she had kept closely guarded. "Well, as it stands, I don't know what my own future holds, job-wise. So, I don't mind giving her all the emotional support I can for now." A gust of wind from the east caused her to lift the collar on her denim jacket.

Grant looked over at her, his gaze steady, his voice strong. "You've got a job here as long as you need it, Tess."

If he had said nothing else during the entire ride, that statement alone convinced her of the goodness of the man. She had a job here as long as she needed it—for as long as Crystal needed a sheltering place, a temporary sanctuary from all the unknowns in her very young life.

Gratitude for Grant's generosity welled up in Tess's throat, leaving her speechless for a long moment. She could only nod in his direction and murmur "Thank you."

Hours later, getting Crystal ready for bed, brushing her hair, helping her into her pajamas, she glanced at the photo of Crystal and Carrie on the bedroom bureau. Settled into a drugstore metallic frame, it was the only remnant Crystal had to keep from her past. Not as much as some Katrina children had escaped with, but at least a visual memory of her closeness to her mother.

Grant's words came to her again: *You've got a job here as long as you need it, Tess.*

No one knew how long that would be, but the offer in its sincerity was a lifeline to her when she and Crystal needed it most.

* * *

In the kitchen the following morning, after breakfast, and after Juan and Carlos had taken Crystal out to the barn

165

to check on Nina, Grant lingered over his second cup of coffee.

Fortunately Tess's coffee making skills had improved and even she enjoyed the fragrant brew to get her going so early each day. She opened her recipe box and fished out the one she was looking for.

Across the granite island, Grant asked with a hint of mischief in his voice, "So, what's Betty Crocker making today?"

She glanced up from the recipe into his interested hazel eyes. "Cowboy chocolate chip cookies." She knew they were his favorite.

His tawny eyebrows raised in appreciation. "Hmm. I approve."

Half-smiling, she wondered what was keeping him here when he usually headed out for the day's chores with the hired men. Something was on his mind, but what was it? Finally, as she took the milk and eggs from the fridge, he shot her a question.

"Would you…would you be interested in going to the Alamosa Lodge next Friday night?"

Taken by surprise, she paused, looking curiously at Grant.

"It's an annual businessmen's event," he continued, a light flush emphasizing his high cheekbones. "Women go too, of course… The food is pretty good and there'll be entertainment." He stopped as if feeling her eyes studying him and set his empty coffee mug on the counter.

Was he asking her on a date? Her boss? No, she was sure he meant it only as a social engagement.

"Well, that sounds nice." Why was her hand slightly trembling as she cracked the eggs into the bowl? "But what would I wear?" She thought of her jeans draped over a hanger in the closet. All her clothes left behind in New Orleans.

"I'll be paying you a month's salary tomorrow." His voice sounded encouraging. "Maybe you can find something in town."

He obviously wanted her to go with him Friday night. Her first night out since she couldn't remember when. A tingle of anticipation danced inside her. "Sure, I'd like to go. And thanks." She smiled up at him. "For everything."

"You bet. I'll pick you up at six o'clock." With a pleasant nod, he was out of the kitchen. The back screen door closed with a smart slam.

Tess beat the eggs into the flour and milk mixture and added a teaspoon of vanilla. Her hand stopped midair. *Who would watch Crystal?* Her mood sank to her knees. She couldn't leave the child alone for that long without someone to stay with her. Shoot! Always a fly in the ointment.

Minutes later, as she slipped the cookie sheets from the oven, a rumbling sound invaded an open kitchen window facing the drive. Peering outside, she saw Jud's battered pickup lumber to a halt in front. A cigarette dangled from the old coot's mouth beneath the brim of his sorry-looking hat. He didn't seem to be in any hurry as he took one last drag then flicked the butt out the window. His sidekick Henry lolled his big yellow head out the opposite passenger window.

Not exactly an answer to a prayer, but perhaps an answer nevertheless. An idea formed in Tess's mind before Jud Pearl could open the rusted truck door, let the dog out, and mosey up the front flagstone walk.

"Hi Jud, any news?" she asked as she opened the front door.

"Nope. Just stopped by to make a social call."

Above his signature faded suspenders, his hair was shaggy, his mustache needed trimming, and he reeked of tobacco. But she let him in with feigned welcome. Today was not the time to be critical of Jud's shortcomings.

He sniffed the air. "Smells good in here. You been cookin'?"

"I just made some chocolate chip cookies. Would you like a cup of coffee?"

He grinned, showing teeth yellowed with neglect. "Don't mind if I do."

Tess turned and led the way back to the kitchen. "Grant just went out to do some chores."

"I'll find him."

These western men were short on words. She went to the coffee pot and poured Jud a cup then scooped up a few of the cookies on a plate and set it on the counter.

After Jud finished one of the cookies and slugged down half of his coffee, he said, "Yer a good cook. Grant's lucky."

She shrugged agreeably. "Thanks. Crystal and I have been lucky too, so far." A twinge of apprehension nipped at her insides, the prospect of what lay ahead always waiting in the corners of her mind.

Jud's expression clouded for a moment. He glanced out the window. "Where's Crystal today?"

"She's down by the barn, visiting that cute filly."

Stuffing the remains of the cookie in his mouth, Jud mumbled, "Mind if I go see her?"

"Of course not. Sounds like a good idea." Getting to know his granddaughter was definitely something she didn't mind. She unplugged the coffeemaker. "I'll go over there with you."

Crystal was chasing Nina around the corral when Tess and Jud approached. She made one more circle then let Nina prance off before skipping over to them.

"Your grandpa stopped by to see you," Tess offered, hoping the two would start bonding on their own.

Crystal greeted Jud with a shy response, her eyes averted.

Jud reached back and pulled a small cloth doll from his back pocket. A doll that had seen better days. Its worn green plaid gingham dress was accented by a frayed collar. Tufts of dark hair stuck out from its head. Wide-open black eyes, two dots for a nose, and bowed red lips animated its painted-on cloth face. "This was your mom's doll…" Jud explained. "She played with it when she was your age. Her mama made it for her."

Crystal's features beamed as she gazed at the doll's face. "What's her name?"

Jud bent down and gave it to her. "I don't know, honey. I found it in an old trunk in the closet."

Releasing an audible sigh, Crystal held the small doll to her chest. "I'll name her." She paused for a long moment. "Crystal."

"Oh…that's nice," Tess said, while she wondered why the child would give her own name to the doll, but didn't want to ask.

Jud chuckled. "Well, now I'll get to see two dollies named Crystal when I come to visit."

Glancing up at him, Crystal smiled. "Thank you." She hugged the doll tighter then asked Tess, "Can I show her to Miss Tabby?"

"Sure thing. Maybe Grandpa Jud will walk us over to the cabin before he leaves."

Jud sent them a quick wink. "Don't mind if I do."

On the way, Tess casually brought up the fact that Crystal needed some friendly company the next Friday night while she and Grant drove to Alamosa. "There'll be hot chocolate for the lucky one who volunteers," she said with enthusiasm.

Jud's mustache twitched and his eyes crinkled up at the edges. "Don't mind if I do."

* * *

"So you're finally going out with Grant." Jenny Stotter, sitting next to Tess in the truck, looked at her with a wide-eyed expression, obvious admiration in her toothy grin.

They were headed over to Lilly's Dress Exchange, a consignment shop run by a woman from Alamosa who owned another shop of "gently-used" clothing there.

Tess huffed at the insinuation of an assumed courtship between her and Grant. "It's not like going out on a date—"

"Well, what is it then?" Jenny's question held an undertone of ever-so-knowing irony. "A date is a date."

Tess pulled up alongside the curb a few doors down from the faded purple awning in front of Lilly's shop. "A social event is not a date." She cut the engine and opened the truck door. Asking Jenny to join her on a dress search may not have been one of her brainier decisions. It had been so long since Tess had shopped for anything besides jeans or sportswear, she'd sensed the need for another woman's company and opinion. Jenny had obliged by recruiting husband Nick to man the daycare for a few hours on his day off.

Inside the cramped quarters, they meandered between the racks of ready-to-wear. With low expectation, Tess eyed the limited selection of blouses and skirts. "Smells kind of like moth balls in here. I don't see any dresses."

A top-heavy saleswoman wearing dangly earrings pointed to the rear of the store. "They're in the back."

Half an hour later, Tess had tried on several dresses: too large, too long, or too weird. She finally found a blue western print with V neck and flared skirt. "It fits pretty well," Tess commented to Jenny from the small dressing room. "But I don't have any shoes to go with it."

"Don't worry about shoes; that dress begs for boots. I've got plenty and we wear about the same size." Jenny separated the divider curtain and poked her head inside the room. "Hey, that dress hugs you," she enthused, approving the fit. "Just what Grant will do when he sees you in it."

"Will you stop?" Tess observed herself in the full-length clouded mirror. The dress did accent her trim waist and hips. But she was no beauty, just a plain-featured woman with self-styled, short-bobbed hair and an average figure.

"The dress also matches your eyes. Nice."

"I like the color…but don't you think the neckline is too low?"

Jenny's eyebrows shot upward. "Are you kidding? All men who're alive from the neck down go for low necklines."

A flush of exasperation burned up Tess's neck. If she could get her hands on a pair of socks, she would stuff one in Jenny's big mouth right now. "I'm not trying to seduce anyone. Especially not my boss."

"Boss—apple sauce. Grant is available *and* he's a great catch!"

"Tess glared back, about to tell Jenny she was blowing this way out of proportion.

But Jenny stepped closer and added in a confidential tone, "The sooner you realize it, the sooner you can get down to business, girl."

Chapter Thirteen

Early Friday evening, Grant opened the truck door and assisted Tess onto the passenger seat. In his tan felt Stetson, a well-fitting western suit, and bolo tie, he made a handsome escort.

His hand cradling hers for that brief moment was warm, not smooth but not rough. He had a fresh-out-of-the shower clean smell about him. She fought a sudden mix of emotions: attraction, nervousness, and anticipation. He gave almost a bow before pivoting, coming around to the driver's side and climbing aboard.

Jenny had insisted that it would be more than *a social event*. But Tess was still in denial about this *date* thing. Admittedly she had spent more time getting ready for this evening than any in recent memory.

"Where are you going?" Crystal had asked as Tess put on the new dress, silvery dangle earrings, and Jenny's chamois leather western boots.

"Oh, just to a business meeting for grownups," she had replied.

Crystal had reached up and touched her earrings. "What's a business meetin'?"

"It's a place where grownups go for dinner and meet new friends."

She'd been relieved when Jud showed up on time, knocking briskly at the door. He'd observed her with a gleam of admiration in his eyes. "Well, don't you look all dolled up." More a statement than a question.

She'd given him a tentative smile, hoping he wouldn't smoke inside the cabin.

By the time Grant arrived, his broad shoulders filling the front doorway, her hands had gone sweaty and she could hardly look him straight on. How ridiculous...her boss.

Journey to Sand Castle

It was obvious they both were feeling somewhat awkward. Holding his Stetson, he'd kind of grinned then grazed his head on the door frame as he stepped inside. Everyone crowded in the tiny front room making her eager to make their exit.

Now in the front seat of the cab, a hint of wildflowers wafted around her. She shouldn't have splashed on Jenny's Floral Interlude cologne so generously, and certainly not have added that extra drop at the base of her throat. What had she been thinking?

Grant turned the key in the ignition, bringing the big engine to life. His large hands on the steering wheel guided the truck onto the dirt road. Tess's stomach fluttered with excitement. Why was she reacting like a teenager on her first date? Couldn't be because this was the first time she'd ventured out with a man to anything social since her divorce over a year ago?

She straightened her skirt about her and glanced back to the cabin where a light shone in the front window, where Crystal and Jud would spend their first time together. "It was good of Jud to babysit," she observed. "Do you think they'll hit it off?"

Grant nodded confidently. "He's her grandpa. It's time they get to know each other."

"Yes, it is." She looked out the dusty side window thinking Grant was right. In his calm, observant way, he sized things up well.

Over to the west, the sun slowly dropped behind the San Juan range deepening shadows across the valley to a purple hue. A family of elk meandered into the rabbit brush some ten yards off the highway. Snow already capped the far peaks.

How could it be that only a few weeks ago she had been a single woman with a job, an apartment, a fairly normal, mundane life? Then she'd been caught up in the

173

worst hurricane New Orleans had seen in almost a century. And now fate had spun her around and changed virtually everything familiar in her life. It didn't seem real: these surroundings, this beauty of nature as serene as a picture post card, this quiet western man sitting beside her.

Grant's voice tinged with a comforting drawl interrupted her thoughts. "You look very nice this evening. I think we're gonna have a good time."

Flattered by his plain spoken compliment and prediction, Tess looked over at his strong profile. "Thank you. I'm…sure we will." She leaned back against the headrest and let some of her pent up anxiety flow away on a sigh.

The parking lot at the Alamosa Lodge was nearly full when they arrived. Inside, guests flowed into a long, narrow banquet hall, impressive for a small town. Older paintings depicting western ranching scenes of cowboys, horses, and cattle decorated the walls. Tess observed them with interest, admiring the ever-present Rocky Mountains in the distance. "Ranching is a demanding kind of work," she commented to Grant at her side.

He nodded thoughtfully. "It's the only kind of work most of these folks would choose."

Along the far wall, a banner read: Ranchers and Businessmen of the San Luis Valley.

Beneath it a long banquet table was set with various appetizers. Tables and chairs were arranged around the room. A cash bar at the rear of the hall bustled with activity.

"What kind of drink would you like?" Grant asked as he steered them back in that direction.

"A club soda with lemon would taste good about now."

"Sure." Grant headed toward the bar.

A middle-aged couple, decked out in western finery, approached before he got far. The man smiled in greeting. "Howdy, Grant, haven't seen you in a spell." His female companion, blond and full-figured, caught Tess's eye with a welcoming glance.

"Gus Garcia. How are you?" The men pumped hands.

Gus's bushy eyebrows lifted, giving him the expression of a happy jack-o-lantern. "This pretty gal with you?"

Grant tilted his head toward Tess. "Yes, this is Tess Cameron. She's my new Girl Friday at the ranch." He introduced her to Gus and his wife Eva.

"Well, you've been needin' someone to help out." Gus grinned with approval at Tess.

"Nice to meet you."

She was glad to have someone to talk to as Grant left to get their drinks. "I like your turquoise necklace," she remarked to Eva, admiring the large oval stone set in a silver pendant.

"Thank you. It was a gift from Gus after I delivered our first calf," Eva said with a slight European accent. "He knew I didn't want to be a rancher's wife…in the beginning. Since then, I've delivered quite a few." Her hearty chuckle intimated she had come to agreeable terms with her position.

When Grant returned with two cold drinks, they mingled among the growing clusters of guests. Tess sipped on her soda, thinking what a contrast there between these westerners and the boisterous New Orleans teachers' social events she'd attended. She liked the comfortable, casual interaction here and the colorful clothing, hats, and boots the men and women wore.

As far as boots went, she had stuffed small wads of cotton in the toes of Jenny's boots since they were a half size too big. So far so good.

From a stage in front of the hall, a Master of Ceremonies introduced the evening's entertainment. "Folks, we're privileged to have with us tonight an award-winning Colorado singer and songwriter, and darn good guitar picker. He's brought a few of his musician friends with him. Let's give Bill Barwick a warm welcome!"

Rousing applause proceeded the entrance of a trio of musicians. Leading the trio was an energetic man with a prominent handlebar mustache. A burly fiddler and a dark bearded bass player followed. From their western hats down to their cowboy boots, there was no question what kind of music these gentlemen favored.

They opened with an old favorite, *San Antonio Rose.*

All around her, people tapped their toes and swayed to the music. Tess delighted in the lively notes of the fiddle. When she looked around the banquet hall, wondering where Grant had gone, she spied him over in a corner with some business men. She turned back to the entertainer and sipped her club soda.

The cowboy singer introduced the next song, one that he'd written. *Carolyn in the Sunset.* His deep baritone voice captured her attention.

"We were ridin' from Durango, back up in Colorado
Somewhere way up on the Great Divide.
We rode through hell and thunder…

Someone filled the empty space behind Tess. When she glanced over her shoulder, Grant winked at her. His close presence, tall and assured, sent a warm flush straight through her.

The cowboy singer strummed his guitar with a bold emphasis on the chorus.

"And he said goodnight to Carolyn in the sunset

He did it every evenin' so they say.

He'd just wander off from us—go to see the stock was fed.

Then we'd see him out against the sky rememberin' what she said—"

A shiver of recognition skittered along her spine. Where would Grant go when he rode off toward night fall?

Then came the refrain:

"When you're tired of ridin' out there all alone

When it's time to put your saddle up, and finally come on home

I'll be here waitin' for ya'; it's a promise that I'll keep

'Cause I'll be there in your sunset when the world goes off to sleep."

The melancholy in the refrain left a sadness in her heart. Lovers parted. Secrets harbored, feelings never spoken. A promise to return perhaps never kept…

Amidst the applause, Tess glanced back at Grant. Looking up into his shaded eyes, she realized how little she really knew about him.

While dining on a flavorful prime rib, there was little opportunity to talk with Grant, seated on her right. Businessmen at the table involved him in ranch conversation while Eva Garcia to her left monopolized her attention. Grant had no doubt been a longtime member of the Alamosa organization, and his opinion was respected. He responded to each man's comments in a thoughtful way.

When Tess and Eva returned from powdering their noses, the western trio had resumed playing. Couples moved around a makeshift dance floor in the front of the hall.

Grant stood up from the table as she approached. "They're playing my favorite—a waltz. Would you like to give it a try?" He angled his head toward the dancers.

A part of her panicked. *No, don't think so.* But another part gave her a shove. "Sure, why not?"

As Grant guided her onto the floor, she prayed that her two left feet would not be too obvious. When he took her in his arms, she forgot she had feet.

Somehow she managed to follow him as they joined the others in a revolving circle. The high sweet notes of the fiddle blended with the rhythmic cords of the bass and Tess's body thawed from frozen to malleable. The warmth in Grant's hazel eyes had something to do with it. His hand on her back was strong, firm, protective.

Dancing was fun! It could become addictive.

"I'm not much of a dancer," Grant confessed as they walked back toward their table.

"You could have fooled me—it's been years-"

A heavy-set man standing by a table across the room called out to Grant. "Wilder, I've got a construction job for you." He motioned with a beefy hand for Grant to come over.

Gus Garcia hustled up to Tess, a wide grin spreading his ruddy cheeks. "Say, gal. I need a partner for this triple step."

Tess let him take her back to the dance floor as Grant disappeared into the crowd.

It was a quick-stepping number. Tess's toes were demolished by the time it ended, but Gus insisted on another dance.

Where was Grant?

Jenny's boots pinched Tess's feet in several places. Her toes crimped in pain. Her patience rubbed thin.

Sitting alone at the large empty dinner table was not how she had envisioned the festivities would end.

Rebuffed, rejected, and riled. She couldn't wait to get back to the ranch and extricate herself from these horrible boots!

Finally Grant made his way toward the table. He wore a casual demeanor. Not a care in the world.

She clenched her jaw in an effort not to snap his head off. "Are we ready to leave now?"

He cocked his head, a surprised expression around his mouth. "Well, if…"

She stood on tortured feet. "I'm ready."

* * *

The ride back was a long one. Tess stared through the windshield at oncoming headlights, her thoughts still agitated. Her toes burned with blisters. "Can't wait to get these boots off," she muttered.

Grant had aided her to the truck as she hobbled along. She'd just pulled her arm away, insisting she could make it on her own. She wasn't an invalid.

"Why don't you take them off now?"

"Yeah. Why don't I?" It was the best suggestion he'd come up with yet. She gave a tug and a yank to each boot and dropped them on the floor of the cab. If she was trying to make an impression, she would have suffered in silence, but now she didn't care—even if her feet smelled odorous in her sweaty socks.

Beneath his Stetson, he released a sigh. "Guess you didn't have much fun tonight." He focused ahead over the steering wheel, but she could sense he was intent on her response.

Well, she wasn't going to sugar coat the fact that he'd left her stranded for half the evening. "But *you did*— chewing the fat with all your business friends." There. She'd let out her complaint and didn't care if he liked it or not.

After a pause, Grant said, "I hadn't seen them for some time..." He swung his gaze to her. "Sorry if you didn't have a good time, Tess."

Her face flushed with an emotion kin to frustration. She wanted to add that it appeared he had invited her to the event simply as a prop, a convenient companion, but bit her tongue instead. The tone of his voice had held a certain sincerity, unlike her ex, who'd needed little reason to vent his volatile comebacks no matter how small her disagreement.

Not sure of how to respond, she fell silent, regretting her mood and the course of the evening.

The silence engulfed them as they drove beneath a sky filled with clouds that masked the prairie stars.

Snatches of possible comments she would make when he brought her home kept popping into her head.

It was a great evening—too bad you missed most of it.

Remind me to burn your toast in the morning.

I spent good money on this dress and shaved my legs for this?

But by the time Grant pulled into the long drive, Tess had almost dozed off, her eyelids heavy as weighted leads. When he opened her door, she tumbled out of the truck and gulped in the brisk October night air.

Grant took her arm. "Do you want to put your boots back on?"

"No. Don't think they'd fit over the blisters. She reached inside the cab and retrieved the discarded boots. Over her protests, he insisted on carrying them.

The cool grass crunched beneath her stockinged feet as they walked toward the cabin. A faint light shone from the front room window. "At least the place is still standing," she said, thinking it could have burned down if Jud had dropped a cigarette in the shag carpet.

"I bet they got along just fine." Grant's tone revealed more confidence than Tess could muster.

To her surprise, when they opened the screen door, both Jud and Crystal were sound asleep on the small sofa. Jud lolled back, snoring loudly, an illustrated story book open on his lap. His arm draped over Crystal's shoulder, her head resting on a pillow next to him, her body curled up like a contented kitten.

Tess and Grant exchanged a questioning glance.

"Should I put Crystal to bed?" he asked in a low voice.

She nodded agreeably.

He set her borrowed boots down by the door. When he scooped Crystal up in his arms, she yawned then frowned up at him. "I wanna go to the meetin'." Her tousled head drooped onto Grant's shoulder as he carried her into the back bedroom.

The tender sight dissolved most of Tess's peevish mood.

After she gently awakened Jud, thanked him and Grant briefly, she bid them goodnight. They disappeared into the darkness, Grant towering beside Jud. Watching them from the door way, she was left with only the dregs of regret.

But how could she and Grant resume the friendly every-day banter that had come to be their normal routine, after the letdown of tonight's *social engagement*?

Chapter Fourteen

Saturday morning started out brisk, with a hint of light sleet on the air. Tess and Crystal, carrying Miss Tabby, entered the kitchen in the main house by the time the sun squinted through clouds over California Peak. The intimidation of a tension headache played at her temples. Saturdays had become a ritual of breakfast pancakes and bacon and, although she wasn't in the mood today, she didn't want to disappoint Crystal.

As least her feet were more comfortable in soft moccasin boots, and her attire of navy sweatshirt and jeans suited her better than dress-up clothes.

Tess handed Crystal a plastic scoop. "You can fill Miss Tabby's dish with those kibbles in the drawer." Thankfully Crystal went about her cat duties with admirable devotion. Tess was glad to have a routine to follow, especially in the rather awkward position she found herself after last night's course of events.

Then what had she expected? An evening out with her employer should have been strictly platonic. Boot heels clicking down the hallway made her nearly drop the milk carton she'd retrieved from the fridge.

Buttoning the top button on a plaid flannel shirt, Grant entered the kitchen. He appeared to be walking on egg shells. Beard stubble accented his jaw and his eyes were still sleepy. Had he slept well after last night's uncomfortable ride home? A grin spread across his face. "Good morning, ladies."

"Good morning," Tess said without facing him. She busied herself mixing pancake batter and making sure the electric grill was hot enough. She wasn't giving him the satisfaction of being Miss Cheerful. She slung a bundle of thick bacon on the grill.

Grant swept Crystal off her feet and into the air. "Hey, pardner, how'd you and Grandpa Jud get along last night?"

She squealed. "Fine. He told me a story about when my mommy was a little girl."

Grant set her down in a chair next to the table. "He sounds like a pretty good guy to have come to visit. Maybe he'll tell you some more stories next time."

Tess raised a brow. *Next time?* "You like Grandpa Jud?"

Crystal nodded in the affirmative, a mischievous twinkle in her eyes. "He's got whiskers—in his ears!"

Grant chuckled and Tess couldn't help smile to herself. She poured coffee into Grant's mug, avoiding his gaze.

He continued his conversation with Crystal. "Did Tess tell you how she danced so much last night that her boots pinched her toes?"

Doing a slow burn, Tess flipped the cakes. How would he know how much she danced?

Crystal's forehead puckered. "She don't like those boots!"

"Maybe I should have put some medicine on her toes. Maybe gave her a foot rub."

Right. Merthiolate and Bandaids would have done the job. Crystal giggled as Tess poured her a glass of milk.

When she served the pancakes, he angled his head, sending her a million dollar smile. And a wink. The kind of a wink that was unexpected. It triggered a blush on her cheeks and she turned away quickly. The pancakes, drizzled with warm blueberry syrup, disappeared fast.

Crystal took a big drink of milk, her attention switching from Grant to Tess and back. "I need a foot rub."

Despite her lingering mood, Tess had to keep her jaw from dropping in amusement. This kid had spunk.

Grant's tawny brows raised a half inch. "Okay. Let's see those toes." He lunged for her foot beneath the table.

With a shriek of surprise, Crystal scooted out of her chair and scampered across the kitchen floor. "Can we play outside?"

"Put on your jacket," Tess called as they disappeared out into the hall. Behind Crystal, Miss Tabby darted, agile on just three paws.

With jerky fingers, Tess rinsed dishes and loaded the dishwasher while Grant wiped off the grill. She could think of nothing worth saying so remained silent, avoiding coming near him, his tall presence now more a disturbance than welcome. When she finished, she wiped her hands on a towel. "See you later."

He followed her out to the back hall and helped her on with her jacket. "Thanks," she said, staring down at the toes of his scuffed boots." Why was he being such a darn gentleman? She wished he'd just stop and let her pretend that last night had never happened.

Grant cleared his throat. "Tess…you know I can only say this straight out. I'm real rusty at this dating thing. Ever since my wife died almost two years ago…" His knuckles grazed her chin with a gentle stroke.

Moisture pricked her eyes. She shrugged, not knowing what to say.

As she opened the back door and stepped onto the deck, he was right behind her. He reached out and slipped his hand around her upper arm. A chilly breeze ruffled her hair, but his fingers sent heat through the fabric of her jacket.

"I just wanted to say I'm sorry about last night," he said in a low voice.

She forced herself to look up into his eyes. "I have to admit, it seemed like it didn't really matter if I was there or not."

"Of course it mattered that you were there. It mattered to me." His hand moved around to her back, a firm warm pressure through her jacket. The touch of his lips brushing her forehead surprised her. "I wanted you to be there."

Her chin tilted upward at the tone of his voice, a sincerity in it which caught her off guard. His gaze traveled over her face, searching in silent expectation. This man's presence disturbed her senses in a way that she could not deny: the silver glimmer in his hazel eyes, the smell of coffee lingering, the way he leaned into her and she did not want to pull away. Even though she knew she should.

The fact that Grant Wilder stood this close to her was surreal. The softness of his lips now gentle on hers made her wonder if it was truly happening. She wound her arms around him, her fingertips touching the smooth flannel of his shirt against the hard muscles of his back. Warm and persuasive, Grant's kiss invited more.

Hormones lying dormant inside her suddenly awoke and unleashed themselves unmercifully through her. She had no desire to leave his embrace, but relaxed further into it.

His breath came warm and moist against her cheek. Her heart raced.

Grant pulled back slightly. His chuckle was low and seductive. "Hey, you've got sparkles on your hair and eyelashes."

She forced her eyes open. "You do, too." Sleet crystals tipped his dark lashes.

"Guess we'd better get in out of this stuff." He released her and smiled.

Reluctantly she agreed. Composing herself, she thought of Crystal and glanced across the yard. The child was scampering back toward the cabin after Miss Tabby.

With one last caress, his fingertips grazing the back of her neck, Grant retreated inside the house.

A brisk wind chased Tess over the deck and across the yard, the sleet stinging her face.

"Brrr, it's cold outside!" Crystal jumped around inside the cabin's small living room like she was on a pogo stick.

Without removing her thin jacket, Tess hurried over and hugged Crystal. "You feel like a popsicle," she said, feeling Crystal shiver in her arms.

Amber eyes gazed up into hers. "Did Mr. Grant kiss you?"

Tess squirmed. This kid had eyes in the back of her head. "Well…I guess he did. Why, were you watching?"

A giggle erupted from out of nowhere. "Yes. I saw him kiss you on the lips. Does he love you?"

Heat crept up Tess's neck and into her face. "Ah, I think Mr. Grant was just being…friendly."

Crystal broke away and began a little dance, the silliest grin lifting her plump cheeks. "Mr. Grant loves you. Mr. Grant loves you."

"No. No, he doesn't." Brother, she'd really fixed things, allowing the kiss to happen within eyesight of Crystal. But what could she have done? Push him back into the house—all six plus feet of him? "We're just good friends," she said, trying to sound more convincing.

Crystal continued her little jig, ignoring Tess.

"I know, let's read a story." Anything to get the child's mind off of Mr. Grant. Unfortunately the sleet continued slapping against the front window with no hint of stopping, so they'd be confined to the cabin for the day.

She went over and plugged in the small room heater by the sofa. "And then we'll have a cup of hot chocolate."

Crystal's eyes widened in anticipation. "Okay, if you let me choose the story."

And so they read stories in the morning, baked cookies in the mini-oven in the kitchen in the afternoon to eat with their hot chocolate, and Tess made hamburgers later for dinner. All the while she kept glancing out the spattered front window to the main house. What was Grant doing up there by himself? Wasn't he lonely? What would he have for supper?

What did the kiss mean?

Why did he kiss her?

Was it simply to show he was sorry for his indifferent behavior last night? Could it have been more than just a kiss? He had followed her outside and coaxed her into his arms. And she'd been more than willing, even in her mood. A man's strong embrace was a foreign thing since her divorce. She hadn't really sought out affection since then. But now she could tell her senses enjoyed it; more than that, they *craved* it.

Even though she knew she shouldn't.

By early evening, the sky cleared, with shafts of light breaking through the clouds. Although still drippy, the night sky beckoned, a few stars peeking out above the valley floor. For some strange reason, Tess wanted to fling the door open and romp through the wet scrub brush.

Later, after Crystal was snuggled under the covers and had drifted to sleep, Tess put on the parka she'd bought at the thrift shop in town and her hiking boots, and quietly went out the front door. She strolled beyond the cabin, listening to the sounds of night: a faint nicker of horses in the barn, the hoot of a horned owl probably watching from one of the looming cottonwoods. She walked, breathing in the fragrant air, misty on her face, toward the flickering lights of homesteads on the distant horizon.

When she stopped, the deep velvet night surrounded her and she stood like a lodestone on the San Luis Valley, compelling the stars to appear to her. The Big Dipper hung right overhead as if all she had to do was climb a ladder to touch it. For a long moment she stared upward in awe wondering what it would feel like to be totally alone in this vast valley. Stretching out her hands, palms open, she envisioned her arms as wide as the valley reaching from the Sangre de Cristos to the San Juans, her fingertips touching the shimmering lights on either edge. Now she was an anchor hunkered down, not a kite, quavering, airborne, erratic in direction with each fickle breeze.

Perhaps she had become an anchor settling into the ancient drifting sands, the waves of recent troubled waters having ebbed away on a faint whisper. But how could she leave her past behind? There were still unanswered questions that directly affected her life.

Shivering, Tess tugged the parka closer around her and turned back. This place of such natural majesty had begun to entwine with her senses: captivating, inviting, like a gift she was not able and not ready to receive.

As she came nearer to the cabin, a coyote howled in the distance. The sensation of icy arrows quivered down her spine. She picked up her pace, more cognizant of sharing this night sky with other creatures of the four-legged variety. A dim light shone from a window in the main house, from Grant's bedroom on the first floor.

Had he been home all evening? Had she heard the rumbling of his truck tires on gravel earlier around dinner time? A sudden clutching at her stomach made her want to kick herself. Why in the world should she care? What Grant did during his free time was not her business.

And wasn't she a rolling stone? New places, new faces—that had been her vow after surviving her divorce. Adventure! Keep to the highway and never look back.

As she approached the cabin, the image of Crystal sleeping securely under the covers came to her. The child was adapting well to these comfortable surroundings. It was a healthy place for her to grow up away from the painful memories of Katrina. She was even beginning to call crotchety old Jud Pearl "Grandpa Jud."

A new small seed of decision planted itself within. As soon as Crystal and Jud bonded further, she would take the next bus out of here—either east or west. One direction would be as good as the other.

She could start over somewhere else, where no man could influence or hurt her again.

* * *

"Hey, you two," Grant called across the drive Monday afternoon to Tess and Crystal as Tess pulled the truck up in front of his garage. She'd just retrieved Crystal from her daycare in town. He strolled over to them, his hat tipped forward jauntily on his forehead, an inviting smile spreading upward. "I'm gonna ride out in the Jeep to check the fences in a little while. Would you two beautiful ladies like to join me?"

Tess's first inclination was to say no thanks. She'd been hoping to avoid Grant for a few days. But, when she glanced into the rear cab at Crystal, the child's features lifted in innocent expectation. "Can we go in the Jeep?"

Grant leaned against the window frame on the passenger's side. "Sure thing. You're big enough now to ride in the Jeep." He gave Tess a reassuring nod. "And Tess can go, too. We won't get a better day for it."

She opened the truck door, let him give her a hand, and hopped down. It was warm and hers was cold. "We'll need to take her car seat."

"You bet."

After securing Crystal in the back of the Jeep, Grant and Tess climbed onto the front seat.

As they drove along the road past the corral, Tess saw Nina gazing out through the fence slats, the foal's dark mane fluttering in the slight breeze. "Look, Crystal. Nina is watching us."

"She's growing so big!" Crystal waved out the window to Nina and Carlos, standing nearby. "Can I play with her when we get back?'

"If it's not too late."

Tess snapped her seatbelt and settled back, imagining a scenic jaunt around the ranch. The leaves had already turned their glorious autumn colors and were blowing away on the wind every day, but some lingered to shine golden in the sun. Grant veered off onto a bumpy dirt trail and she swayed closer to him as he swerved to avoid gaping chuck holes.

She tried not to think of his kiss yesterday morning on the deck. But a sliver of memory flashed into her mind…his hand firm on her back, his breath warm on her cheek, his lips….

She looked out the window, recalling Jenny's questions at the daycare center. "Did you have a good time Friday night? Is Grant a good dancer?" Like a Jewish mother, she persisted. "Did you get home late?"

Tess had dodged, skirted, and glossed over the answers when she returned Jenny's boots. "Thanks, they were great at first, but then they pinched." She had let her know about the blisters, but downplayed her disappointment at being left alone toward the end of the evening. After all, Grant was still her employer and she didn't want to paint him in a too negative light.

"The dinner buffet and the western singer were the best parts of the evening."

Jenny had looked crestfallen. "He didn't even *try* to kiss you?"

"No, he didn't," she'd replied truthfully. "Hey, remember I told you this was a social event, not a date." As for the morning-after kiss—all she needed was for word to get back to Grant about that.

Gazing out the windshield to the snow-tipped Mt. Blanc, Tess half-smiled to herself. Jenny was such a romantic. Too bad Nick was driving the company truck on the road so much.

"Hey, look at those pronghorn deer over there by the Aspen grove." Grant pointed to the nimble-hooved animals just as one broke from a small gathering and started chasing two others.

Tess took in the stand of orange-leafed Aspen and the three pronghorns. "They're fast little guys."

Grant tilted his felt brim a little higher on his forehead. "This is about the end of their rutting season. The young bucks defend their territory with a vengeance."

"What are young bucks?" Crystal piped up from the back seat.

Grant's expression was almost gleeful, making Tess slightly uncomfortable. She hoped they wouldn't run into a rutting display within Crystal's view.

"Young bucks are young deer, kinda like young boys—full of mischief," Grant answered, "they like to tease the girl deers."

A silence from the back seat. Then, "You mean like Butch and Sam at Jenny's house? They like to tease me a lot."

The front wheels hit a bump and Tess knocked against Grant's firm, muscular shoulder. "Yes," she answered, catching her breath. "Kind of like that. It means they like you."

"Oh." A short pause. "Well, I don't like them—they pull my hair!"

Grant made several stops to check the fence line, making notes on a clip board which he shoved into the glove compartment. Then, for no apparent reason, he looked over at Tess and patted her knee in a friendly, almost comforting way. Before she could react, he focused back on the trail.

She studied him thoughtfully for a moment. He was indeed an ever changing mystery.

Suddenly his eyes narrowed and color marked his high cheekbones. "Hey, there's that blasted coyote."

Up ahead, Tess spotted a large animal loping along the fence.

"That pesky no-good bandit! He destroyed my neighbor's goat and ambushed Tiger, my barn cat, last spring."

Tess leaned forward, peering out the front window. "He's bigger than I would think—looks more like a wolf."

As they approached, the coyote darted its steely-eyed gaze at them. The late afternoon light illuminated its mottled gray coat and taut-muscled body.

"Let's chase him off." Grant pushed the accelerator toward the floorboard and the Jeep surged forward.

Tess didn't favor that idea. "We'll never run him down." She thought of Crystal in the back seat.

But Grant was determined. The trail became an obstacle course of rock and ruts, the Jeep bouncing over them like a rubber ball. Grant's eyes stayed glued to the trotting, four-legged *bandit*. "Maybe not, but we can let him know he's not welcome."

Careening off a large rock, the Jeep tilted to the left. Tess's sunglasses slid down the bridge of her nose.

"Whoa!" came a holler from the back seat.

"Hang on, Crystal," Tess called out.

The coyote sped up, but the Jeep caught up even with it. Tess saw its shaggy head pointed straight ahead, its long legs expanding into a faster sprint. Grant laid his hand on the horn, belting out a robust blast.

Her insides turning to jelly, Tess held onto the edge of the seat, scared at the unpredictable chase and mad at Grant for making her feel like a speeding bullet. Was this the way men acted out their frustrations in the wild west? *Juvenile.*

Crystal must be terrified in the back seat.

Another pot hole and Tess's stomach did a double flip. Dust kicked up thick around them. She turned to see if Crystal was all right, but everything around her blurred.

Just as she opened her mouth to shout *stop!* the coyote leaped the fence and shot off into a gulley, headed in the opposite direction.

Grant let up on the gas, but her stomach was still clenched tight. Dust grated her eyes and clogged her nose. "Well, I hope you're satisfied," she choked out. "That was dangerous!"

Grant shook his head. "Naw, we weren't in any danger. This Jeep is in top shape."

She let out a ragged breath, hating to think how their crazy chase had affected Crystal. If the child was emotionally overwrought and had more bad dreams, she'd really let Grant have a piece of her mind. She loosened her seatbelt and turned to the back seat, bracing herself for what she would find.

"Are you all right, pardner?" Grant called, looking into the rear view mirror.

To Tess's surprise, instead of tears, a grin spread from ear to ear across Crystal's face. "Did the coyote get away? That was fun! Can we do it again?"

Heat rushed up Tess's neck, feeding her resulting embarrassment. Here she was shaking like a leaf and

Crystal wanted to 'do it again'? She swiveled a look at Grant. "We've got to get back."

"Sure thing." He slowed, did a rocky U-turn and drove back toward the ranch.

Tess stared straight ahead, still grumbling inwardly at Grant's cavalier attitude. About half a mile ahead, from the corner of her eye, she spied that same coyote, hunkered down on a hillside, staring at them. His ears were pricked forward and she could swear he wore a wide, self-satisfied grin.

As they turned onto the ranch road, an old truck spun up a cloud of dirt in front of them. "Looks like Jud's pickup," Grant observed. "Wonder what brings him over this way?"

"Maybe he's stopping in for supper." Then she hoped not because she didn't really feel like fixing supper for anyone tonight. She just wanted to jump into a hot shower and unwind with Crystal and a pizza, maybe listen to the scratchy jazz station on the old radio.

Jud waited beside his truck as Grant pulled to a stop in the drive. From the look of him, Tess sensed this was not a social call. A slouch hat slanted down over his forehead, hiding his eyes, a cigarette dangled from his lips beneath his long gray mustaches. His head jerked up when Crystal called, "Grandpa Jud" out the back window.

It was then that she saw his eyes, red-rimmed, and the tremble of his unshaven jaw. A dull ache of foreboding gathered in her chest as she got out of the Jeep and climbed into the back to help Crystal unbuckle her seat restraints.

"Where's Henry?" Grant asked, coming around to greet Jud.

"Left him at home," Jud mumbled and flipped the cigarette stub across the gravel.

Crystal hopped down from the Jeep and ran to her grandpa. "We chased a coyote!"

Jud gazed at her with a strange pained expression then patted the top of her head.

Tess guided Crystal to the front of Jud's truck. "The grown-ups want to talk now, honey.Why don't you go play with Nina and I'll come get you in a little while?"

Crystal started to balk, but Tess added, "Hurry—I'll bet Carlos has some sugar cubes you can feed her."

With a quick pivot, Crystal scampered off toward the corral.

When Tess turned and walked back to the men, and saw the mask of anguish on Jud Pearl's face, she knew why he had come. Her heart beat quickened.

"I got a call from New Orleans," he blurted out. He swiped at his eyes with the back of his hand. "They found Carrie," he rasped. "They found my little girl."

Tess swallowed over the knot of despair in her throat. "I'm so sorry, Jud." The day she had dreaded had finally arrived. The day they all had dreaded—the day they hoped would never come.

Her eyelids and throat burned with hot tears. She choked them back. Across the yard, Crystal cavorted with Nina inside the corral. Who would tell Crystal that her mommy was never coming home?

Chapter Fifteen

A kick to the gut couldn't have been any harder to take. Tess hadn't known Carrie that well, but she'd become a surrogate mother to her daughter, in the hope that Carrie might still turn up somewhere. Perhaps a missing person who had temporary amnesia. Any number of possibilities had crossed her mind in the days leading up to today. She moved closer to Jud, wishing she could find the right words to express her sorrow.

Grant placed a large hand on Jud's slumped shoulder in a gesture of sympathy. "That's tough news, Jud. Real tough."

Jud sighed raggedly and pushed his slouch hat brim off his forehead. His heartrending stare toward the corral cut Tess to her core. "I don't know what to say to Crystal." He drew a faded red handkerchief from his back trouser pocket and blew his nose.

"Let's go inside and I'll make some coffee," Tess offered.

They walked to the house through shafts of waning afternoon sunlight. Tess felt palpable dread surrounding them and knew their conversation would be a difficult one. Once inside, the house was chill and cavernous in its cheerless welcome.

In the kitchen, she measured coffee grounds into the coffeemaker, put some ginger cookies onto a plate, and noticed her hands were shaking. The sound of the coffee brewing, even its aroma, did little to warm her. They fell in around the kitchen table.

Across from her, Jud dropped his head into his calloused hands, mumbling, "I can't hardly believe Carrie's gone... All these years I been so angry at her for leavin' me after her mama died." He dabbed at his eyes with the crumpled handkerchief. "Now, it don't seem real that she's—dead. Poor girl."

Helplessness filled Tess. She couldn't ease Jud's pain. But she sensed it must be healthier to talk about his grief than to let it fester inside. "I'm so sorry."

Grant leaned toward Jud. "Did the authorities tell you how they found her?"

Uunruly gray brows hitched above Jud's glazed eyes. "They found her in her car. I guess the water forced it into a creek…and she couldn't get out. Just drowned when water flooded through the windows." He groaned like a sharp knife had twisted inside him. "Several other cars was piled up all around hers in knee-high mud."

Grant averted his gaze to his coffee cup and fell silent. From the corner window, Tess saw Crystal skipping across the side yard. She turned back to the men at the table. "Crystal's coming." The palms of her hands grew clammy at her sides. "We'll have to tell her."

Like he'd been poked with a hot cattle prod, Jud shot to his feet. "I can't—I can't tell that child." His red-rimmed gaze swung over to Tess, desperation rife in his voice. "You can do it, Tess. Yer close to her."

Her nerve endings tingling with sudden panic, Tess stared back. "Jud, you've got to help explain—"

With an abrupt wag of his head, Jud backed away from the table and bolted out of the house.

Sweet Lord. She leaned against the granite island, icy against her fingertips.

The back door opened then banged shut and Crystal bounded into the kitchen. Her glance took in Grant and Tess, and the empty chair hastily vacated moments before. "Where's Grandpa Jud?"

The sound of tires spinning up gravel came from out front as Jud's pickup lurched down the road. *The coward.*

Tess's stomach clenched as she attempted a response to Crystal's question. Thankfully, Grant scooped Crystal up in his arms and nuzzled her neck. His tender gesture, at that moment, allowed Tess to release a deep breath and steady herself.

Crystal giggled and hugged him, then asked Tess, "Can I have some hot chocolate?"

Hot chocolate. It would be warm and soothing, and comforting. "Sure you can." But not here. Now that it was up to her to break this sad news, she wanted to be alone with Crystal, let the child feel free to meet her grief in a completely private way.

"I think we'd better go make it at our place, so Mr. Grant can finish doing his chores." When she looked into Grant's eyes, she saw that he understood, and was grateful.

He walked them to the front door, his arm lightly around her shoulder, his strength passing through to her at the very time she needed it most. "I can rustle up some chili if you two want to come back for supper later," he offered as they left.

"I appreciate it," she said, looking back at him standing tall, his broad shoulders filling the front doorway. "I'll let you know."

The log cabin waited at the edge of the property, shadowed a mottled brown in the early evening light. As they moved through the dry leaves, beneath crooked limbs of the nearly bare cottonwood trees, Tess reached down and slipped her hand in Crystal's. The child's fingers were cold, and so were hers. A strange heaviness gathered in her chest.

How would she tell Crystal this terrible news? All of her educational background and teaching experience had never prepared her for such an emotional challenge. A silent prayer formed in her heart. *Please help me say the right words.*

Beside her, Crystal kicked up leaves in their path then stomped them under her small shoes. The crunching sound broke the silence around them. "Let's stop here a minute," Tess said, coming to a halt beneath a cottonwood. She took a deep breath and looked upward. "Can you see the leaves falling from those tall branches?"

Crystal craned her short neck, gazing up at the old tree. "Yes."

"You know, we call this time of year the fall because the trees drop their leaves and seem to die."

"What does that mean?"

"Well, the trees aren't the same as they were in the summer when their leaves were beautiful and green."

"Where do the leaves go?"

"The leaves go into the earth and help the grass to come back in the spring—and the trees to grow their leaves again."

"Hmm." Crystal's forehead crinkled. "Why?"

Before Tess could answer, Crystal broke free and raced to the cabin's front door. "Com'on, let's have some hot chocolate," she called.

Shivering, Tess hurried to join her and they hustled inside. In the front room, she turned on the lamp and the room heater, filled the tea kettle in the kitchen, and turned up the burner underneath. Her mind whirled with the immediate challenge of sharing her life-changing news with Crystal.

When the hot chocolate was ready, Tess carried two steaming mugs out to the small table in front of the sofa where Crystal played with Miss Tabby. After they sipped on their drinks for a while and Miss Tabby had curled up in the corner of the sofa next to Crystal, Tess gathered her courage. "This afternoon when Grandpa Jud came over to see us he was very sad."

Crystal glanced up from petting the cat. "Why was he sad?"

"Because he got a phone call from New Orleans. A doctor called and told Grandpa Jud that your mommy was in a car accident when Hurricane Katrina came. You remember all that big rain?"

Crystal's dark lashes flew up, her amber eyes startled. "Mommy got hurt in her car?"

Tess nodded slowly. "Yes. She—the rain came into the car. She couldn't get out...and she died." The last words wrenched themselves from her tongue.

She heard the sharp intake of Crystal's breath. "Mommy died? Where did she go?"

A knot forming in her chest, Tess moved closer on the sofa and stroked Crystal's arm. "She's gone to a place where good people go when they die. She went to heaven to be with God, who loves her."

Even as she watched the child's features crumple in despair, Tess knew her words had caused pain—and were painfully inadequate.

Crystal's eyes pooled with tears. "Can't the doctor make her better?"

Tess shook her head. "I'm afraid not."

Crystal jumped to her feet. "No! I want mommy to come *here* to live with us on the ranch!"

Reaching out to her, Tess tried to embrace Crystal, but she would have none of it.

Crystal glared back as tears streamed down her plump cheeks. "I don't want Mommy to be in heaven—I want her to come *here*!"

Her heart rending in sympathy, Tess felt hot tears prick her own eyelids and threaten to overflow. "I'm so sorry." She went to Crystal and put her arms around her.

Small fists pummeled her chest, and she caught them for a moment, but the child broke away and ran into the bedroom sobbing.

Tess chased after her and stumbled on a lumpy throw rug in the dwindling light. Crystal huddled in a dark corner, a small trembling thing, moaning into her cupped hands.

"Oh, baby. Oh, baby." Tess did the only thing she knew to do—went to her and guided her over to the bed. "It's going to be all right. We love you," she whispered.

She sat Crystal at the edge of the bed, removed her shoes, and her own, and slipped her under the bedclothes. Tugging the comforter over them, she pulled Crystal into her arms, half sobbing, half crooning to her. She rocked them both to ward off the pain that cut like a shard of obsidian glass—that howled like a beast of prey. *Life was unfair. Unfair. Unfair!*

Their tears drenched the pillows and still Tess rocked this bereft little one until, warmed by each other's body heat and exhausted by grief, a fitful sleep washed over them.

Sometime later, Tess lay staring at the ceiling shadows, listening to the rise and ragged fall of Crystal's breath. Why on earth did Carrie's life have to end so swiftly...as others had during the devastation of Katrina? Why was she, Tess, here in her place struggling to make sense of it all? A dull ache bound her forehead replacing the tears, now dried tracks over her tight cheek bones.

Her thoughts reeled, bringing back snatches of various spiritual philosophers she'd read over the years. Joseph Campbell had spoken incessantly about the "soul's journey" on a physical path. But was each soul's life on earth predestined? The exact length determined at conception?

She recalled the words of the great Lebanese philosopher, Kahlil Gibran: "For life and death are one, even as the river and the sea are one." The visual image of Carrie floating from a sparkling river into the vast welcoming sea soothed her.

Her mind finally compromised on the belief that Carrie's death was an accident—and not any form of celestial punishment. God's love must surround her.

Later, during the night, Crystal moaned in her sleep and Tess pulled the comforter over her shoulders. How could she translate more positive feelings about the afterlife journey to a four-year-old? This child had suffered enough loss in her short life. Let her go forward with a bright rather than a hopeless view of her mother's death. Better to tuck away a pearl than a stone.

Faint rays of light split through the crack in the window curtains. In the early morning stillness, a horse neighed somewhere in the barn and Crystal tossed off the comforter. A small hand reached out and shook Tess's arm. "Where did my mommy go?"

Tess cleared her throat and answered softly. "She went to heaven."

Innocent, sleepy eyes searched her face. "Where is heaven?"

A vision of the rippling dunes, like the sea, pastel beneath a warming sun, became vivid to Tess. She said, "It's a special place—like the Dunes."

"Can we go there, too?"

Tess paused, thinking. "Yes."

"Will Mommy be there?"

She hesitated then answered as truthfully as she knew how. "We can send a message to her there. We can think about heaven when we go there."

Beside her, Crystal released a long sigh. "When can we go?"

Tess enclosed her small hands in her own and gave them a tender squeeze. "Soon, honey. Soon."

* * *

Tess jumped down from the truck, her boots hitting asphalt with a thud. She had fifteen minutes before having to pick up Crystal from daycare. That would be just enough time to give Jud Pearl a piece of her mind.

She opened the door to the tobacco shop and stepped past Henry, snoring in a sprawled heap a few feet away. One eyebrow raised slightly, a blood-shot eyeball flickered open then drooped downward. The shop was empty of customers. Only the twangy voice from a western station on Jud's radio in the back room greeted her ears.

"Jud!" Tess trudged toward the sage green curtains pulled across the doorway, the air thickening with a smoky smell. "Jud?" She pulled the curtain aside and blinked into the gray haze.

"Yeah? Who is it?" came that familiar graveled voice.

To her right, she saw him slouched in a faded, maroon plaid recliner, a coffee mug on the table next to him. A brown cigarillo dangled from beneath his unkempt mustache.

She charged into the room. "It's Tess. Who did you expect? The tooth fairy?" She coughed on an inhalation of foul, stale air and choked out, "I want to talk to you."

He eased forward to an upright position. "Guess I know what it's about—Carrie."

He blew out a puff of smoke, still not making an effort to move from the chair.

She stood planted in the center of the small room, furnished meagerly with aging furniture, the window shades allowing only slants of light to enter. "Yes, I want to talk about Carrie, but can we get some air in here? I don't see how you can breathe."

He nodded. "Suit yerself."

She opened two of the windows enough to let in a cool breeze from the mountains. Then she turned and vented her frustration. "Why didn't you stay and share the burden of telling Crystal about her mother's death?"

His body gave a shudder and he averted his gaze. "I didn't know how to…"

Tess wanted to shake his bony shoulders. "You're her grandfather, Jud. She needs you now—more than ever!"

He looked up at her through pain-filled eyes. "I ain't been much of a grandpa so far." He stubbed out the cigarillo in an already full horseshoe ash tray and sat forward in the chair. "And I don't know where to start."

Her anger subsided at the mournful sight of him, bent like a fragile twig. "Have you made arrangements yet?" she asked softly. "Do you want to have a service for Carrie?"

"A funeral? I s'pose it would be the right thing to do…even though I ain't much into religion." His eyes welled up. "Just can't face it." He angled his bushy head in the direction of a nearby sofa. "Have a seat."

She plopped down onto a rump-sprung cushion. For a moment, silence hung in the air between them, thick as the lingering haze.

Jud slowly glanced over at her. "Will you help me?"

Ever since Crystal had entered Tess's life, she had somehow known she must be strong for her. She met Jud's imploring gaze. "I have an idea. It will take both of us…and Grant, too."

~*Grant*~

Chapter Sixteen

The breeze of an unusually warm October morning wafted through the front seat of Grant's Jeep, lifting Tess's hair at the nape of her neck. She tugged the brim of her baseball cap over her forehead and looked through the windshield to the approaching dunes. Beside her, his hands on the steering wheel, Grant hummed softly. In the rear view mirror, Tess saw Crystal stare with solemn eyes at the cloth doll Jud had given her then hug it to her chest.

Crystal had wanted to bring Miss Tabby, but Tess had said no. The cat might wander off. The dunes were no place for a cat. Crystal had pouted for a while then salved her disappointment by bringing her mother's doll.

Behind them, Jud meandered along the road in his dilapidated truck. Henry's straw-blond, canine head bobbed next to Jud in the passenger seat. Two old pals. Jud wore a beat up western hat and sunglasses, a cigarette stuck in the corner of his mouth. Oddly enough, she could imagine Henry wearing a similar hat and goggles, and snapping a photo of them to send as a joke to…someone. The thought nearly made her smile.

But this was not the time for playful thoughts, nor was this a lighthearted trek they were on. Today they had set out on an important mission in memory of Carrie Pearl. Tess had planned it with all of them after Jud returned from Louisiana with Carrie's remains. Although, she hoped their spirits would not be dragged down by the ceremony but uplifted.

Tess held her worn Bible in her lap, the Bible salvaged from her belongings sent from her New Orleans apartment manager. Its gilt-bordered pages were as thin as delicate flower petals. The book's leather cover pressed smooth and comforting beneath the palm of her hand.

"Are we almost there?" Crystal whined from the back seat.

"Almost," Grant said as he turned into the parking lot.

It was the last week that the park would be open to the public until spring. Tess was relieved to see only two other cars parked at the far end of the lot. Once out of the Jeep, Tess took Crystal's hand and gazed across Medano Creek. Wave upon wave of sand-capped peaks stretched before them, cradled by the deep lavender-hued Sangre de Cristos beyond. Surrounding the middle island, the creek had dwindled to a muddy bed of clay.

Overhead clouds floated by on the near-blue sky like ships with billowed sails. The group made their way down the sloping bank and onto the creekbed, the rubber treads of their boots making sloppy prints in the mud. Once on the island, Tess turned and looked behind, watching as Jud took up the rear, his hat brim slanted down over his craggy features. With care, he held a small square box. Henry loped beside him, tongue lolling out of one side of his open mouth.

Carrying a wicker hamper, Grant led the way. A tall beacon, sure-footed, his facial profile sharply pronounced against the island's stand of cottonwood and ponderosa ahead. When she had first asked him to be a part of Carrie's memorial at the dunes, he'd immediately agreed. He had known Carrie since she was a kid.

When they had walked further into the trees, Grant stopped. "Is this far enough?"

Mid-morning sun splashed through the ponderosa, and Tess shielded her face, breathing in the dusky sweet pine fragrance. "Let's go to the other side where we can be closer to the dunes."

He nodded and went ahead.

Tess let go of Crystal's hand and let the child run through the clustered trees. Henry sidled up to Tess then romped over to check out a sharp-eared, black squirrel scurrying up a cottonwood. Jud caught up with her, slightly out of breath. "I kinda forgot what I was goin' to say... You know, for the service."

Tess held up the good book. "That's okay. There are plenty of helpful hints in here."

On the sand bank, they gathered in a circle. For a moment the only sound on the island was the wind skittering down from the rolling dune field. All eyes rested on Tess. She gathered her thoughts for a moment. "Let's think about something special we remember about Carrie," she said. She glanced over at Jud. "Would you like to start?"

He removed his hat. "She had beautiful dark eyes like her mother."

Tess prompted Crystal. "What do you remember about your mom?"

Crystal frowned, concentrating. "She liked music." She kissed her cloth doll's painted-on face and held it close.

"I recall she could play the guitar pretty well..and sing," Grant added.

Jud sighed audibly. "Yep. She wrote some of her own songs."

Tess smiled. "And Carrie was an excellent teacher, devoted to her students."

After several more memories were revealed, Tess handed Grant the Bible. "Would you like to read first?"

"The 23rd Psalm," he said, and proceeded to read with a clear, strong voice. "The Lord is my shepherd; I shall not want. He maketh me to lie down in green pastures; he leadeth me beside the still waters."

When he had finished, he closed the Bible and gave it back to her. She held it at her side. Before them the sand dunes rolled in silent waves. She breathed deeply. "Lord, we know that Carrie is gone from us, no longer on this earth. Now she dances with the wind—and sings with joy. She soars beyond the sun and the stars.

For she is spirit, unbounded, like a bird carried on wings to your eternal love. She is *free*."

"Amen," said Grant.

"Amen," Jud rasped.

Crystal sniffled quietly.

To complete the ceremony, Tess glanced over at Jud. "Jud wants to share this part of Carrie's memorial with us."

He knelt down to the box he'd set on the ground, but a questioning look filled his eyes when his gaze switched from her to Crystal.

"Your mommy gave us a special gift when she died, Crystal." Tess reached into the hamper basket and retrieved four large plastic cups. She gave one to each of them. "Carrie was born on this land and we want to send her gift back to the land and to God."

Jud's eyes watered and he sniffed back tears as he opened the box and took Crystal's cup. Her expression grew surprised when he scooped some of the gray ashes from inside the box into the cup and handed it back to her. He repeated this action for Tess, Grant and himself.

"Now each of us is going to decide how to give back Carrie's gift," Tess said. "And we are going to do it with gladness in our hearts, instead of sadness." But tears came to her eyes as well, and she brushed them away with her sleeve.

Jud fished out a handkerchief from his back pocket and blew his nose loudly. Grant's expression softened behind his sunglasses and Tess wondered if he was thinking about Laura.

Crystal tugged on her jacket. "Can you help me do it?"

"Of course, honey." Tess turned and gazed down the creekbed. "Let's go skip over the beach." Before she could start out, Crystal leaped ahead, carrying her cup like a torch, her doll left behind on top of the hamper.

Grant snapped a lid on his cup. "I'm going up the dunes. You want to come?"

"Maybe… I want to stay with Crystal for a while."

"Okay." With an understanding smile, he set off across the muddy creek bed.

Ahead, Crystal sprinted along the meandering beach, Henry trotting along beside her, tongue lolling, eyes fixed on the mysterious cup. Probably thinking it held a tasty treat, Tess mused.

Crystal held her cup out at arm's length, tilting it, letting the morning breeze carry its freed ashes into a golden trail behind her. *Was Carrie watching?*

Off to the side, Jud ambled from tree to tree, spilling portions of his cup around their base as if to use Carrie's ashes as a nutrient, allowing them to work down into the dry soil and nourish the dormant roots. Certainly this gesture would bring him some inner peace.

When Crystal came back, breathless and begging for a drink, Tess poured lemonade from a pitcher in the hamper. "You did a good job for your mom," Tess said and hugged her close.

"Yeah, I did." Crystal's thick hair was dusted with sand and smelled of pine. "What are you gonna do with mommy's gift?"

"Well, I thought we could build a sand castle."

"Hmm. A sand castle?" Crystal gazed up at her with wide eyes. "That sounds like fun."

Glad that they wore their work clothes, Tess set about to find a good sunny spot on the beach. The damp sand was just the right consistency to mold and shape beneath their hands.

Within a short time, she and Crystal had scooped and patted a sizable castle, complete with a draw bridge and moat.

"Come on, Grandpa," Crystal called from her squatting position on the sand. "Help us build this."

Jud ventured over and observed their progress. "I'd like to, but my knees wouldn't let me get up once I wallowed around in that mud."

Tess commiserated. "I'll be ready for a long shower at the end of this day." She formed a central turret and poured her cup's ashes into it. Crystal watched in fascination. "Now when spring comes, the icy streams will flow down from the mountains and the ashes will float away with them," she explained to Crystal.

The remains of one life joining the flow of life.

Small furrows appeared in Crystal's forehead. "But then our sand castle will wash away."

"That's okay. We can build another one." She smiled reassuringly at the child and got to her feet. "I think this one is beautiful, though. Don't you?"

"Yes, but I want to put a princess in the castle." She turned and ran a ways to the hamper.

On a distant rise of dune, Tess saw Grant surrounded in shimmering sunlight. He stood, moving his arm back and forth as if ringing a bell. She imagined Carrie's ashes as musical notes, lyrical, in tiny tinkling sounds, singing over the crest of each ivory-hued dune. Her heart soared with them.

Beside her, Jud met her inspired gaze. Neither spoke, not wanting to spoil the dignity of the moment.

"Here's the princess!" Crystal bounded down the sloping bed and placed her mother's doll in faded plaid gingham dress atop Tess's turret. She patted Crystal's shoulder. "Now our castle is perfect."

Later when Grant returned from his climb, they all sat beneath the clustered trees and shared a picnic lunch. Sliced beef sandwiches and potato salad satisfied their hunger, the sun overhead warming their outstretched bodies. After feeding Henry, Jud and Grant drank strong coffee from Jud's thermos, and Tess and Crystal shared lemonade.

"Well, let's head 'em out," Grant called to Crystal after they had cleared up the remains. He hoisted Crystal onto his back, piggy-back style, and picked up the hamper basket. Tess hurried to catch up to his long stride while Jud followed behind, Henry trotting happily alongside.

Grant's strong presence buoyed Tess's spirit. He was like one of these tall ponderosa that she could lean on for support, his roots growing deep below the plain.

Crystal hung on with glee. "Giddy-up, horsey!" She had fetched her doll princess from the castle turret at the last moment, not wanting to leave her behind, and placed her inside her zipped-up jacket.

Watching Crystal so at ease, hugging Grant's neck, the burden of her mother's death not such a sad burden now, Tess sensed a release of Carrie Pearl's spirit. It was a comforting thought that Crystal would not have undue painful memories of saying goodbye to her mother.

Gazing back to the purple Sangre mountains, Tess thought of her own mother in Germany and knew she would soon have to call her to update her living situation. Where Tess's ultimate residence would be was still a puzzling question.

Jud's footsteps came up beside her. "I'm sure glad we brought Carrie out here," he said, a wistful tone in his voice.

"I am too, Jud. It just felt right, didn't it?"

He wagged his shaggy head. "Yeah. Now when I come out here, I'll think about her..." He choked back a sob. "She finally came home."

Emotion gathering in her chest, Tess reached out and rested her hand on his shoulder. "Yes, she did."

None of them would ever see this ageless, magnificent place again in quite the same way.

They loaded up and headed back. Jud followed them to the county road then turned off toward town. He honked and waved as Henry's bony head hung out the front side window.

Tess remarked to Grant, "Jud should get a doggie seat restraint if he's going to let Henry sit up front."

Grant raised an eyebrow above his sunglasses. "Sounds like a good idea." Then he fell silent behind the wheel.

In the back, Crystal sagged against her booster seat cushion, dozing, a peaceful softness to her features.

The end of a rewarding day left Tess with unanswered questions. Now Crystal needed a strong adult guardian more than ever. Jud couldn't possibly fill that position. Could he ever? She'd come to like him, even understand his sometimes crotchety demeanor. He'd lived alone so long, he'd become very set in his ways.

She turned to Grant. "Thanks for being there for Crystal today...for Jud and me too."

"I was glad to do it." He smiled that familiar warm smile she'd come to know. He was an admirable man, loyal to his friends and his beliefs. For a moment, she thought he might reach over and touch her hand. She wished he would. But his gaze moved back to the road ahead.

* * *

By midweek the days had begun to feel more winter-like; frost rimmed the windows inside the cabin and

213

blustery winds whipped across the valley. Tess added another heavy blanket to the bed and kept the small room heater on all night. She and Crystal snuggled up to keep warm, but by early morning Tess found herself hunting down their new knit caps to pull on under the covers.

She made no complaint to Grant. She was used to making things work on her own. If need be, she would find heavier pajamas at the town thrift shop for her and Crystal.

Wednesday morning winds howled at the cabin's windows and front door. The brittle chill in the air cut through them as Tess hurried Crystal up to the main house to fix breakfast for the men. Juan and Carlos worked only occasionally now on the ranch, preparing the barns and horses for winter months.

Grant greeted them at the back door with a smile and a frown. "Get in here, you two," he commanded as the howling wind chased them inside. "I put on a pot of coffee."

"Thanks." Tess removed Crystal's coat and hat, and unwrapped herself from her parka. "It smells good." She smiled up at Grant as he assisted her and hung her parka on a hall peg, then glanced away for fear of showing her growing affection for him. Too many times lately, she remembered his tender kiss on the back deck and how it had felt to be in his arms…for just a short time. It was foolish to think of it, she knew. But the mind had a way of flashing back to the very things one should put aside.

Crystal shivered. "Can I have some hot chocolate?"

"Sure, honey." Tess quickly made her way to the kitchen and got to work on the breakfast menu. She'd fixed the hot chocolate, mixed up the pancake batter, and heated the griddle when Juan and Carlos rumbled through the back door. Their faces were flushed from the cold winds.

"Help yourself to the coffee," she said. "Grant made plenty."

Juan smiled broadly beneath his dark mustache, beard stubble dotting his full jaw. "We can use some. It's really cold this morning."

Grant joined the men and refilled his coffee mug. "We'll put the horses in the barns, brush 'em down, and check for any new injuries."

After breakfast, Tess cleared up the dishes while keeping an eye on the storm clouds gathering over the mountains. "Guess you won't be going to preschool today, Crystal," she said with conviction. "It's not a good day for driving."

Grant shrugged into his sheep-lined coat in the hallway. "That's for sure." He stepped into the kitchen to go over the call he wanted her to make on a ranch construction job. "We'll be back for lunch unless those winds blow us down the valley."

"Be careful," she said with some concern. She'd heard about the ferocity of winter storms through the San Luis Valley. After experiencing Katrina, the prospect of any violent weather left her in a quivery physical state.

Through the morning, she busied herself with office work and reading an alphabet book to Crystal. When the men came in for lunch, sloppy Joe fixings simmered in the crock pot and an apple cobbler bubbled in the oven. She'd laid out a platter of large hamburger buns alongside pickles, olives and chips. Everyone helped themselves.

Her fragrant cobbler desert, golden-brown and still warm, brought approving comments.

Grant wrapped his arm around her shoulders. "Tess, you've become one terrific cook since you started working here. Hope you plan on staying on with us." He winked at her, an unabashed satisfaction in his eyes.

Her self esteem hiked up a notch. The genuine sincerity of his appreciation was not wasted on her. Watching them all dive into the sloppy Joes and the cobbler like her cooking was world class gave Tess a sense of fulfillment she hadn't experienced since teaching her first graders in New Orleans. As they sat at the long kitchen table, talking and joking, despite the frigid weather outside, it felt like being with family.

After Juan and Carlos went back out to finish tending to the horses, Grant lingered, helping with cleaning up the kitchen. "You know, that storm could get worse. Why don't you and Crystal come on up to the house tonight?" he finally asked.

She folded a dish towel and laid it on the counter, weighing his suggestion. "Oh, we're fine…"

"I'll bet that little room heater doesn't give off enough heat to keep a rabbit warm."

Outside, sleet tapped against the kitchen windows. She wavered for a moment, dreading another night of chattering against the cold.

"You can stay in the front guest room. You can turn the heat up as much as you need it." He stood in front of her, all six-plus feet of him, his mind obviously set.

Across the room, Crystal watched with interest. How could Tess say no when she must consider Crystal's well being? She nodded in agreement. "Thanks. I'll go pack some things for overnight."

About half an hour later, as Tess finished putting together a satchel of nightclothes and other necessities, a knock came at the cabin door. When she answered, there stood Grant, snowflakes battering his cowboy hat and heavy jacket. "I've come to help you up to the house, ma'am," he drawled, bringing to mind a towering John Wayne out of some long ago Western film.

His expression was almost comical, but then again, it was sweet.

Miss Tabby loped up behind Tess and peered out between her legs. "Gosh, I almost forgot the cat. Come inside and I'll get her travel cage." She caged Miss Tabby, wrapped in a doll blanket, and slipped on her parka. "Good thing you showed up, Mr. Wilder."

He gave her a casual smile as he lifted the cage. "Please, call me Grant."

He offered his arm, she took it, and they hurried through the driving wind and white stuff to the welcoming ranch house.

* * *

After a hearty soup supper, Grant, Tess, and Crystal gathered in the large family room in front of the stone fireplace that reached to the beamed ceiling. Grant had lit the logs and now a fire crackled before them in flames of blue and orange. Crystal dragged a catnip mouse across the Indian print hearth rug, tempting Miss Tabby who leaped to the bait.

"Will you be comfortable in the guest room?" Grant asked from the E-Z Boy recliner next to the sofa. He'd removed his boots and wore large-sized moccasin slippers.

"I'm sure we will. That bed will feel very roomy after the one we've been sleeping in." Tess referred to the queen size, knotty-pine poster bed. "And the bathroom is great…that shower and tub will spoil us."

Warm hues of the firelight played across Grant's features. "If there's anything you need, just give a holler."

Tess sank back into the cushy sofa pillows, a mellow mood surrounding her. "Thanks. You've been very kind to Crystal and me."

"No, it's the other way around," he said. "You two have definitely livened up this place. You've helped me

217

out a lot." His gaze held hers for a long moment causing a warm flush to flow through her.

Crystal bounded onto the sofa next to Tess and laid her head in Tess's lap. Tess reached behind Crystal and slid a crocheted throw over her. "That's nice," she said. "I'm goin' to sleep."

"Do you think you'll like sleeping in that new bed?" Grant asked Crystal, with a wink to Tess.

Crystal's small head popped up as if on marionette strings. "Yeah. It's got big pillows."

Grant chuckled. It came from deep in his throat, a pleasant manly sound. A comforting sound.

Outside snow continued to fall, an erratic wind moaned and groaned. Cocooned in a warm, safe place, Tess laid her head back on the sofa, drifting along on a sense of being protected from earthly cares. At least for now.

Grant got up and went over to the fireplace to lay another log on the fire. When he returned to the recliner he said thoughtfully, "You know, that old cabin isn't built for winter living, Tess. If you and Crystal want to stay on, and I hope you do, maybe you two can move into the guest room."

Somehow she hadn't expected this invitation. Even though she knew he was right. They couldn't continue to live in the drafty, unheated cabin. It made sense, but the offer still caused a disturbing sensation in her midsection. Could she become too dependent on this strong western man? She was used to making her own way, especially after her divorce.

She hesitated, torn by conflicting emotions. First thing, she had to conquer her involuntary reactions to that gentle, caring look of his. But for Crystal's sake… "You're right, Grant. For Crystal's sake, I think we probably should.   At least until her future is more definite."

Glancing back to the fire, Tess avoided looking into his questioning gaze. Duty prompted her to do what was best for the girl. Her own future must be set aside for a while longer.

Chapter Seventeen

The late autumn days took on a sense of normalcy, as normal as this unusual situation could be. Tess kept to a busy schedule of fixing breakfast and dinner, taking Crystal to preschool three days a week, and helping Grant in his office. He was currently working on a construction project at a neighboring ranch which made her grateful. That meant there wasn't a lot of time spent together. Being near him caused unwanted feelings and thoughts to enter her mind.

Evenings occupied her with reading to Crystal, bathing and early bedtime.

She wondered if Jud would approach her on the subject of Crystal's future; where she would eventually live, who would be her legal guardian, but he didn't. She figured he needed time to work through his grief over Carrie's death.

When Jenny announced that the preschool group would be taking a field trip to visit "the goat lady," and asked Tess to join them, Tess welcomed the opportunity for a day of serendipity.

They bundled the kids into two vehicles, dividing up the boys so as not to avoid back seat bickering. "Boy stuff," as Jenny called it. Butch and Sam had taken to punching each other in front of the girls. Not an especially attractive activity to be around.

The goat farm was situated off the county road near Mosca. Fanny Flanagan, the "goat lady" stood in her front yard, holding a small, black-and-white goat in her sturdy arms as they drove up the gravel road. Tied in a bow beneath her angular chin, a blue gingham bonnet framed her long oval face. Tufts of steel-gray hair poked out around her weather worn features. "Howdy!" she called cheerily. The goat bleated, squirming to get down in the mud.

"Baaaa!" Butch hollered in a macho, six-year-old voice as he, Crystal and Erleen climbed out of Grant's Jeep. Sam and the Robles sisters, Teresa and Anna, tumbled out of Jenny's SUV, adding to the vocal entourage of little people. A multi-colored Australian sheep dog trotted up to investigate. First eyeing the animated group with suspicion, he then barked a deep throated warning.

Tess and Jenny attempted to keep everyone together. "No running near the goats, guys!" Jenny instructed, noticeably concerned about disturbing the dozen goats wandering in the nearby corral.

"Oh, it's all right to come closer," Mrs. Flanagan said. "Bailey just takes his guard job seriously with new visitors." She smiled a wide toothy greeting as she maneuvered over to them. "He barks like he's protecting Fort Knox."

Jenny introduced herself and Tess to the woman. "Meet Mrs. Flanagan, kids, she's the owner of this farm," she continued. "She'll tell us all about how she raises her animals."

Crystal's small hand shot up. "Can we pet your goat?"

Fanny Flanagan beamed down over the children. "Yes dear. This is Gwendolyn. She is one of the youngest of this year's does."

Six eager hands reached up to simultaneously pet Gwendolyn's head and soft white coat.

"I name all of my sheep and goats, so I can keep track of them."

"How many animals do you have?" Sam Stotter asked, standing on tip-toe to stroke Gwendolyn's black ears.

The goat lady guided them over toward the corral. "Well, we have about twenty goats and fifteen sheep. Of course, that changes in the spring…when new kids arrive."

While twisting a strand of her pale blond hair, Erleen looked up at her. "Do new kids come live here then?"

Mrs. Flanagan's chuckle rippled over her intent audience. "Goodness no, dear. I meant the new baby goat kids arrive then."

To be perfectly clear, Jenny added, "That's when the momma goats have their babies."

Tess looked over and smiled at Crystal, gave her a shoulder hug. She hoped Crystal would assimilate all this birthing with moms and kids in a positive way.

Mrs. Flanagan opened the corral gate and let the kid jump out of her ample arms. It bawled energetically and romped over to join the others. "Would you all like to learn how to milk a goat?"

Half a dozen voices chorused, "Yes!"

Like a pied piper, the bonneted goat lady turned and led her guests into the barn. Once inside, she caught an unsuspecting doe and hoisted her up on a milking stand. With nimble fingers she demonstrated how to trap the milk in its udders and squeeze it out into a bucket.

Oohs and aahs accompanied her instructions. "Would any of you like to try it?" she asked, righting herself to stand over them.

The boys pushed forward along with Crystal. Erleen and the Robles sisters hung back, somewhat intimidated. With a curious pride, Tess watched Crystal take her turn squeezing the goat's teats. The animal seemed used to the pulling and tugging as it munched on a wad of grass.

"Hey, you're not doin' it right. I'll show you how." Butch nudged against Crystal, his pudgy hands stretching out to take hold of the goat's udders.

Crystal ignored him and only appeared to squeeze harder. Then a mis-aimed squirt of milk missed the bucket and shot directly into Butch's eye. He reared back, swiping his fingers across his offended eye. "Hey! Stop it!"

Delighted squeals came from Teresa and Anna. Sam guffawed loudly and Erleen took it all in with a quizzical frown. Tess turned away, trying not to laugh out loud.

Head down, features concentrated, Crystal kept on pulling and squeezing. "Plink, plink, plink" went the milk as it landed in the metal bucket.

His male pride wounded, Butch lunged at Crystal, his cheeks flushing as red as the roots of his hair. One fisted hand raised to chin level. "I can punch a girl…"

"Don't think so." Jenny latched onto Butch's shoulders and pulled him back a few steps. "Not unless you'd like to go sit in the Jeep for a time out."

"Nah." Butch made a face and slunk off to the sidelines.

"Let's all go inside for goat's milk and pumpkin cookies," Mrs. Flanagan suggested brightly. "I just baked them this morning." She scurried toward the rear of the two-story farm house, the group close on her heels. "Please leave your shoes on the porch," she called before disappearing inside.

"She doesn't want us to track in sheep poop," Jenny explained as they all lined up their shoes next to the screen door.

After they had finished their sweet snack in Mrs. Flanagan's tidy kitchen, the children were eager to explore the sheep corral. Tess and Jenny lingered by the corral fence musing over each child's unique qualities.

"This venture has brought Crystal away from some of her sadness over losing her mom," Tess observed. She'd briefly told Jenny about the memorial service that she,

Grant, Jud, and Crystal had shared at the Sand Dunes. "I'm glad we came out here today."

A northerly breeze blew wisps of Jenny's loose ponytail around her face. "Me too. I think Crystal will do just fine. You can tell she's got some spunk. None of those boys are going to push her around."

"There's a new twist, however." Tess glanced sideways at Jenny, knowing she'd have to reveal the new living arrangement sooner or later. "Grant invited us to move into the main house for the winter months. It's just too darn cold to stay in the old cabin."

The beginnings of a knowing smile lifted the corners of Jenny's mouth. "So...well, maybe it's about time. You're sure to get better acquainted up there."

Tess sighed audibly. "I don't think...that isn't my intention. Crystal's welfare is more of what's on my mind."

"Oh, of course. Has Jud said anything about what he would do for her?" She shook her head. "Sure can't see Crystal living with him, though. Can you?"

"Not really. That store is no place to raise a child. You know he smokes like a chimney."

"Yeah, he does." Jenny leaned back against the corral fence railing. "Besides, Grant needs some company. He's got to be lonely routing around in that big house by himself. And he and Crystal hit it off well, didn't you say?"

"Very well. He has a patient nature with children."

"He's a good, honest man," Jenny added.

"She's never had a positive adult male influence in her life."

Jenny gave Tess that straight-on look she'd come to recognize. "Kind of like a *dad* influence?"

Tess stared back in mock exasperation. "Jenny! You never give up, do you?"

A nonchalant shrug lifted Jenny's shoulders. "Don't want anyone to pass up a good thing—that's all."

* * *

A few nights before Halloween, Tess helped Crystal carve a smiley face on a large, round pumpkin on the kitchen table. The wide mouth came out rather lopsided which gave the face a humorous effect. No trick-or-treating was in store, but Tess thought a lighted jack-o-lantern on the front porch would add a festive touch to the celebrated autumn ritual.

Grant stepped into the kitchen from the hall and observed their handiwork. "Well, that's a good looking fellow. Maybe Jud could loan you one of his pipes to stick in its mouth."

Crystal shook her tousled head. "No, we don't want him to smoke."

A shared smile passed between Tess and Grant. "I'm going out to the barn to check on a couple of the horses."

Crystal jumped down off her perch on the chair, her eyes wide. "Can we come, too? I want to see Nina."

Tess looked up to see Grant pause just inside the doorway to the hall. "I don't think-"

One tawny eyebrow lifted. "Sure. You're both welcome to come out and tuck them in." He pulled on his sheepskin jacket while Tess hurriedly cleared up the pumpkin carvings.

The barn smelled sweet with fresh hay, and a slice of light from the nearly full moon streamed through the side windows above the stalls. Grant was in a rear stall, checking on Sugar.

"Nina!" Crystal called, running to greet the foal.

Tess caught up and pulled some sugar cubes from a pocket in her barn jacket. Actually, it was Grant's old jacket he'd let her wear when she helped out with barn chores. The sleeves were rolled up twice and the hem hung down almost to her knees. "You can give Nina a sweet before bedtime," she said, offering them to Crystal.

Big eyes sparkling, Nina happily accepted the treats from Crystal's outstretched palm then nuzzled her cheek. Crystal giggled and, on tiptoe, stroked Nina's nose. "She's growing so tall!"

"Yes, she is. You'll be able to ride her by spring," Tess mused. Then the thought hit her: *Will we be here in the spring? Will I be here in the spring?*

After Grant finished with the horses, they walked out into the crisp evening. A sky black as velvet and glowing with stars canopied the valley. The moon shone so brightly it was piercing. Tess absorbed the vastness of it, reveling in its awesome beauty. She breathed deeply. "How can anyone describe the wonder of this place?"

Beside her, Grant gazed upward. "I've asked myself that question many times."

In no hurry to go back to the house, they strolled a ways out onto the prairie. Tess pointed to a constellation above them. "That must be the Big Dipper."

Crystal craned her small head. "What's a 'Big Dipper'?"

Tess darted a look at Grant. "I'm sure you're the expert on the stars."

"Well, all I can tell you, Crystal, is that when God made that great big sky, He threw out a whole lot of shiny stars, and some fell into different shapes. The one called the Big Dipper looks like a big water dipper that the cowboys out West used to get a drink from the rivers." Grant pointed upward. "And there's the Little Dipper right nearby."

"Hmm." Crystal observed the shimmery display with keen interest.

Just then, half a dozen colored lights of flame-red, green and yellow streaked down across the southern sky. Crystal jumped up and down. "Wow, look!"

Tess sucked in a breath of surprise. "What are those? Falling stars?"

"They look like stars, but it's a meteor shower," Grant said. "They're particles of comet debris that enter the earth's atmosphere."

Crystal ran over to Tess and hugged her legs. "Will they fall on me?"

Grant grinned from beneath his hat. "No, honey, they'll vaporize…just disappear before they come to earth. They do put on a pretty show, kind of like falling fireworks."

"What's that star?" Crystal asked, gazing up above the Sangre de Cristos.

"It looks like the brightest star, doesn't it?" Tess knelt down on one knee and slipped her arm around Crystal. "And it's shining right down on you…kind of like your mom, always looking down from heaven, beaming her love light on you."

Crystal's face took on a glow. "It's a special star."

"Let's call that star the Carrie star, okay?" Crystal nodded vehemently.

Tess glanced over at Grant who stood close by observing them quietly. He pulled out a folded handkerchief from his back pocket and wiped his eyes.

They walked back toward the house, Crystal chattering about the special star. Grant strode at her side, his hand protectively at her elbow. A thoughtful gesture. Warmth from his hand traveled up her arm. She looked into his shadowed features, welcoming the firm strength of him.

A twinkle of moonlight reflected in the deep blue of Tess's eyes as she gazed up at Grant. Of all the admirable qualities Tess had shown since she had entered his life, the way she had just given Crystal an imaginary lifeline to her mother affected him the most strongly.

For a child, faith was easy to grasp onto. Loss and fear could quickly be replaced by their positive imagination. A man could not replace his previous faith so easily. The loss of a loved one—especially the sudden loss he had suffered—could take years to resolve within himself, if ever. His belief in a higher power could be so challenged that his long held concept of God might evolve into something different.

Even mentioning God as a creator of the heavens to Crystal now surprised him.

Beside him, Tess spoke in a low voice. "Well, that was an astronomy lesson she'll never hear at school. It's better to have a little faith than none, isn't it?"

Grant smiled, not knowing how to answer her question. "Guess we gotta have some or we wouldn't bother getting out of bed in the morning."

One thing he did know, he was more than glad to have Tess and Crystal staying under his roof even if it was temporary. They made his days less lonely. His nights less filled with bitter thoughts and nagging guilt. That mean lingering guilt.

Could he have prevented Laura's death? Could he ever forgive himself?

Such questions had twisted sharply inside him like a jagged stick for too long—until Tess walked into the Java Jug in town, with the sad-eyed little girl and her three-legged cat.

Right out of Hurricane Katrina and into his life. She needed a job, needed a roof over her head. Her ward, the child of mixed race, apparently an orphan. He could tell by Tess's faltering answers to his queries that she couldn't cook, probably hadn't done much office work. Not that she wasn't intelligent and pretty as a summer mountain Columbine, but he hadn't cared.

Truth was he had needed them as much as they needed him.

* * *

Tess was cleaning up the kitchen counters after lunch the next day when the back door slammed and Grant entered the kitchen. His face flushed from the brisk afternoon wind, he carried a large object under his arm. She thought she recognized it as the cradle she'd seen him working on. "Where's Crystal?" he asked, looking around the large room.

"I'm here." A tousled head poked out from under the kitchen table. "I'm playing with Miss Tabby." Her eyes rounded when she saw Grant. "What's that?"

He walked over and set the cradle down on the table. Stained to a light tan, it gleamed with a soft sheen on its rockers. "It's a cradle for your dolls. I was going to wait and give it to you for a Thanksgiving present, but you might as well have it now."

Crystal jumped up from under the table and stared. "For my dolls? Wow!"

Suddenly buoyant, Tess moved quickly to stand beside him. "It's beautiful, Grant. You made this for her?"

Grant's voice held a quiet pride. "Yep. I like to do woodworking projects and I thought Crystal's dolls could use a bed too. It's made of sturdy pine so it should last a while."

Tess smiled up at him. "What do you say to Mr. Grant, Crystal?"

Hopping first on one small foot then another, Crystal chanted, "Yes, yes! Thank you! Can I put them in it now?"

"Sure you can. I'll take it to your room."

Tess and Crystal followed behind him as he carried the cradle to their front bedroom.

After seeing that Crystal's dolls were introduced to his handiwork, Grant excused himself to run an errand to a neighbor's. From the bedroom window, Tess watched him drive off in the pickup. She recalled seeing him work on the cradle in his workshop in the barn. He must have spent many hours of labor putting together, sanding and staining the gift. A deep emotion had inspired him to make the cradle. It had seemed a sad emotion.

Whatever had inspired Grant, whatever caring or reasons he had for giving the cradle to Crystal touched Tess in a way she had not known before. No man in her life had given such a gift to her or anyone she knew. He could have brought Crystal a new doll or toy, another gift that a little girl would like. This gift was indeed special.

Later, when Grant returned, Tess put on his barn coat and went looking for him. The steady wind swooping down from the Sangres lifted her hair, pushed her toward the barn. Inside, she saw him brushing down a black gelding in a rear stall. The horse had never been as hardy as the others, having recurrent digestive problems, so Grant kept it in the barn on colder days.

His broad back was to her as she approached, but when he heard her boots on the planked wood floor, Grant turned from his grooming. He glanced over his shoulder. "Did I get a phone call?"

"No," she said, finger-combing her mussed hair away from her face. "I just wanted to thank you for giving Crystal the doll cradle. She loves it."

He stood, the brush suspended in his hand. "Good. I hoped she would." He gave her a tentative smile then resumed grooming the animal.

She reached out and stroked the horse's shaggy black mane. "How's he doing today?"

"As well as can be expected. He's about twenty-five years old, I'd say."

She withdrew her hand, stuck it in one of the large front pockets. Gazing at his hands as they worked confidently, brushing the horse's coat to a luster, she said, "I saw you working on the cradle once in the barn. You seemed…sad that day."

He paused in his grooming, a melancholy expression passing over his angular features. A palpable silence fell between them. A discomforting silence that made Tess wish she'd kept her comment to herself.

Then, as if Grant had made an internal decision, he set the brush on a side shelf and swung around to face her. "I started the cradle when Laura told me she was pregnant. But after the accident…I had to put it away."

Stunned by his revelation, Tess stood speechless.

His face clouded with uneasiness but he continued. "I had intended the cradle to be for our baby. Laura was just four months along when…the accident happened. She was driving the old truck on the county road. It was sunset. She ran a stop sign." He released a ragged sigh. "A tanker truck plowed right into her."

Like a lightning rod, a hot chill skittered down Tess's spine. "Oh no."

He sagged against the side of the stall, his eyes averted to the hay strewn floor. "The highway patrolman at the scene told me it happened so fast, she didn't know what hit her. Knowing that was the only thing that let me keep living from day to day…"

Compelled to step toward him, Tess placed her hand on his shoulder then lifted it to his warm cheek. Emotion caught in her throat, preventing her from saying all of the comforting words she wanted to say.

He drew her to him and held her close for a moment, his face in her hair.

His embrace, firm and needful, implored her to speak. "I've never known what it's like to lose a child, but I can understand your pain," she said gently.

Rising from the depths of his sorrow, his sigh was heart wrenching.

"I'm so sorry, Grant."

He lifted his head and braved a smile, but his eyes could not hide his anguish. "Sometimes it seems like it happened just last week."

"No one gets over such a loss quickly," she said. "But you will one day." Her eyes met his in a meeting of sympathy.

His lips brushed her cheek and then found her lips. She welcomed his tender kiss and returned it with compassion and a longing she'd buried inside for too long. They held each other, each having known loss and the stark reality of having to go on alone.

Tess held back the tears pricking her eyelids, threatening to overflow. She braced herself as Grant withdrew his arms from around her, stepping back a space. "Thanks for being here, Tess." His gaze embraced her.

She nodded slowly, attempting not to let him sense the heaviness in her heart. "Any time you need a shoulder, I'm available." A gust of early winter wind blew through the barn causing her to shiver. "Guess I'd better get back to the house."

He gave her upper arm a squeeze before she turned and left the barn. Unwanted tears trembled on her lashes before slipping down her cheeks. Grant's revelation had shaken her faith once more when she had just begun to heal from Katrina's devastation and the closure of Carrie Pearl's untimely passing.

Could she ever look upon Crystal's cradle without experiencing a flash of pain instead of joy?

Not long after she'd entered the house and turned on the lights inside, preparing for the evening hours, Tess saw Grant from the family room window. He rode out of the barn on his palomino, his Stetson pulled down over his forehead, a long duster whipping about his legs.

She hugged herself as he disappeared down the dirt road along the fence line. He would be gone until early night fall.

Childhood memories of her father leaving the house, always leaving her and her mother behind, came flooding back into her mind. Dressed in his Air Force uniform, his pants crisply pleated, his perfunctory kiss on her forehead, and the purposeful set of his shoulders as he strode out the front door.

Feelings of loss, frustration and fear gathered inside her. She had no control over Grant's lone rides, any more than she'd had over her father's departures, could only guess where Grant went and what drove him to go.

But why should she care? Was it possible that she was falling in love with him?

With a moan of distress, she turned away. The familiar scenario felt just like the haunting words in the western song she'd heard when she and Grant were at the Alamosa Lodge that night. How she wished he would "hang his saddle up and finally come on home."

Chapter Eighteen

For the next several days, Crystal was obsessed with her new cradle. Every morning after helping Tess set the table and clear up the dishes after breakfast, she would race back to the bedroom and put her dolls in the cradle, cover them with a folded pillow case, and rock them "to sleep". When she returned from preschool, she would do the same, some time singing a lullaby to them of her own creation. When she could catch Miss Tabby, she'd lift her up and settle her into the cradle beside the dolls, which meant the dolls had to sit on each other's lap. Miss Tabby's cradle visits didn't last long, and she would leap out and lope away, usually to take cover under the bed.

Observing from a safe distance, in order to give Crystal the privacy she needed, Tess took mental notes and was encouraged. The doll playtime gave Crystal real joy and she came away more serene than Tess had ever seen her. A definite change in her demeanor since those first weeks after they arrived at the ranch when the child had displayed worrisome agitation and fear.

One afternoon during the week of Crystal's routine, as Tess finished changing the pillow cases on their bed, Crystal hopped up on top of the quilt. Holding her Carrie doll in one hand, she focused a bright gaze on Tess's face. Tess put her arm around Crystal's shoulder. "You and your dolls are enjoying Mr. Grant's cradle, aren't you?"

"Uh-huh!" Unmistakable enthusiasm in Crystal's reply. She tipped her head in an almost flirting way. "Will you be my mommy now?"

The question hit Tess so quickly, the breath went out of her. Hesitant to give the wrong answer, she struggled to right herself. "Well...I...I want to take care of you, honey."

Dark-fringed eyes peered into hers. "But will you be my mommy and take care of me?"

Tess balanced precariously between the real and the surreal. She should have anticipated this question sooner. Admittedly she had avoided it in her mind. How could she in all honesty make such a promise? She could not explain the complex legalities she would face if she decided to proceed with adopting Crystal. Nor could she fathom them herself in her current emotional and financial state.

Yet how could she refuse being at least a surrogate mom to this vulnerable, endearing child? She loved Crystal perhaps as much as she would a child of her own.

Hugging Crystal to her, feeling her small heartbeat against her breast, she said in a voice choked with emotion, "We can pretend that I am your mommy for now…and I will never leave you, Crystal."

Her promise seemed to comfort Crystal, and she returned to doting over her dolls. But a few minutes later, she approached Tess again. This time with a more monumental question. "Will Mr. Grant be my new daddy?"

Tess floundered, a gamut of perplexing emotions colliding inside her. How could she have been so naïve to think Crystal wouldn't have noticed the sometimes erratic adult interactions surrounding her? Even though she'd tried her utmost to treat Grant with a neutral but friendly demeanor while around Crystal. Of course, there was the kiss on the back deck that she had witnessed….

Well, she simply could not allow Crystal to fantasize about any such possibilities. Attempting a firm reply, Tess said, "Mr. Grant and I are friends, Crystal. He thinks you are a special little girl. But, I don't think he wants to be a daddy."

The expectant expression left Crystal's face and she went back to her doll cradle.

Tess sighed uncomfortably, a brief feeling of emptiness washing over her. She returned to her household tasks and pushed Crystal's question to a far corner of her mind. Romantic notions would only frustrate the situation further. There was nothing to be gained in dwelling on anything that farfetched. First things first, and Crystal's welfare was definitely in that category.

* * *

Winter descended upon the valley, with the days beginning in frigid temperatures and nightfall coming too soon. Tess layered her clothing and Crystal's. She was glad for the consignment shop in town where lightly worn children's clothing could be found. Warm sweaters and sweatshirts guarded against the cold. Even the horses' coats grew thicker, almost fuzzy, protecting them, too.

"Look!" Crystal exclaimed one morning in the barn, trolling her hands along the foal's side. "Nina's wearing a sweater."

Smiling, Tess pulled her coat collar up around her neck. "Yes, she is." It was obvious both child and horse were growing as well.

Tess loved these mornings, as crisp as they were. It gave her a chance to take in the breathtaking beauty of the surrounding Sangres and their snow-covered peaks jutting into the Colorado sky. How vastly different this setting was from the muggy, cloudy New Orleans winter days. Not that the Big Easy didn't have its own natural attraction, but now it seemed only a shadowed memory in her past where pain had existed. She often thought of the people living there and hoped sincerely that they could rebuild the city and their lives.

Living so close to nature did have its drawbacks, however.

Loud clattering, banging, night sounds jolted Tess and Crystal from a sound sleep later that week. It came from the far side of the house. Crystal grasped Tess in the dark. "What is that?"

Tess sat straight up, listening. "I don't know?"

The racket continued, like a bucket of bolts being shaken.

Reaching for her robe on the armchair next to the bed, Tess slipped her bare feet down to the throw rug. She hurriedly shrugged into the robe and headed for the closed bedroom door. "Stay there, Crystal. I'll be right back."

She made her way across the icy tile floor in the short hallway and through the front room. Surely Grant had heard the noise. What was it? A wild animal or someone attempting to break into the house?

Rounding a high-backed chair in the dark, she stubbed her big toe. And yelped. A tall man appeared in silhouette in the hallway to the kitchen. Her heart leaped to her throat before she realized it was Grant.

"Tess?" he called.

She limped up to him. "What is that sound?"

"I'm going to check and find out." He turned and disappeared into the mud room and she followed, wishing she'd had time to put on her slippers. She saw the outline of a rifle Grant held in one hand. He set it against the wall for a moment before jerking open the back door, grabbing it up again, and heading outside into the frosty night.

More calamity came from the side of the house. Nerve ends tingling up and down her arms, Tess pulled her robe more tightly around her. Small hands suddenly clung to her legs. Frightened eyes looked up at her in the shadowed hallway. "Honey, you should have stayed in bed."

"I'm scared!"

Taking Crystal's clammy hand, Tess led her into the kitchen. "Grant went outside to look. Come on, we can peek out a window. Maybe we can see something."

Together, they scurried across the room as the night exploded in a thunderous *bang*.

Wild wails nearly shattered Tess's eardrum. Like tiny talons, Crystal's fingers tightened their grip on Tess's hand.

Her heart thudding like a sledge hammer, Tess guided Crystal over to a window where they peered out into the darkness. A yipping came in the distance followed by eerie howling. *Coyotes*. It had to be.

"Do you see anything?" Crystal's question was quivery.

The back door closed followed by the firm click of the lock. Grant rounded the doorway into the kitchen and flipped on the light switch. In the light, he stood broad-shouldered, his collar-length hair ruffled about his head, his eyes squinting at them above a beard-stubbled jaw. At the sight of him, with his coat half buttoned unevenly, horse print pajama bottoms stuffed into old work boots, Tess was struck with near amusement. She bit her lip and straightened, letting go of Crystal's hand. "What happened?"

His sleepy features grimaced. "Coyotes. I scared them off…this time."

Crystal moaned and hovered closer to Tess. "Will they come back?"

Grant shook his shaggy locks. "They better not. I'm gonna tie up those trash cans so tight they'll never get them undone."

Even though Grant followed through on the trash cans, and built a cozy fire in the front fireplace the next few nights, Tess moved through the house as jumpy as a cat after darkness closed in. Imagining hungry coyotes and bears, before their winter hibernation, prowling nearby was not comforting. At least the thought of Grant's loaded rifle standing ready, out of sight, but where he could reach it, soothed her nerves.

She made hot cocoa and read stories to Crystal on the sofa while Grant relaxed in his recliner. He didn't mind her reading aloud. It settled him into a peaceful mood, his gaze falling on the flickering logs. When Crystal's eyelids drooped and she fell asleep beneath a blanket, Grant would carry her off to bed.

The three of them blended together as a temporary family, she thought. Albeit an unlikely one. Her former life as a rolling stone had left her dubious of having another marital commitment; her current guardianship of Crystal was still precarious. Not that Grant wasn't a salt-of-the-earth kind of man. She admitted that at times she wouldn't have minded slipping into his arms in the recliner. Just for a few moments. A strong man's arms could ward off many fears and let her release some remaining sadness from her recent past.

Of course, that wasn't possible. Grant had carefully hidden his own grief, revealing only a part of it in the barn that day. She questioned how long the current reverie would last.

* * *

Later in the week, at breakfast, Grant made a suggestion that surprised her. "I guess Thanksgiving's coming up. Would you and Crystal like to have some of her friends here at the house?" He finished pouring coffee into his mug and sat down at the table across from her. "I'll buy the turkey."

Tess rolled his question over in her mind. "That sounds like a good idea. I'm not exactly a turkey chef, but it shouldn't be that hard."

"I've helped cook many a turkey," Grant boasted. "You can count on me." He sent her a wink to seal the deal, drained his coffee mug, and sauntered off to do chores in the barn.

Just like a man—suggest a project and then leave. Yet he was enthusiastic enough about it that she was pretty sure he'd follow through on the *you can count on me* part.

As the back door closed, Tess was already eyeing the collection of cook books lining the upper kitchen shelf. High altitude birds… The secret was how to cook the gobbler and have it come out tender. Not tough and not raw.

By Saturday morning, she'd planned her invitation list and the holiday menu. She told Grant while she added eggs to a bowl and he watched the English muffins in the toaster oven.

"I've invited Jenny and Nick Stotter. She was so glad for the invitation. Her folks are down in Dallas and his dad's in a nursing home in Ohio, so they're usually on their own for the holidays. Sam is excited, too. He wants to ride Nina, if it's okay with you and Crystal."

"If I get to ride her first," Crystal insisted from under the kitchen table where she and Miss Tabby had camped out.

Grant shoved a swath of tawny hair off his forehead. "Nina is still too young to ride. Sugar would be a good ride, instead."

Although his hair needed a trim, he'd shaven. Tess always appreciated a clean shaven man.

"Who else is invited?"

"Jud, of course. And Roy, your hired man. They can keep each other company. Imagine they've got some tall tales to tell after living in the West all these years."

Grant pulled the muffins out of the toaster oven and slathered them with butter. "Oh, they've got lots of stories, all right."

"That will be eight, counting you and me." Tess whirled milk into the eggs in the frying pan, a funny little twinge prodding her stomach. She'd hesitated saying, *We'll be the hosts*. Too intimate somehow.

The glow of his smile charmed her; the hazel-gray sparkle in his eyes made her turn back to her work. She dished up bacon warming in the microwave and the eggs, and they sat down at the table to discuss more of the holiday details.

They had just finished breakfast when a knock came at the back door and Grant hollered, "Come on in."

Boot heels clacked along the back hall then Jud poked his grizzly face around the corner and ambled into the kitchen.

Grant raised his hand. "Hey, Jud. Coffe's still hot. Want some?"

At the sight of Jud's disheveled appearance, Tess just smiled and pointed to the coffee pot on the kitchen counter. "Help yourself. There's more English muffins."

"Coffee's fine." He removed his worn sheepskin jacket, hung it over a chair, and poured himself a mug.

"We're talking about Thanksgiving. You want to come?" Grant asked as Jud sat down and joined them.

Crystal hopped out of her chair nearby and went over to him. Her braids, which Tess had tied with red bows, framed her plump cheeks. "Will you come, Grandpa Jud?"

Jud cocked his head, resembling an old bloodhound, jowls and mustache drooping over his faded brown pullover sweater. "Hmm. Sounds good. Don't mind if I do."

Then they talked about the weather and the coyote visit while Tess cleared the breakfast plates. Grant grinned as she picked up his, saying, "Anything you want me to do?"

Jud's bushy eyebrows lifted noticeably. "Things are gettin' pretty domestic around here." He snickered half to himself.

A warm flush crept up Tess's neck and she busied herself for a minute rinsing the plates before setting them in the dishwasher. The old coot. He was more in tune to the situation than she'd guessed he could be. A thought struck her and she straightened and glanced over at him, sitting so smugly at the table. "Now that you're here, Jud, how about a hair trim? Looks like yours could use it."

Dark eyes squinted out of a surprised face. Jowls quivered. "Well...I hadn't planned on it. You know how to cut hair?"

"Sure do. I've been cutting mine and my friends' hair for years. I'm pretty good at it."

Jud laughed out loud, showing his tobacco-stained teeth. "Well, ain't that somethin'."

Tess whipped out a clean kitchen towel from a side drawer. "I'll get my trimming scissors and be right back." Not giving Jud a chance to object, she raced down the hall to her room, fetched the shears and two combs, and returned in a flash.

"Let's move your chair over by the far window where's there's some light," she suggested. "Grant can give you a hand."

A bemused expression on his angular face, Grant hoisted the chair high and set it down in a corner where sunlight flooded through window glass. "Now this I've gotta see."

Tess snapped the towel and placed it over Jud's shoulders thinking, *Don't get too big for your britches, cowboy. You'll be next.*

Wasting no time, she parted, combed and cut Jud's unruly thatch. Snipping here, clipping there, her scissors sheared the coarse steel-gray hair that had grown for months on Jud's head. Despite the lingering odor of cigarette smoke emanating from Jud, she hummed softly, content to see a new man emerging from her efforts.

Grant occupied Jud with talk about local news on the Zapata and commiserated on the shortage of tourists in winter until he asked for a mirror, "so I can see you're not scalpin' me, gal."

Crystal giggled and sang as she danced around the table, "Grandpa's getting his hair cut, Grandpa's getting his hair cut."

"Go get the hand mirror off our dresser, please," Tess asked Crystal. "I'm almost done."

Not much later, Jud squinted into the mirror approvingly. "Hmm. You do a darn good trim, for a city gal." His droopy mustache twitched. "Matter of fact, first time a gal barber has ever trimmed my hedge." His deepset eyes glimmered.

"Even your sideburns look good," Grant observed, eyeing them critically.

Tess wasn't through yet. "But there's still that overgrown mustache."

Jud reared back in the chair. "Not my coffee brush, ma'am!"

She planted herself squarely in front of the stubborn codger. "I'll make you a special pumpkin pie at Thanksgiving—if you'll just hold still for a second." One hand on his prickly jaw and the other holding the scissors, she eliminated half the scraggly gray caterpillar, then stepped back to study her work. "If I do say so, Jud, you look years younger."

Grant chuckled with approval. "Young enough to give the ladies from miles around a run for their money."

Eyebrows wagging, Jud peered into the mirror. "I feel a mighty cold breeze on my upper lip."

"At least you won't be dunking that mustache in your coffee now." Infectious laughter surrounded her as Tess removed the towel and brushed the remaining hair off Jud's shoulders. "How about a shave?"

"Nope." Jud hoisted himself out of the chair. "That'll be enough, thanks."

"Well then, you're next, Mr. Grant."

"Oh no. I don't need one." Grant started to back away, but she and Crystal tackled him and pushed him down into the chair. It was a task similar to tackling John Wayne, but he didn't offer too much resistance. "Yes, you do," both Tess and Crystal chorused.

Compared to Jud, Grant was a massive figure seated in the chair. Tess needed a folded table cloth to reach across his broad shoulders. Although he had the craggy look of an unfinished bronze sculpture, she was aware of his natural attitude of self-command. He crossed one leg over the other and relaxed back toward her. In the sunlight cast from the window, his hair was a thick, tawny-gold. It waved downward just over his collar.

Strangely Tess hesitated before touching his head, as if to do so would cross a barrier she'd not yet done. Bracing herself, she took in a deep breath and raised her comb.

"Now don't give me a Mohawk or a buzz cut," he challenged good naturedly.

She handed him the mirror. "I'll just trim it up, if that's what you want."

He held the mirror's long handle awkwardly in his big hand, his gaze meeting hers over his shoulder. "That's good. Just remember, I know how to use a pair of shears too."

Jud cut in. "You mean those big ol' sheep shears?"

It took a moment for Tess to comprehend Grant's tease. "Ho, ho. Well, I can run faster than a sheep."

"So can I." He winked in jest at her in the mirror.

"You two gonna talk all day?" Jud paced behind Tess. "By the time you get started, his hair's gonna grow another half inch."

She didn't need Jud's cattle prod to dive into her work. Matter-of-factly, she snipped away. Where Jud's hair had been thinning and coarse, Grant's was thick and wavy, curling around her fingers above his ear. She dared not admit to herself how smooth it felt, how her fingers reveled in its texture.

Grant made a shivering motion as her scissors skimmed his nape. "Hey, that tickles!"

Her hand jerked, nearly nicking his earlobe. "Now hold still—or your ear will be next."

Watching from the sidelines, Crystal objected. "Tess, don't cut Mr. Grant's ear."

Jud leaned in and tweaked one of Crystal's braids. "Shucks, he can get by with one."

Grant folded his arms across his muscular chest and let out a long sigh. "Speak for yourself, Jud. Say, when's this torture gonna be over?"

"Torture?" Tess finished trimming the back of his neck and blew away the hair cuttings.

"I'm only turning you into a well-groomed cowboy." With a flourish, she whisked away the table cloth and draped it on the back of another chair.

Grant unfolded his long limbs and stood before them, a grin on his face. "What do y'all think?"

Jud peered at him like he was judging a prize bull. "Well, you wouldn't scare off a bear."

Crystal giggled. "You're handsome!"

With the sun shining in the window, highlighting Grant's newly shorn locks, Tess was pleased with her work. He was definitely handsome—in a way that she didn't want to admit. "Here, take a look for yourself." She picked up the mirror and handed it to him.

Despite his nonchalant stance, admiration shone in his eyes when he viewed his new image. "Hey, thanks Tess. How can I thank you? Maybe a kiss."

Clapping her small hands, Crystal jumped up and down. "Yes!"

It was Tess's turn to pedal backward. "No…" She didn't need to compound the temptations she'd begun to feel when around Grant. "No thanks. Just…be sure you find me a big turkey for the Thanksgiving party."

Jud started to open his mouth and Tess squelched his comment before he could make it. "Which shouldn't be hard to do, considering there are plenty of wild turkeys around here."

Chapter Nineteen

The weeks that followed were full to the brim with preparation for Thanksgiving. To Tess, this holiday would be one of the most important of her life because it mattered so much to the people surrounding her. For Crystal, it would be the first Thanksgiving without her mother. For Grant, it would be a chance to find a sense of family with local friends, and to connect with himself. To make peace with himself.

As for herself, with her future comparable to an unfinished jigsaw puzzle, Tess sensed that she was here to find the missing pieces. One holiday probably would not complete this task. But what were the missing pieces and where would they fit to make her life puzzle complete? It was a simple yet profound journey she found herself taking. Not initially of her own free will, but now a goal.

On the hair cutting day, Jud had left behind a generous check in an envelope for Crystal's preschool through the end of the year. He'd thanked her for the hair cut and added, "Thanks for taking such good care of Crystal. I'm workin' on her mom's estate, but it'll take some time."

She knew Jud would be there for his granddaughter, but who could predict Crystal's long term future? Tess had promised that she'd never leave Crystal as long as she needed her.

Fortunately Jenny Stotter and family were coming to the Thanksgiving gathering. "I'll bring a couple of side dishes," she said over the telephone when Tess had offered the invitation. "My mom, rest her soul, left me a great recipe for pecan pie." Her voice had held mischief. "It's got a secret ingredient I think you'll like."

Just like Jenny to have a surprise. "Great. We'll love it, I'm sure." Tess had smiled to herself. One less pie to make. "Mrs. Libby shares a terrific pumpkin pie recipe with me at Thanksgiving."

"Mmm…who's Mrs. Libby?"

"You know—the canned pumpkin pie filler? Libby's recipe always makes the best."

"Oh, yeah. Well, Nick and Sam are looking forward to it. Okay if Sam brings his new truck? It's got rubber wheels so it won't scratch the floor tile."

"Sure, that's fine." Tess had ended the conversation relieved. A girlfriend in the kitchen would be welcome.

Roy Briggs, the hired rancher, was coming too. His wife was caring for her sister over in Durango and he would be glad for the company. He said he'd bring his guitar; he liked singing old western songs at family gatherings.

Music would liven the evening. The Wilder home could do with some merriment that had been missing since Laura Wilder's departure.

Tess called Juan Rodriguez to extend an invitation also, but he and son Carlos would be with their large family over the holiday. She had assumed as much, but wanted to let them know they were invited.

* * *

On Thanksgiving Day, Tess awoke early to light snowfall outside. Her agenda was full: to assist Grant with the twelve-pound turkey he'd bought from a rancher in the valley, bake a pumpkin pie and finish setting the long dining room table, rarely used except on special occasions.

Her heart was light in spite of her heavy schedule. Beyond the bedroom window, nature in all of its wonder was on display. A pair of red-winged blackbirds perched on a spruce branch, their chests puffed up against the chill morning. Looking for breakfast. A reminder to throw out stale bread crumbs. Crystalline flakes sparkled on the tree branches dancing beneath an eastern sun that peeked through silvery clouds.

The thought struck her that she hadn't spoken with her mother since shortly after arriving at the ranch. German time was hours ahead of Colorado time, but she chanced it anyway. It was good to hear her mother's voice and tell her about the planned event she was partially undertaking.

"Tess, I can't believe you're doing all this. Cooking and everything." Admiration tinged her mother's voice over the wire. "I am proud of you."

It was amazing, Tess had to admit. Even a year ago, she would have been planning a day out with single friends in a New Orleans eatery. Choosing from a menu of turtle soup to shrimp gumbo. "Thanks, Mom. I hope you all have a wonderful Thanksgiving!" She knew her mother and stepfather would celebrate with their American friends on the base.

Toward noon Jenny arrived carrying a pie and a side dish. The first thing she said when she entered the kitchen was, "Where's the bird?"

"Already in the oven." Tess welcomed her with a quick hug and relieved her of the food offerings.

"Must be a big boy." Jenny bent to peer into the oven's front window. "Umm, yes he is." Her eyes the color of nutmeg and fringed with mascara crinkled at the corners.

"Grant helped me get him dressed for dinner. I made the stuffing. It's in the fridge."

Jenny raised a dark brow mischievously. "Sounds like you're putting the guy to work—good for you! Nick couldn't boil an egg if his life depended on it."

"Where are your guys?" Tess craned her neck to see out a front kitchen window.

Leslee Breene

"They'll be here in a couple hours. Nick got in late last night from L.A. on the red eye shift. He didn't want to miss today." Jenny shrugged good-naturedly. "He treasures these holidays home with us."

Tess put her arm around Jenny's shoulders. "Well, of course he does! Crystal is so excited about having a Thanksgiving party and playing with Sam."

"If she can tear him away from his new truck." Jenny put her pie in the fridge next to the stuffing. "Well, hand me an apron and show me where to start."

"I guess we could start peeling the potatoes. My favorite job." She made a face and so did Jenny. They both laughed.

Midway through the food preparations, Jud showed up at the front door, Henry loping behind him. A frosting of snow covered his hat and coat and mustache. The first thing Henry did was to shake the moisture on everyone around him then pad down the hall to the kitchen to sniff around. "Thought we'd get here a little early," Jud said. "Need any help?"

"Not just yet," Tess replied, taking Jud's coat and hat. "Grant is out checking on the horses. He'll be in shortly and you can ask him."

Before the words left her mouth, loud barking came from the kitchen and a whirl of tabby fur, followed by a dog in pursuit, streaked past her.

"Hen-ryyy!" Crystal wailed, trailing behind them. "You leave her alone." She shot through the family room and into Tess and Crystal's room.

Tess tensed then chased after them. A dog and cat brawl was not what anyone needed on Thanksgiving Day.

Frantic barking preceded her. "Miss Tabby ran under the bed," Crystal moaned as Tess entered their bedroom. "Henry's scaring her!"

The big yellow lab burrowed his long nose under the dust ruffle, more than eager to catch the cornered cat. His barking ratcheted around the room making Tess's eardrums quiver.

"Jud!" she called into the family room.

Jud ambled into the foray, and, with strong persuasion and a strong arm, managed to wrestle Henry out of the room. "You're goin' outside, fella." Looking back at Tess, he said, "I'll take him out on the deck for a while so he can cool down."

Tess released a long sigh and braced herself. She had visualized this as a memorable holiday. Hopefully it wouldn't turn out to be a disaster.

Minutes later, Roy Briggs arrived carrying his guitar case and a jug of "homemade apple cider." Grant came in from the barn, the aroma of hay and the crisp outdoors on his jacket. His presence buoyed her self-confidence once he entered the kitchen after he'd washed up, and offered to help with any last minute tasks.

When Nick and Sam joined the guests, the turkey was browning nicely. Jenny passed around a tray of appetizers to the men in the family room while Tess made sure the cranberry sauce was on the table and filled the water glasses. Crystal was momentarily distracted by Sam's new truck which kept her out from under foot in the kitchen.

Through the doorway, Tess heard Roy proclaim, "Here's to good weather and healthy horses." Mugs clinked. She guessed the men were toasting with his cider.

Amazingly everything was ready on time. Grant seated at the head of the table said a thoughtful grace then carved the turkey like a pro. Jenny served up the mashed potatoes and gravy. Tess's stuffing recipe turned out quite well, despite her opinion that it could have used more seasoning. Everything disappeared in minutes. Not a single dinner roll was left behind in the serving basket.

After dinner they moved to the family room, where Grant set the logs ablaze in the fireplace, and relaxed before desert. Light snow still cascaded past the windows outside. The pine cones tossed on the fireplace logs gave off a fragrant woodsy aroma. Tess sat in a cushioned armchair, enjoying a moment off of her feet. Crystal soon climbed up on her lap. Wrapping her arms around the child, Tess allowed a mellow mood to surround her. Grant propped his feet up in the recliner across the room, observing them quietly, his gaze shifting to the fireplace when her eyes met his briefly.

Roy Briggs hunkered down on the long sofa next to Jud. Both of them rested their manly hands on filled stomachs, Roy's a bit more prominent than Jud's. "That sure was a fine meal, ladies," Roy addressed Tess and Jenny.

On the floor a few feet away, Sam glanced up from his new truck. "My mom made a special pecan pie."

"And my Tess made a special pumpkin pie," Crystal countered.

"We'll have some in a while," Jenny said from the other end of the sofa. Nick sat in an overstuffed chair next to her looking half asleep.

Tess squeezed Crystal. "Yes, when we can find some room."

"Wonder if we'll have more snow by mornin'," Jud pondered as he stared out the far windows.

"Tonight kinda reminds me of a night a couple years ago when I was makin' a late check of the 'heavies'—you know, the pregnant cows in the calving lot," Roy said. "It was in the early spring. The wind was whippin' snow around and it was cold. Every cow wore a white blanket of snow on her back.

As usual this brown heifer met me at the gate, followed me on my rounds like a shadow. My wife called

252

her Bess. She was one of those cows that took it upon herself to check into everybody's business.

Well, when dawn came up, I hurried on out to make my next check and let most of the cows out of the gate to graze. One older cow was on her side, her eyes glazed over. She'd calved and evidently died right there. I looked around, expectin' to find a frozen calf—no baby could have survived the cold without its mama cleaning him up or givin' him milk."

Tess noticed how the children had become still, listening intently to Roy.

"Well," he continued, "oddly enough, there was Bess layin' in one corner. She was maybe ten to twelve days away from calvin'. As I went over, she stood up big as you please and right behind her was a new baby calf!"

Sam left his truck and moved closer to the sofa. "Was it still alive?"

"Well, ol' Bess mooed kinda soft-like to the calf, which had been cleaned up, and by gosh, it stood and started to nurse." Roy shook his head from side to side as if still amazed.

"It was the strangest thing. Bess wasn't close to calving her own. Sometimes a cow gets confused, you know, and claims another cow's new baby as her own— but Bess had just saved that little calf's life!"

Crystal tilted her chin in Roy's direction, her expression expectant. "Did she keep her for her own?"

Smiling, Roy dipped his head slightly. "Well, honey, she did mother that new calf. And, after Bess had her own little one a few weeks later, those two critters played together like brother and sister." He winked at the adults around the room.

Crystal's eyes glowed when she looked up at Tess. Whether Roy's story was completely true or not made no difference. He had warmed their hearts with a touching story of caring, of surrogate love.

Grant arched a look over toward Roy's guitar case. "You going to honor us with a few songs, Roy?"

"That's what I brought it for." He opened the case and lifted out a long-used guitar. "Now, if Jud will help me out…"

Jud cleared his throat. "Well, sure will try."

With an obvious love of his subject, Roy strummed on his guitar and offered a collection of old western ballads. Jud harmonized with him in a throaty baritone, complementing Roy's straight-forward tenor. Other voices chimed in.

To her surprise, Tess connected immediately with the lyrics of these heartfelt songs: *Along the Navajo Trail, Cool Water, Happy Trails to You.* A way of life was inherent in all of them. A way of life that reached back to generations before this generation.

After an enthusiastic round of applause for Roy, Tess called out "Okay, who wants pecan and who wants pumpkin?" before heading to the kitchen. Jenny was already slicing wedges and sliding them onto plates.

"They do look good! What's your secret ingredient?"

"A splash of brandy," Jenny confided.

Tess hovered over the pies. "I'll have a piece of pecan. A big piece."

Jenny scooped out a large spoonful of Cool Whip and plopped it onto a pumpkin slice. "Your pumpkin for me," she said, licking a smudge of the creamy stuff from her finger.

Tess grinned. "That makes four pecan and four pumpkin."

"I think you could get used to this family holiday routine, huh?" Jenny gave her one of those knowing glances.

Leave it to Jenny to get to the center of things. "I'm enjoying tonight," she said. "Crystal is too. Who wouldn't with great neighbors like you all?"

"Uh-huh. I was thinking you might be enjoying Grant's company as well. He's been looking your way all evening."

Tess gave Jenny's shoulder a little shove while hoping the sudden warmth climbing up her neck wasn't too obvious. "Oh, stop. We haven't had time to think about... Well, you know."

Jenny's chuckle was a mocking tease. "Right. You two just haven't had any time to think about—"

"Say, ladies," Grant's voice interrupted them. "How's that pie comin'? Need any help?"

Hoping he hadn't heard their conversation, Tess quickly grabbed up a few desert plates. "Here, you can bring these out to the crowd, if you'd like."

"Yes ma'am." He grinned, took the pie plates and disappeared into the other room.

Jenny raised a mischievous brow.

"Just keep cutting that pie!" Tess ordered before Jenny could make another wise remark.

* * *

At evening's end, all company departed into the light snowfall, Crystal cuddling her favorite doll and sound asleep in her bed, Tess joined Grant in the family room. She sat down on the long sofa and watched him add another log to a dwindling fire. As he arched over the wrought iron screen on the stone hearth, completing a task that he'd no doubt donc many times, she admired his rugged physique that truly fit this western environment.

She settled back against the welcoming cushions. A quiet comfort melted into her bones, an indefinable feeling of rightness. Instead of climbing into his recliner, Grant sat down on the sofa, propping his boots on the coffee table of smoothly finished barn wood. His quietly imposing presence was reassuring, so opposite from the agitation surrounding her whenever she'd been in the same room with Howard.

The difference between the men, it seemed, was that Grant was confident with his place in the universe. He was not a rolling stone as she and Howard had been.

"Well, nobody went away hungry tonight," Grant said, interrupting her thoughts. "That turkey was about the best I've ever had."

"Thanks to your help, and Jenny's."

"Your pumpkin pie was great, too." The firelight cast a warm glow over his high cheek bones. "Your cooking has come right along since you started."

She smothered a chuckle. "I guess it was pretty bad at first, huh?"

His answering gaze left no question of his sincerity. "You're a fine cook, Tess. Makin' dinner for a lot of people isn't easy, but you managed the whole thing like a pro." He reached over and squeezed her arm gently, his hand sliding downward to press warm against hers for a brief moment.

Leave your hand longer, her senses implored.

Grant's strong shoulder was not that far from hers. If she leaned just a bit to the right…she could lay her head there. If she only knew what he was thinking now. If she just had a clue of how he felt about her. He was such a gentleman. A gentle man. Never once since she'd come to the ranch had he ever made a wrong move toward her.

As if reading her mind, Grant remarked, "This could get to be a habit…sitting in front of the fire…in the evening."

She met his gaze then self-consciously swung her focus back to the fireplace. "It could…" She sighed, uncertain of where the conversation might be headed. "It's so peaceful here. A fine resting place."

"You can stay as long as you like."

Her heart rate picked up. "I can't thank you enough—for everything."

His expression grew intent. "You've thanked me enough. It's been a two-way street, as far as I'm concerned."

She shook her head sleepily. "I'll always be in your debt, Grant." And if she wasn't careful, she'd be tempted to lean over and kiss him goodnight. Which might lead to more kissing—and that wasn't on the agenda.

She eased forward on the sofa and got to her feet. "Happy Thanksgiving," she said, certain that her smile reflected a growing affection for him.

Grant rose to his feet at the same time. His voice was low and filled with emotion. "You and Crystal made it the best Thanksgiving I've had in a long time." His arms came round her in a tender embrace and she was held in a circle of strength, protected from every fearful thing her mind could ever imagine. Her eyes closed and she savored the moment where just the two of them stood in this place, this ancient valley where hunters, settlers and wanderers had ventured through past centuries. This place that held one as in a dream. This place that invited, no tempted, one to stay and make that dream a reality.

With a reluctant sigh, Tess pulled away from him and said goodnight. Later, as she slipped beneath the bed covers, and the pine tree outside the window swayed in the night wind, unrelenting questions kept her from sleep. When was the last time she'd truly enjoyed being with a man, in a group of people or sharing a quiet moment? How many men had commanded her respect and admiration as much as Grant?

A small kernel of hope unfurled inside her, a realization that there was a special quality about him. No longer could she deny her attraction to him or ignore the evident affection he showed her. They each had suffered a loss in a relationship. Yet she believed both she and Grant possessed the ability to love again—deeply.

Could they find the love together that had escaped them in the past? Grant would have to reveal his inner feelings before she could ever invest her complete self in their future.

Chapter Twenty

Grant stood at the far kitchen window looking toward the eastern range. Sleet and mist shrouded the valley on the heels of a winter snow warning. His half empty coffee mug still radiated some warmth in the palm of his hand, but the outside chill of this mid December morning nagged at him like an old wound.

"Think I'll ride out and bring the horses in from the south pasture," he said to Tess as she finished clearing up the breakfast dishes.

She glanced at him across the room. "Do you want me to call Roy to help?"

"No. I should be able to handle it." He took one last swallow from his mug and brought it over to the sink. "Just want to be sure they're all close to home, in case this one turns big."

Her reassuring smile deepened the dimple in her right cheek. "Sure. Wish I could ride better. I'd go out with you."

He strode toward the hallway. "No problem. You will some day." He shrugged into his heavy sheep-lined jacket and pulled a longer rain slicker over it.

"I'll keep the coffee on," she called from the kitchen door.

He nodded agreeably, noting the blue spark in her wide set eyes. An urge to draw her to him for a sweet goodbye kiss came over him and he had to back toward the door to dissuade himself. "Thanks," he mumbled, shoved on his hat, and dodged outside into the thickening sleet.

Since Thanksgiving, he and Tess had given each other more space. An unspoken agreement of proprietary boundaries. He knew her working for him could be a temporary arrangement—convenient for both of them.

Still, he'd grown used to having Tess and Crystal in his house. Nearby. A bond had ultimately formed between the three of them. How could he go back to his old life routine without Tess? He had to kick himself in the rear lately as a reminder that she was his employee and tamp down the notion that she could be more.

When Laura was taken so suddenly, he'd vowed never to love anyone again. The pain of her loss was something he could never endure twice.

Driving sleet, turning to stinging snow, prompted Grant to hurry to the barn.

* * *

To make use of indoor time, Tess put together a spice bread, popped it in the oven, then got out the crock pot from the cupboard. She added broth, a cut up chicken dusted with herbs, pearl onions and chopped carrots. It was an easy dinner to make ahead.

Every so often, she glanced out the kitchen windows and was surprised at how quickly the sleet had turned to snow falling steadily in the yard. The white Sangre de Cristo peaks reminded her of ghostly pirate ships rising from a turbulent sea.

Crystal hovered by the windows, her nose inches from the glass, watching the snow and obviously wishing she could go out and play in it. Snow was still a fascinating phenomenon. There had been nothing like it in New Orleans.

"Maybe we can make a snowman," she pleaded. Then, "Can I go out to the barn and see Nina?" And, "When is Mr. Grant coming back?"

"Questions, questions," Tess responded. "We'll have to see when the snow stops…maybe after lunch." She began watching for Grant by midmorning. If only he'd had one of the men to help him bring in the horses. Juan and Carlos had started a snow removal service during the winter months and weren't always available. If the snow kept coming, she would have to call for their assistance.

Visibility now was limited in all directions. Heavy snow blustered past the windows, piling in drifts along the road. The temperature dropped into the teens. Where was Grant?

When the spice bread was ready, she removed it from the oven and set it on a counter rack to cool. She fixed hot Ovaltine for Crystal and tried to ignore the badgering nervous twinge in her stomach.

Finally a muted nicker of horses sent her racing to the windows at the other side of the house. She could just make out frosted equine shapes moving toward the corral. *Thank heaven,* Grant had driven them back to safety.

Minutes later, the back door swung open and a snow-laden giant she barely recognized stomped into the hallway. Beneath the white encrusted hat brim, Grant's wind-reddened face revealed the misery he'd confronted. "I've searched the whole pasture to hell and back—and I can't find Nina," he ground out through ice-rimmed lips.

She shuddered at his revelation and the desperate glare in his eyes. "Oh, no." Rushing to him, Tess helped unbutton his slicker as he made a fumbling attempt with frozen fingers. "Let's get these wet clothes off then you can tell me about it."

Crystal's small frightened voice came from behind Tess. "Nina's lost?"

"Mr. Grant will tell us more, but he needs our help now." Tess continued aiding Grant get out of the heavy barn jacket after she hung his slicker on a wall peg. He had plopped his dripping hat next to it and stood like a sagging fence post in a water puddle, now spreading out around his muddied boots on the tile floor.

Crystal shied back, a small sob catching in her throat. Part of Tess longed to go to the child and assure her of the foal's wellbeing, but Grant needed her right now.

He shivered and rubbed his large hands together. "Gotta call Roy—see if he can come over here."

"I will call Roy." She went to the kitchen and grabbed a clean towel from a drawer. "You'll probably want to use this." He wiped off his face and hair while she went to make the call. "Maybe you should change into some dry clothes," she suggested, her tone gentle.

He nodded with a weary smile. "Yeah—they're soaked."

On her first attempt to call Roy Briggs, his line was busy. When she got through, he gave her bad news.

"Roy slipped on some ice last night and sprained his arm badly," she told Grant when he came into the kitchen in a fresh shirt and jeans. "He's sorry he can't come over."

Grant blew out a long breath. "I understand. Everybody's got their own troubles."

He pulled out a chair from the table and slumped into it. "Something sure smells good."

"I'm heating some beef soup, and I made a loaf of spice bread."

A glimmer of appreciation lighted his tired gaze. "Man, I fell into a tub of butter when I hired you, Miss Tess." His mussed hair gave him a boyish expression, almost made her chuckle.

They ate lunch and Grant related his futile search for Nina. "I know she's out there somewhere. I found her mother with some of the mares, but the snow was whipping in my face… I couldn't see more than five or ten feet in front of me." He shot a look outside where the wind keened like a howling wolf and snow piled higher in the yard.

Sitting across the table from Tess, Crystal fought back tears. "Can she find her way home?"

"We hope so." Tess reached over and placed her hand on Grant's. "You've done all you can for now."

He stared out the window and shook his head. His forlorn expression tore at her heart. Bracing herself, Tess announced, "I'll ride out there with you and we'll find her."

Grant's hand slammed down on the table. "No, you won't. You can't ride in this blizzard."

Taken aback by his unusual temper, Tess softened her approach. "I can ride Sugar. She's gentle and she knows that pasture like the back of her…hoof."

He managed a lame grin at her attempt at humor. "I appreciate your grit. But it's no use. Not in this weather."

* * *

By mid afternoon the deluge subsided enough to see up the road and a ways into the south pasture. Grant paced back and forth in front of the kitchen windows. "Those drifts are nearly four feet high in some places. The forecast predicts another foot over night." He stopped and glanced back at Tess. "Think I'll take Buck out this time for another look. He's strong and sure-footed."

Tess bolstered her courage. "Let me take Sugar and come with you. If Nina is hurt, you might need some extra help."

An uncertainty crept into his expression, but she didn't back down. After a long pause, he said, "Well, okay, but if the weather gets worse, we head back."

"Agreed." She didn't give him a chance to change his mind. In five minutes, she was bundled up and ready to go.

"We're going to find Nina and we'll be back as soon as we can," Tess explained to Crystal before she left.

"I want to come, too."

"Not this time. It's a job for grownups."

When Crystal's forehead began to pucker in objection, Tess added, "You can play with Miss Tabby and watch your favorite TV program."

Tess grabbed a plaid wool neck scarf hanging on a hall tree beside Crystal's forest green hat, closed the back door tightly and hurried to join Grant at the main corral. It was difficult to leave Crystal behind, knowing she couldn't comprehend the possible dangers in the outdoor elements, but the child would have to learn to follow adult rules while living on the ranch.

A westerly wind from the San Juans blew with renewed vengeance as Tess, riding Sugar, followed Grant, astride Buck, from the corral. Wet clots of snow pelted them mercilessly, distorting their visibility.

"Stay close," Grant called from up ahead.

"I will," she answered from beneath her brimmed felt hat, glad that she'd tightened the hat strings and tucked the wool scarf inside her coat collar.

They plodded along the roadway, the horses stepping through knee-high drifts. Tess's face stung from the raw, biting cold and she shivered against the whistling wind. At least Sugar knew her way. The mare's steady footfalls eased Tess's initial unease.

Grant's big buckskin quickly became a blurred shape ahead. Tess urged Sugar on, but the horse was unwilling to move any faster. She prodded Sugar with her boot heels; falling behind Grant was not an option. Sugar picked up her speed, but not by much.

The snow closed in around them. Here they were on a vast plain and it felt like they were confined to a shrinking space. Ice trickled off her hat and down Tess's neck, dampening her scarf. Although her long coat covered her knees, the wind snuck inside her layered clothing, freezing her inch by inch. Mother Nature in the West exhibited her own kind of fury.

She had no idea how far they had traveled when Grant's whistle reached her ears. Then he began to holler, "Nina," followed by an imitation of a horse nicker. It sounded pretty authentic. He must be thinking the foal would hear and respond.

The only guide now in the continuing storm was the hazy fence line to the left. Tess was gratified to have it. She recalled reading accounts of western ranchers stringing ropes from barn to house in the winter for the simple reason of aiding them through such a blizzard if someone got stranded outside the main house and couldn't see to get back. A literal lifeline.

She thought of the six-month-old foal. Separated from her mother and the rest of the herd. Alone in this strange white world. Trembling in the cold. A mean, twisting knot formed in her midsection. *Please hang on, Nina!*

The buckskin's big head and powerful chest plunged from the snow curtain in front of her. Grant's eyebrows, eyelashes, nose and mouth emerged ice-encrusted. "You doin' okay?" he called against the wind.

She brushed some of the snow from her hat brim and peered up at him. "Yeah. We're doing all right."

"I'm going to keep following the fence line for a while. It's the logical place a horse might wander to in this mess."

She nodded in the affirmative. "Okay."

Grant moved the buckskin up the road, or what had been the road. So high were the drifts now that it was impossible to find one's direction without the fence. Tess gave Sugar a little nudge and the horse obediently kept up the pace. Her black mane and mahogany coat were a frosted white, blending in with everything around them.

Grant gave out another loud nicker. A soft equine nicker responded.

Tess's heart skipped a beat. *Nina?* If only she could see anything five feet beyond Sugar's bobbing head. She leaned forward in the saddle, straining to hear.

Silence. Then…another faint nicker.

"I found her!" Grant shouted.

Thank heaven. Tess dug her heels into Sugar sides. "C'mon, girl. Go. Go!" They plowed ahead until Tess caught sight of a small ghostlike creature hobbling alongside the fence. Nina! Tears of joy welled up inside her.

Grant dismounted and went to her. He began talking to the foal in a calm voice as he examined her. Soothing her.

But waiting for Grant to determine Nina's injuries made Tess miserable. "How is she?"

"Well, her eyes are nearly frozen shut…and it feels like she's injured her right rear leg. Probably fell in a gulley near the fence. "

Tess shuddered against the cold. "How will we get her back to the barn?"

"I've got an idea." Grant pulled a coiled rope from his saddle and tied it around Nina's neck. He led her over to Sugar. "I'm going to tie her up to your saddle. Nina knows Sugar. She trusts her. It'll be slow going, but she'll make it."

Tess looked back at the pathetic little foal and said a prayer that she would.

Grant mounted Buck and came up beside them. "We'll be right next to you. Let's go."

With the wind at their backs, they started up the rough trail they'd made. Nina slogged through the knee-high drifts behind them. Minutes passed like hours. Several times Nina stumbled and Tess pulled Sugar to a halt in order to give Nina a rest. Knowing the foal was in pain with each step weighed heavily on her own spirit. *God be with us* became her continued mantra.

Grant's presence on Buck gave her reassurance. The big buckskin was powerful and surefooted. Grant gave the animal a firm lead. Steam from the horses' breath flumed out around their nostrils and their hooves made crunching sounds in the snow.

When the weary caravan came within sight of the barn and corral, several horses nickered as if in greeting. It was none too soon. Even with Grant's assistance, Nina could barely hobble into the barn

Frozen to the bone, Tess couldn't wait to get inside the main house and fix a pot of hot tea. "We're back, Crystal," she called when she entered the hallway into the kitchen. Peeling off her jacket and boots, she thought it odd that Crystal hadn't come running to meet her at the door.

She padded on tender, frozen, stocking feet toward the inner family room. Miss Tabby lay curled up on the long sofa sound asleep. But where was Crystal?

"Crystal, where are you?" she called twice before realizing the house was empty.

Hurrying back down the hall, she noticed that Crystal's jacket and hat were missing from the wall pegs. A terrible dread swept through her.

Tess rushed out the rear door and into the unrelenting snow. "Crystal! Crystal!" The sound of her hoarse voice hit up against a wall of white, dissipated into nothingness. Her soggy, stocking feet crammed into wet boots, she sank down into a drift off the deck. In her limited vision, there was no sign of Crystal.

Like trudging through thick molasses, she made her way over to the main corral. Horses clustered together, their backs blanketed in white, their large eyes downcast and framed in eerie ice-sickle lashes. "Crystal's missing—I can't find her," Tess blurted out to Grant when she saw him in the first barn stall.

He looked up from tending to Nina's rear leg. Surprise mingled with disbelief in his expression.

"She must have gone looking for us..." A heavy cloak of helplessness weighed her down.

Grant straightened and came to her side. "She couldn't have gone far. We'll find her."

They headed out of the corral. "This snow would come up to Crystal's hips in some places," Tess worried. "I hope she wore her boots... Where should we look first?"

Grant tugged his sheepskin collar up around his neck. "Let's go toward the south pasture from the deck. That's probably where she'd look for us."

Tess started out walking beside Grant but quickly fell behind. She couldn't match his long-legged stride.

They passed the cabin hovering cold and dreary beneath the mounting snowfall on its roof. Grant's timbered voice broke through the whirling flakes, his wide-shouldered form silhouetted ahead of her. "Look over near the house, but try to stay in line with me," he called back to her.

That would be a challenge, staying in line with him. Tess forced her boots ahead, making a zigzag trail. Where would Crystal go? How far could she get? A sudden gust whirled frigid pellets against her cheek. She tensed against the onslaught, her gaze searching all around the back yard. "Crystal!"

When they reached the south corral near the stables, Grant motioned toward the front drive. "You can check the front of the house and I'll go behind the stables."

"Okay." Ice crystals soaked her knit hat and slipped down her neck as she scoured the area on the side of the garage. Her heart leaped when she saw a few small prints but fell when they disappeared near a snow drift. "Grant!" she hollered. Unfortunately he was out of hearing range now. The prints went off in the direction of the front driveway so Tess hurried her pace.

A temporary break in the downfall opened a window clearing in the front yard. If Crystal's trail had existed, none was visible now. Only a pristine blanket of white draped across the yard and driveway, or where the driveway used to be. A definitely difficult terrain for a child. If she had managed to head south from the house, could she have wandered toward the fence? No, the snow was simply too deep.

Oh, Lord. Where was she?

Chapter Twenty One

Whispering a prayer for Crystal's wellbeing, Tess turned and began the arduous effort of putting one boot in front of the other toward the south corral and stables. Maybe Grant had had some luck. Crystal had to be close by…somewhere.

The gray sky toward the San Juan range brightened a little as she neared the corral. Snow streamed off her jacket in watery rivulets. She unwittingly thought of Katrina and the wall of water invading New Orleans not that long ago. The waves of misplaced people literally flooding into her elementary school. Hadn't Mother Nature taunted man and beast whenever she pleased? The only thing a human being could do was to struggle and fight back.

And the only tangible thing one had to fight back with was hope.

Yet her patience was wearing thin. "Crystal!" she cried out one more time, a lump forming in her throat. She admonished herself for not staying with Crystal and letting Grant go out in this miserable, bone chilling weather to find the foal.

From the rear of the stables, Grant rounded the corner. Alone. Tess's chin trembled and tears stung the back of her eyelids when she saw him. She trudged over to Grant, unable to stop tears of frustration from spilling over her cheeks. "Where can she be?"

He clasped her shoulders. "Get a hold of yourself. She's got to be close by."

Tess wiped her eyes with the back of her glove, choking down a sob. "I don't know if she wore her boots—"

His features were red-raw with cold, but his voice held encouragement. "We're not giving up."

270

She shook her head vehemently. "No. We're not. Where should we look next?"

"I'll head back around the other side of the corral. You go round this side and we'll meet at the far end. Stay close to the fence." He patted her arm, a smile fanning out from his eyes. "I'll holler if I find her."

"I think I'm losing my voice," she rasped.

"Wave your arms above your head."

She nodded then watched him move away in the opposite direction.

A burst of icy wind cut through her. The snow fell steadily around her, shrouding the landscape in a sullen silence.

Was this a cruel game fate was playing? She had avoided committing to a mother role to Crystal. For several reasons. What if the child went missing in the storm? A surge of horror bolted from her diaphragm to her belly. What kind of a mother would she have been at any rate—leaving her child at a time when she needed her most?

Don't waste time beating yourself up. Find Crystal.

She squinted against driving white flakes, trying to discern snow drifts from any possible movement, like a snow-covered child. Holding onto the top corral railing, Tess plodded slowly, her feet turning numb from the cold. Across the corral, Grant's tall frame was a silhouette against a vacuum of white.

"Crystal!" Tess croaked into the wind.

A nicker in the distance answered her call. She winced at the irony. The horses all tucked away comfortably in their stalls, safe from the elements. The child was wandering about…who knew where?

Chances were they might stumble over her, frozen stiff as a board. A myriad regrets assailed her, pricking her chilled body like a thousand tiny needles. She squeezed her eyes shut against mounting anxiety.

A faint moan pierced the silence. Her eyes flew open.

A flash of forest green, like a cork, bounced atop the white snow blanket. Several yards ahead, a small almond-hued face bobbed beside the corral railing. Tess rocked sideways into a knee-high drift, her mind roused from its gloom.

With a hoarse whoop, she pushed forward. Like a towering giant Grant reached the child first and scooped her into his arms. Breathless, Tess closed the distance between them. Her voice was a ragged remnant filled with joy and relief. "Crystal! Where have you been?"

Tears tracked down the reddened cheeks. Small arms reached out to her. "Mommy!"

In a crushed embrace, Tess grasped the child into her arms, hugging her as close as breathing would allow. Her knees wobbled and she leaned into Grant, her heart too grateful to describe.

"Where's Nina?"

"She's safe in the barn." Tess held Crystal at arm's length. "Why did you go outside when I told you to stay? That was dangerous." She stared at Crystal's chafed red hands. "And you forgot to wear your mittens."

More tears flowed from Crystal's swollen eyes. "You left me…I was afraid."

Tess brushed the tears away, another sting of guilt dissolving her reprimand. "Let's get you inside before you freeze into an icicle!"

The three of them plunged back along the haphazard tracks across the back yard. Halfway to the deck, Tess slipped in the snow and she and Crystal fell into a drift. Grant's helping hand reached down and lifted them to her feet. "I'll take Crystal from here, ma'am," he said in his big western sounding voice.

Miserably cold and soaked through, all Tess could do was manage a relieved smile.

Crystal giggled, despite a lingering hiccup. "Carry me!" Her arms went around Grant's heavy coat collar like a young koala bear would fasten onto its papa.

Once inside, a mad race to tear off sodden outer clothes ensued. Crystal's toes were a frigid beet red. "Please don't EVER scare us like that again, young lady," Tess commanded as she led Crystal toward the linen closet and warm, dry towels. "Mr. Grant and I were very afraid you were lost and we might not be able to find you until the snow melted." She called to Grant, "I'll put on some hot water for tea in a minute."

The tea kettle was already simmering when Tess reached the kitchen. Her shoulders sagged with fatigue inside the dry sweat suit she'd quickly pulled on. Grant's eyes were wind-burned and he looked beat, but he'd changed into a clean flannel shirt.

"Would you rather have coffee?"

"Yeah. I'll fix some instant."

"There are some chocolate chip cookies in the cookie jar."

"Bring them out to the family room and I'll make a fire to warm our bones," he suggested with a weary smile."

Tess brought out a tray with the hot drinks and cookies and set it down on the large knotty pine table in front of the sofa. She'd made Crystal cinnamon herbal tea with honey and added extra milk. Before long a roaring fire heated the room, its flames leaping upward inside the chimney. The hot aromatic tea and cookies satisfied her immediate hunger. Crystal snuggled against her, her head soon in Tess's lap. "Nap time, honey," Tess said, slipping a lock of hair from her forehead.

"I'll take her." Grant carried Crystal into the bedroom. "She was asleep next to Miss Tabby before her head hit the pillow," he said when he returned and slid into his recliner.

"Thanks." Tess stared into the fire, aware of the silence between them. She was becoming all too comfortable with their familial fireplace gatherings. She wondered how Grant felt about them, but didn't dare ask. Instead, she cocked her head in his direction, another question rising to the moment. "Why don't you have a dog, Grant? Seems like every rancher should have a canine companion."

He stared at the crackling fire, but his eyes seemed to be looking into the past. "I've had dogs before but I haven't since… I don't want to love anything so much again that I can't lose it."

"I see." Tess dropped her gaze to her tea mug, an unsettling ripple of sadness traveling through her. Even though his wife had been gone for almost two years, Grant still grieved for her and the life they had shared. "You must miss Laura a great deal." For some reason, speaking Laura's name out loud was more difficult than she could have imagined, but she continued because she needed to know. "Did you have a dog then?"

A muscle quivered in his jaw before he answered. "We had several dogs." He ran his hand through dampened hair. "She had a golden retriever. Scout, a beautiful, sweet animal. He'd follow along when she went riding. We both suffered when Scout had to be put down."

That afternoon in the barn when Grant had revealed the circumstances of Laura's accident came flooding into her mind. How much more devastating it must have been when he lost his wife *and* their baby. "You have lost much these last few years." Her voice quavered and she paused, not wanting to upset Grant further.

His features were tired. His sigh was audible. "The losing is one thing…the guilt is another."

"Guilt? Why should you feel guilty?"

He sat forward in the recliner, his elbows propped on his knees, the light from the fire emphasizing his wind-burned eyes. "When Laura left the ranch that day, she was angry. We'd had a small disagreement. I can't remember what it was about. I blame myself for not stopping her. She ran a stop sign, but maybe she *couldn't* have stopped. Were the truck's brakes working? I kick myself about that." He shook his head soberly. "The truck was totaled in the wreck, so I'll never know."

An acute sense of loss overwhelmed Tess, left her floundering for the words to salve Grant's wound. He rose to his feet, went over to the fireplace and placed another log on the two dwindling logs. His back was turned to her as if he preferred to hide his grief. "You shouldn't blame yourself," she said, rising from the sofa.

He swept the back of one hand across his cheek, perhaps wiping away tears. "The only thing that helped was getting off the ranch sometimes, riding out on Sonny."

She moved over to him, stroked his arm gently. "I wondered when I saw you ride away…and you wouldn't come back for a long time."

He half turned, still not looking at her. "When I ride out there, looking up at the mountains, it makes me feel freer from the guilt. It frees my spirit."

Silently she nodded. "I understand. I'm sure God rides with you." She swallowed over the lump in her throat. What had made her say that? Because she knew he was a God fearing man? Because down deep inside somewhere she believed it?

They stood for a long moment. Tess fought back moisture brimming in her eyes and the burgeoning pain in her heart. Beside her, Grant leaned against the mantel.

Unlike their previous moment in the barn, he did not reach out to her. Nor draw her near in a mutually comforting embrace, a tender kiss.

Neither seemed to have the right words. The healing words to help each other surmount this great barrier between them.

Doing the only thing that made sense to her at the moment, Tess left his side and gathered up the tray on the coffee table. Before taking the tray back to the kitchen, she said in as light a tone as she could rally, "At least we found Nina. That little foal seems indestructible."

She didn't add that they had also found Crystal, her most precious possession. Crystal was, for now, her responsibility, not his.

He nodded agreeably. "And Crystal. Those two are tough little gals."

His inclusion of Crystal showed his caring for her which pleased Tess.

She went back to the kitchen and left Grant by the fire to ponder his thoughts and memories. She hoped his self blame would ease, but how much longer would it take? Months? Years? Melancholy over the loss of a loved one could hobble one's life.

* * *

While washing their mugs at the kitchen sink, Tess weighed the events of the day in her mind: the battle against nature's elements, against time to find Nina and Crystal and bring them in from the storm. The battle raising her ire was with Grant. Not really with him as with the demons that plagued him. He seemed to be stuck in a time warp of the past where he was happiest—with Laura. A time warp that could only bring pain to her and Grant if she continued to stay on the ranch, seeing him every day, working in close proximity.

The reality was Grant still missed Laura.

Did he think of her when he rode out on Sonny? Did he think of her riding beside him, her blonde hair framing her fine features?

Tess sighed, attempting to find one thing Grant liked about her. He had sincerely complimented her on the Thanksgiving dinner. Although she'd bet he missed Laura's cooking.

And in his bed... Their bed. Did he still long for her arms around him in the darkness of night, when persistent winds blew down from the Sangres and sighed against his bedroom window? The question sent an arrow through her heart.

She gripped the edge of the counter, its granite chill forcing her to banish the badgering thoughts. She must not allow them to antagonize her further.

When the storm had subsided and early shadows crept across the snow fields in the front yard, they sat down to bowls of tomato soup and cheese sandwiches burned to a crisp in the toaster oven. Tess's energy level hovered close to fatigue and she didn't offer to remake the sandwiches. Grant ate quickly and went out to the stables to take care of the horses, leaving her with a subdued Crystal who picked at her burnt crust and wasn't interested in finishing her milk.

A cold draft invaded the kitchen when Grant opened and shut the rear storm door, raising goose bumps along Tess's arms. She watched him from the side window plowing through a maze of drifts, his hat pulled forward, his wide shoulders set against the frigid air, set in the routine of his nightly chores. Changeless.

After this afternoon's conversation with Grant, her feelings toward him had grown more confused. How could a woman possibly fall in love with a man who was still in love with his deceased wife?

Her usual sense of direction wavered, her head swirled with doubts. What had happened to the level-headed woman of yesterday? Had she *ever* been level-headed?

Her unresolved feelings toward Grant left her senses blurred. At bedtime she crawled under the cold covers and moved close to Crystal, clinging to the child's warm body like she would a lifeline. Still, long after Crystal's breathing slipped into the soft rise and fall of sleep, Tess lay wide awake staring at the shadows on the ceiling.

Crystal's voice calling her "mommy" earlier in the day floated in and out of her memory.

By morning her head ached, but she met the day with new resolve. After breakfast, she dressed herself and Crystal in their work clothes and they began clearing off the deck. While she shoveled a path out to the yard, Crystal used a small broom to whisk snow from the covered table and chairs. In the front, Grant worked with Juan and Carlos to clear the drive and roadway. Even though Juan's pickup was equipped with a huge snow plow, it was slow going.

By noon, Tess had talked on the phone with Jenny and fixed sandwiches and coffee for the men. Everyone dragged inside dripping snow puddles in the back hall. She insisted they remove all wet boots and only allowed them to enter the kitchen in stocking feet. As long as she was the hired cook, she would make the rules in the kitchen. Their empty stomachs foremost in mind, no one grumbled too loudly.

The apple cobbler, still warm from the oven, brought enthusiastic reviews. Although the cobbler's aroma was enticing, she could only manage a few mouthfuls due to the duress she'd been under when she made it.

After lunch, Juan and Carlos returned to their work. When Grant finished putting on his snow boots, Tess met him in the hallway. What she had to say would not be easy, but she approached him with as much conviction as she could muster.

He smiled as he shrugged into his heavy coat. "Your cobbler was great."

"Thanks." The palms of her hands were sweaty and she jammed them into her back jeans pockets. "Say, I wanted to thank you for all you've done for Crystal and me—"

By the slightly surprised expression on his face she knew she'd gotten his attention. "But I've decided it would be best for her sake and mine to leave at the end of the month."

His jaw dropped as if he'd been hit by a fly ball in the midsection. "Leave? I thought you liked working here."

"I do—I mean I have, but under the circumstances, I think—"

He stepped toward her, placing his large hands on her arms. "Tess, if there's anything I've done, anything I've said…"

She moved back slightly, causing him to drop his hands to his sides. "It's difficult to explain, but I-I don't feel comfortable staying." His eyes implored her while her ribcage tightened as if in a vise. "I'm just not good at living with ghosts, Grant. I talked with Jenny today and we'll be moving in with the Stotters after the holidays until I find another job."

He shook his head, a baffled expression in his eyes. "At least you'll be here for Christmas…" The faltering of his voice shattered her heart.

"Yes, we'll stay until Christmas," she heard herself reply in a raw response before she turned and left him standing by the door.

Chapter Twenty Two

Tess was leaving. She was taking Crystal and moving out of the house.

We'll stay until Christmas, she'd said. Only until Christmas.

What had he said? What had he done for her to make such an abrupt decision?

He chewed over the impending dilemma as he trudged out to the stables, his boots stamping down hard-crusted snow. A steady throbbing pain started over his temple adding to his growing misery. He'd obviously done something to offend her, set her mind to leaving and taking a different road, away from him.

When he got to the stables, he went again to Nina's stall midway back. Earlier this morning, it had been too dark to see much. Since her eyes had been nearly frozen shut yesterday when they'd found her, he feared they might have some kind of permanent damage, and he wanted to check her over for possible sprains or other injuries. She raised her tawny head in greeting, her eyes open and clear when he approached. She was definitely friskier than he'd thought she'd be after what must have been a frightening experience lost in a blinding snow. He examined her limbs for tenderness or swelling and found none, which was a relief.

A ray of Colorado sun broke through the clouds and slanted across the stable highlighting Nina's furry back. She nuzzled his coat pocket, sniffing for a treat and he slipped a few sugar cubes from it into the palm of his hand. She nibbled them up gratefully. He began brushing her thinking how much Crystal loved this little filly. The two had built up a natural fondness for each other.

Pain pinged like a hammer on his temple. How Crystal would miss Nina. And how he would miss the spunky little girl he'd come to care deeply about, almost as if she were his own.

His mind went back to his conversation with Tess yesterday in front of the fireplace and he knew what had triggered her sudden decision to leave. Some things he'd said about Laura. His guilt feelings about her fatal accident. Maybe his grief had been too much of a concern for Tess. She already carried enough of a load on her shoulders. He never should have revealed that hidden place in his heart to her. He never meant to burden her with his demons.

As he brushed Nina, he reflected back on his marriage to Laura. Had he been a good husband? People in the valley had a tradition of not speaking much openly about how they cared about each other. Husband and wife usually kept those thoughts private, saved them for behind the bedroom door. He'd been selfish with his verbal support or displays of affection to Laura. Not that he hadn't felt affection toward her.

At times she had seemed distant, going off by herself. He would see her standing at the bedroom window, her eyes fixed in a blank stare or riding out on her horse, her mouth set in a tight line. She was a quiet woman or so he'd thought. Maybe she would have been more open, partook of life on a larger scale if he'd encouraged her. It pained him that he could not recall much laughter between them during their life on the ranch. Perhaps she'd been lonely in this wide valley with few neighbors in either direction.

His mother had been a quiet, reserved woman yet she and his father always appeared to be loving companions throughout their marriage. Few words were needed between them. A loving embrace on a winter's gray day, a gentle touch on a shoulder after a hard day's labor conveyed warm memories of his parents during his childhood.

Marriages had just worked out, he had always assumed. Like the seasons: a promise of nourishment and new beginning in the spring; searing heat in summer, frigid, sometimes isolated, days of winter. So the moods and variants of a man and woman's life together.

He'd had a lot of time to think about it since he'd been alone on the ranch.

And then came Tess.

Walking into the Java Jug toting a bewildered little girl and a three-legged cat—three refugees fresh from the ravages of Katrina. Tess, with her tomboy face, short-cropped hair and dimple in her cheek. Despite all of her hardship, she had an air of calm and self-confidence which caught his attention and wouldn't let go. Something about her outward sense of determination made him want to help.

Her obvious lack of culinary skills made no difference. One look into those deep blue eyes brought out the sucker in him. That she had quickly mastered the job of cook and office assistant still amazed him. At the time, he'd thought she might last a week or two. At the time, he'd had no idea that he would come to love Tess in a completely different way than he had Laura.

Her reassuring smile brightened his day from the minute he entered the kitchen each morning. When he poured his coffee into his mug, he would watch her busily fixing breakfast, see the exposed nape of her pretty neck and have the strongest urge to kiss her there, tenderly. Tess, his new riding partner, his evening companion in front of the fire, casting a soft gaze over at him. She had shown empathy for him in her caring touch.

God had created no finer, more admirable woman.

And now she was leaving.

Journey to Sand Castle

* * *

Christmas was a week away. Only a week away!

Tess rolled out cookie dough then called Crystal from the family room to help cut various shapes in holiday cookie patterns. Snowmen, angels and stars were carefully laid out on a set of cookie sheets and popped into the oven. Later, the snowmen were given green gumdrop eyes and a row of cinnamon candy smiles.

"I want to put yellow dresses on the angels," Crystal announced as she set the last candy smile on a snowman.

Tess added a few drops of food color to the vanilla icing and let Crystal dress the angels with ruffled gowns. The stars soon shone with rainbow sprinkle candies.

When finished, they each chose a favorite cookie and devoured it, chased down with a glass of milk. Crystal licked her lips after gulping down the last bite. "Yum. I love Christmas!"

A sharp little pain pricked Tess's heart as if a tiny arrow had struck her. She wanted this to be a beautiful Christmas for the child, even if it would be her last on Wild Pine Ranch. She hadn't yet found the courage to tell Crystal about their move to the Stotters.

Let her enjoy every special moment here until the time came for them to leave.

The sound of the back door swinging open and Grant's voice calling "Anybody home?" entered the kitchen.

The timbre of his familiar voice made Tess slightly weak in the knees. "Just us elves," she answered.

Crystal rounded the doorway into the back hall, Miss Tabby loping on her heels. Then she squealed in surprise. "Come quick! Mr. Grant brought us a Christmas tree!"

Tess and Crystal watched as Grant set up the six-foot evergreen near the fireplace. He'd found a dusty cardboard box filled with ornaments in the garage storeroom. When Tess placed a skirt of green embroidered felt at the tree's base, Crystal hopped around it like a prairie rabbit. "Christmas is coming, Christmas is coming!" she sang out.

Grant stood back several feet, eyeing it critically. Its piney fragrance filled the room.

Crystal stood on tiptoe, her arms outstretched toward the top.

"It's not too big, but not too small," Grant observed. "It's just your size, cowgirl."

The box once opened emitted a musty smell. "This is the first time I've put up a tree at Christmas in…" His features crumpled slightly. "In a few years."

Crystal squatted down next to the box and peered inside. "What's in here?"

Grant handed her a tissue wrapped object. "Open this one and find out." He pulled out two more and gave one to Tess.

A flurry of wrapping paper disappeared, revealing ornaments that had seen many holidays past. Tess discovered hers was a small white church with stained glass windows and an arched front door. "How lovely," she said.

Observing the little church, Grant beamed with satisfaction. "I made that church years ago in my workshop."

Tendrils of warmth encircled her insides. The piece was a keepsake, especially if Grant had carved and painted it himself. She hung it on a branch in the front of the tree.

"You got a horse!" Crystal came over to get a closer look. "His head looks too big."

Grant laughed a full throaty laugh. "This is a replica of Sonny. He'll keep watch over the tree…and the presents."

Anticipation glowed in Crystal's eyes. "Here, look at mine." She held up a glittering gold star.

"Awesome! Now that should go on the top." Grant lifted her to the highest branch and Tess watched with joy as Crystal carefully hung the sparkling star.

His mood was buoyant as he reached back into the box and doled out several more ornaments.

Yet mixed emotions reverberated through Tess when she imagined the happy memories each ornament evoked in Grant. Memories of past Christmases he'd spent with Laura.

* * *

After an early Christmas Eve supper, Tess drew a jacket on over her cranberry wool dress and bundled Crystal into her coat, hat and mittens. Grant had pulled the truck around in front of the house and waited for them.

"Hurry, honey, or we'll be late for church." She closed the front door behind them and led Crystal over the shoveled path to the truck, the exhaust from its tail pipe billowing into the crisp air.

Realizing this would be the child's first visit to the town's church, Tess felt a pang of guilt. For any number of reasons, including her spiritual numbness since Katrina, she had failed to set aside a Sunday to take Crystal to church. And she had hesitated asking Grant to leave his ranch chores.

What're we gonna do in church?" Crystal asked with tentative enthusiasm.

Once they'd climbed into the truck, with Crystal fastened in her safety seat in the rear cab, Tess turned her question over to Grant. There was an inherent strength in his face when he answered. "We're gonna do some singing and celebrating." He smiled at Tess as he turned out of the driveway and onto the road. "And we'll be hearing about how the Lord was born in a stable—"

"A stable?" Crystal echoed from the back seat.

"That's right. Probably like the stable we've got out back for the horses."

Tess was surprised at Grant's apparent renewal of faith. And the way he described the stables made Tess feel a part of the ranch. How strange that she would *not* be a part of it for much longer. She fell silent the rest of the way into town, gazing up at the cascade of stars through the wide windshield.

On a pine-studded lot at the edge of town, The Church of the Dunes welcomed them. Grant assisted Tess and Crystal down from the cab and they walked toward the traditional white structure. He took her arm with gentle authority. She laid her fingers over his for a moment in a gesture that seemed perfectly natural.

Community members ascended the front steps into the small, bright sanctuary. Tess recognized Roy Briggs, one arm in a sling, and his stout wife sitting in a front pew. Jenny, Nick, and Sam Stotter greeted them inside. Sam grinned at Crystal, his electric hair standing on end as usual, his cheeks flushed red from the cold. Grant removed his hat and shook Nick's hand.

Lighted candles glowed on the altar amidst fragrant pine boughs. Familiar hymns lifted on heartfelt voices. Several times during the service, Tess found Grant gazing at her and she looked away, the tenderness in his eyes making her heart ache. Between them, Crystal sat attentive, listening to the beautiful story of Christmas. Tess squeezed her hand, grateful for this priceless moment.

Later at the ranch, Grant wished her and Crystal a "Merry Christmas" in the front room before saying goodnight. He reached out and gently touched Tess's fingertips, the pads of his fingers warm on hers. She tried to avert her gaze, but could not. The unspoken words in his eyes and on his lips were palpable. *Don't go*.

After tucking Crystal in bed, Tess lingered at the bedroom window. Stars flickered above the Sangre de Cristo peaks then blurred against the sky. Melancholy surrounded her instead of the expectancy she'd always known on every Christmas Eve since childhood. Why was she so unlucky in love? She'd chosen the wrong man the first time around. She could not choose another who was still in love with a woman no longer on this earth.

In the quiet darkness of the room, Crystal drifted in peaceful sleep, likely envisioning Santa Claus and his reindeer flying on course toward the San Luis ranch. At least there would be presents under the tree in the morning.

Regret consumed her. Regret that the past few months of coming to know and love Grant, and the ranch, were skidding to an abrupt halt. Regret that she could not have eclipsed Laura's memory from Grant's mind. Regret that she would soon be forced to take Crystal from this loving place.

* * *

Christmas morning. The sound of hurried footsteps rushing into the room and the pounce of a three-legged animal using her curved back as a springboard across the bed woke Tess with a jolt. "Tess, come see what Santa Claus brought me—a baby doll almost as big as me!" Crystal exclaimed, her eyes wide with excitement.

Swinging her legs over the side of the bed, Tess sat up. "Santa came already?" It must have been the wee hours of the morning. The bedside clock revealed the time as seven-thirty. Lord! She'd overslept.

"There are lots of presents still under the tree and Mr. Grant said to get you up 'cuz he's making scrambled eggs and bacon for breakfast. My favorite." Crystal prattled on as Tess jammed her feet into slippers and headed for the bathroom to wash her face.

Fifteen minutes later, she'd thrown on a comfortable emerald green sweat suit, finger-combed her hair, and followed her nose to the inviting smells wafting from the kitchen. Coffee bubbled in the coffee maker. Bacon sizzled in the pan. Crystal was busy setting napkins at the table settings.

Grant looked up from buttering the Texas-sized toast. "Mornin'. Hope you gals are hungry. If not, we'll have to give this grub to Santa's reindeers."

Crystal snickered and ran up to him on tiptoe. "No! We're hungry!" She threw her arms around his legs and he patted the top of her curly head.

Tess fought the urge to give him a hug. "Thank you for doing my job on Christmas," she said instead. "What a great gift!"

He sent her a spontaneous wink. "Think I saw another one out there for you."

She smiled, knowing she would miss his good-natured winks. Hopefully he hadn't spent much on a gift for her. After all, she was leaving him without a cook or an assistant which put her on a guilt trip. Even though he'd had enough experience around the kitchen to get by until he found another.

A soft blue neck scarf waited under the tree for Grant. He deserved more.

At least he appeared in a congenial mood, not overly concerned about her departure. No knots in his stomach; he likely suffered no regrets. Although the food smelled enticing, when they sat down to eat Tess found it difficult swallowing over the lump in her throat.

Grant and Crystal's appetites made up for hers, and they cleaned their plates swiftly. She was relieved when breakfast was finished and they could make haste to the Christmas tree.

A three-foot doll waited on the sofa, dressed in western fringed shirt, blue jeans and boots. Her red cowgirl hat accented her dark braids and sparkly brown eyes. There's my new doll!" Crystal bolted to the sofa and hopped up next to her. "I'm gonna name her Bonnie June."

Tess had no idea where the name had originated in Crystal's imagination. Perhaps in New Orleans? It didn't matter—as long as it pleased her.

Wrapping paper scattered in all directions. Grant tore the paper off his gift from Tess. He held the enclosed scarf to his cheek. The warmth of his smile echoed in his voice. "I'll definitely wear this on a snowy day." He handed her an obviously man-wrapped gift held together with large pieces of transparent tape.

She opened the package and found a delicate heart-shaped wooden box inside. Her breath catching in her throat, she carefully removed the box.

"It's a keepsake box, for jewelry and ladies trinkets."

She traced the smooth wood grain beneath her fingers. She opened the lid and inhaled the pure fresh aroma of new wood. "You made this, didn't you?"

"I did. In my workshop. That ponderosa is sturdy—should last almost a lifetime…"

A self-conscious rush of heat warmed her face. "What a beautiful gift, Grant." Tears pricked the back of her eyelids, threatening to spill over. "I'll always treasure it."

Why hadn't she given him a meaningful gift to remember her by?

The sound of a horse's nicker and commotion from the front yard distracted them.

Crystal darted a look at Grant. "What's that?"

"Hmm." He rose to his feet. "Must be the last gift."

Scooping up her big doll, Crystal raced to the front door. Tess and Grant followed.

When Grant swung the door open, Tess and Crystal both let out sighs of amazement.

"A sleigh," Tess observed.

Crystal pointed with glee. "Horses!"

A light snow had fallen over night, making everything fresh, the air crisp. Shimmery sunlight accented the thick manes and coats of two roan geldings standing at attention in the driveway. An old fashioned sleigh beckoned. Grinning from ear to ear, Carlos sat on the seat holding the reins.

Crystal's imploring gaze centered on Grant. "Can we go on a sleigh ride?"

He slid his arm casually around Tess's shoulders. "If it's okay with Tess."

She agreed wholeheartedly. "What is Christmas without a sleigh ride?"

"Can I bring Bonnie June?"

"Sure. There's room."

"Go put on your boots, honey."

While Crystal went to the back hall to find her boots, Tess felt Grant's arms go around her and her knees threatened to buckle.

"Merry Christmas," he murmured and kissed her softly on the lips. "You know I'd give you everything on this ranch AND myself if you would change your mind and stay."

Her mind whirled with Grant's unexpected proposal. All she could manage in reply as he drew her closer was a hushed "I don't know what to say."

"Tess, I've given the idea a lot of thought and I *know* it could work. I love you so much."

Through misted eyes, she looked up at him. "But what about Laura?"

"Laura has passed on, God rest her soul. We are here. We can make a new life—clean and true."

"You'll keep riding off to find her somewhere out there—"

Grant sighed deeply. "I don't need to do that anymore. I've decided it's time to give up my grief and move on." He held her gaze, revealing his soul. "I'd be a fool to let you and Crystal leave this place. You two own my heart."

A sudden shuffle of boots on the hardwood entryway snatched their attention. Wide-eyed, Crystal stared up at them. "Why are you crying, Tess?"

Tess wiped away moisture on her cheeks and laughed. "I'm crying happy tears because I want to tell Mr. Grant that I love him very much."

Grant held Tess closer. "You can be my witness now, Crystal, when I ask Tess to marry me."

Crystal's forehead puckered. "Do you want to marry me, too?"

Grant bent over and lifted Crystal onto his hip. "Tell you what—let's talk about it on the sleigh ride."

Minutes later they climbed into the roomy sleigh, Crystal nestled in the middle with her new doll in her lap. Carlos handed Grant the reins and, as he wished them a "*Feliz Navidad,*" Grant urged the big roans forward.

Small golden bells jingled against the horses' harnesses, their thick manes catching the brisk morning breeze. Heavy hooves crunched on snow making a new trail up the road.

"Well, are you gonna marry me too, Mr. Grant?" Crystal insisted.

He cast a mischievous glance over at Tess. "Honey, I'm hoping Tess wants me to marry her first; then we can live on the ranch as a family." He leaned over Crystal and gave Tess a warm kiss. "Will you give me an answer Ms. Cameron?"

She touched his cheek with gloved fingers. "My answer is *yes*, Mr. Grant."

His smile broadened in approval. The snow-capped Sangre de Cristo peaks rose alongside them like sentinels, majestic and strong. Tess rested back against the seat, a blissful glow flowing through her. The man she had come to love and trust guided the sleigh, the abandoned child who had captured her heart sat beside her. She gloried in their future journey together to a place where each would feel safe.

A place in the heart.

A place called home.

Epilogue

Spring had come early this year. Out for a nature walk, Tess and Crystal explored the southern acreage. Blooms of lemon yellow, prickly pear cactus and spiked blue larkspur caught her eye. God's touch was everywhere. On their honeymoon, Grant had told her that spring would be glorious in the San Luis Valley.

Six million years ago, the landscape had looked much the same as it did today. Volcanic remains had formed the San Juan Mountains on the west and to the east, the high peaks of the Sangre de Cristo Range.

Overhead she saw a flock of at least one hundred sandhill cranes in flight beneath magnificent billowing white clouds. Long necks outstretched. Powerful wings spread wide in a rhythmic rush. The sky was filled with the "khrrrr, khrrr"of their tremulous cries. Sandhill cranes had existed then as well, but probably not in the San Luis Valley. Now they were the oldest living avian species.

For a brief moment, her heart soared upward with them, in sync with their journey. They would court and mate in the valley's wetlands. She recalled that time last fall, just after arriving from the devastating reality of Katrina, when she and Grant had first watched the cranes as they left the valley to fly south for the winter. Shaken by the recent past and unsure of the future, she had exclaimed her wish to be one of them.

But now, inhaling the ponderosa-scented air, Tess felt her oneness with this place. Her heart was here. Her roots would grow deep into this ancient soil.

Crystal frolicked amidst a cluster of Indian paintbrush, crimson in the sun. She bent down to examine something then ran toward Tess, pigtails bouncing, amber eyes bright with discovery. "Look, Mommy." She held aloft a sprig of white-blossomed rabbit brush. "I found a shiny caterpillar!"

Was it more than an irony? That Carrie Pearl had left the San Luis Valley in search of a new life, and Tess had been forced to come here—and found hers.

She looked over to the dunes, still mysterious, ever beckoning, always flowing like the sea. Then she looked back to the child, the tie that would always bind Carrie and her together like kindred souls. Carrie's gift. And Jud's.

Closer than Tess's own blood and bone.

Crystal.

About the Author

Leslee Breene, award-winning author of novel and short fiction, takes pride in being a Denver native. She lives beneath the Colorado Rockies with her husband and, hopefully soon, a beloved rescue canine.

Ms. Breene attended the University of Denver, received a Denver Fashion Group Scholarship, and graduated from the Fashion Institute of Technology, New York City. For several years, she worked as a newspaper fashion illustrator in San Francisco.

During leisure time away from the computer, she enjoys scouting for book settings with her husband in the Colorado Rockies. Some memorable research sites are Leadville, the Sangre de Cristo Mountains, the Colorado Sand Dunes, and Jackson Hole, Wyoming.

Ms. Breene is an active member of Colorado Romance Writers and Women Writing the West. She is available for Denver/suburban area library and group speaking engagements. She welcomes visitors at her website: www.lesleebreene.com and www.facebook.com/lesleebreene/.

"JOURNEY TO SAND CASTLE takes the reader on a journey of discovery of caring for someone other than yourself. Tess must put her own life's decisions aside for a small child and finds a life more enriched than she could have foreseen. Ms. Breene restores your faith in the goodness of people."
~Joan Clayton, Executive Assistant Director, Englewood Public Library (retired)

Leslee Breene

Book Club Questions

1. Tess Cameron was compelled to make a life-changing decision regarding orphaned Crystal Pearl. Have you ever been faced with a foreboding decision that turned out to be a godsend?

2. Was the San Luis Valley effectively contrasted to the aftermath of Katrina? Did you feel you were actually there with the characters?

3. Was Jud Pearl a convincing character? Why did you sympathize with him, or not?

4. Were the scenes where Tess and Crystal face prejudice convincing and compassionate?

5. Grant Wilder struggles with inner pain and guilt regarding his wife's accidental death. Did you empathize with his resulting actions?

6. The memorial at the Sand Dunes. Was it a meaningful and effective setting to say goodbye to Carrie Pearl? Did you inwardly share the way each character demonstrated their way of letting go and expressing their love for her?

7. Tess found love and her spiritual home in the San Luis Valley. How did the characters change through the book?

CPSIA information can be obtained at www.ICGtesting.com
Printed in the USA
LVOW01s1613070314

376486LV00016B/579/P